THE GHOST

WHO LIED

HAUNTING DANIELLE

THE GHOST OF MARLOW HOUSE

THE GHOST WHO LOVED DIAMONDS

THE GHOST WHO WASN'T

THE GHOST WHO WANTED REVENGE

THE GHOST OF HALLOWEEN PAST

THE GHOST WHO CAME FOR CHRISTMAS

THE GHOST OF VALENTINE PAST

THE GHOST FROM THE SEA

THE GHOST AND THE MYSTERY WRITER

THE GHOST AND THE MUSE

THE GHOST WHO STAYED HOME

THE GHOST AND THE LEPRECHAUN

THE GHOST WHO LIED

THE GHOST AND THE BRIDE

THE GHOST AND LITTLE MARIE

THE GHOST AND THE DOPPELGANGER

THE GHOST OF SECOND CHANCES

THE GHOST WHO DREAM HOPPED

THE GHOST OF CHRISTMAS SECRETS

HAUNTING DANIELLE - BOOK 13

THE GHOST
WHO LIED

BOBBI HOLMES

The Ghost Who Lied
(Haunting Danielle, Book 13)
A Novel
By Bobbi Holmes
Cover Design: Elizabeth Mackey

ROBETH
PUBLISHING, LLC

ISBN-13: 978-1547113583
ISBN-10: 1547113588

To all the dogs and cats who've been in my life over the years. You didn't just provide unconditional love, you inspired me—helping me bring Sadie, Max, Hunny, and Belle to the world of Haunting Danielle.

ONE

JULY 1, 2015

I f he grew weary of property management, perhaps he should consider a career as a private detective. Adam Nichols chuckled at the thought, and then he remembered the private investigator who had been murdered in Frederickport not that long ago—shot by his own client. Of course, in that instance the PI had turned hit man, which was not a career path he would want to venture down. Adam wasn't overly fond of firearms. Fortunately, today's mission didn't involve guns, and he was confident no one was going to get killed.

Hands on hips, he stood in the center of the room, surveying his work. Smiling in satisfaction, Adam congratulated himself on the superb job of concealing the cameras. This wasn't his first foray into espionage. He had installed his first hidden security camera over a year ago in his office. That ended up saving Danielle Boatman's butt when it had captured her attorney attempting to plant evidence.

The second time was a favor he had done for an old friend, Jason Baker. Jason wanted a way to keep an eye on his restaurant employees when he wasn't there. If they weren't doing their work, he wanted to know. What they ended up capturing, within an hour of installing the cameras, was evidence of an attempted murder.

Adam's cellphone began to ring. Pulling the phone out of his pocket, he looked at it. It was his assistant, Leslie.

"Yeah," Adam answered the phone.

"You told me to call you when she picked up the key," Leslie told him.

"When was she there?" he asked.

"She just walked out the door."

"Did she say when she was going to the house?" Adam asked.

"I did just what you told me to do. I gave her the key and then asked when she was going over there."

"What did she say?"

"She said she had to pick up something first, but then she was going right over there."

"Perfect," he muttered.

"What's going on, Adam?"

"Nothing. I just wanted to make sure she got the job done. I might have someone who wants to look at the property tomorrow."

After the phone call ended, Adam used the app on the cellphone to test the cameras. Satisfied they were working correctly, he turned off the phone, slipped it back in his pocket, and locked up the house.

Adam arrived back at his office ten minutes later. As he breezed through the receptionist area, he told Leslie, "I don't want to be disturbed; hold my calls."

Leslie glanced up from her desk, only to see Adam hurry by and disappear down the hall to his office. "What's with you today?" she muttered after he was out of earshot.

Once alone in his office, he shut and locked the door. Taking a seat at his desk, he grabbed hold of his mouse and moved it. His computer was already on. The screen lit up. Smiling, Adam activated the software for the security cameras. It was possible to monitor the cameras with his phone, yet today he preferred to use the larger screen for a better view. A moment later, the interior of the rental house was live streamed onto his computer monitor.

"Good, she isn't there yet," Adam muttered. He watched and waited.

It was taking her longer to arrive than he had anticipated.

"She obviously did more than just pick something up," he grumbled. Adam glanced to the clock. He had been sitting at the computer for over thirty minutes. Growing restless, he reached for his cellphone. But then he noticed motion on the monitor. Someone was coming in the front door of the rental house.

"It's about time." Adam abandoned his cellphone. He leaned toward the computer monitor and watched.

"What the…?" Adam frowned. "I don't think so."

He continued to watch. Minutes ticked away.

"Where are you going now?" he mumbled. His gaze never left the screen.

Minutes later, he began to chuckle. "Well, I'll be damned. I wouldn't have believed it if I hadn't seen it for myself."

DANIELLE THOUGHT she was alone in the parlor. Pulling the blinds to one side, she peeked outside. It looked as if someone was on the porch swing. Focused on trying to see who it was, she was not prepared when a male voice whispered *boo* into her left ear.

Letting out a screech in surprise, she turned abruptly to the source and found herself staring into the twinkling blue eyes of Walt Marlow.

"Dang you, Walt, I hate when you do that." Danielle stomped one foot in protest.

"Do what?" Glancing down, he was momentarily grateful he didn't have any mortal feet for her to stomp.

"Stop acting like a ghost, you brat."

"You know I hate that word." He didn't seem particularly upset. Walt leaned to the window, trying to see what Danielle had been watching.

"Don't act like a ghost, and I won't call you one."

"Why are you spying on Lily?" he asked, still looking out the window.

"Is that who it is?" Danielle peeked out the window again, her head next to Walt's.

"I was in the attic when I saw her coming across the street from Ian's."

"I wondered who it was." Danielle turned with Walt into the room. "I thought it might be one of our guests. Is Ian with her?"

"I don't think so. I didn't see anyone else when she was crossing the street." Walt walked over to the sofa and sat down. He watched as Danielle went to the door leading to the hallway. She shut it.

"I really don't need one of our guests to hear me talking to myself," she whispered when she returned from the now closed door and took a seat on the sofa next to Walt.

"You aren't alone," he reminded her with a smile.

"So tell me, why the *boo?*" she asked.

Walt shrugged. "No reason. I'm just in a good mood."

"Any special reason for the good mood?"

Walt let out a satisfied sigh and leaned back comfortably on the sofa. Outstretching his legs, he crossed them at the ankle. "I suppose I'm looking forward to the open house."

Danielle grinned. "I seem to remember a time you opposed the idea of turning this place into a B and B. Now you're looking forward to the party?"

"Mostly, I'm looking forward to seeing you all dolled up and wearing the Missing Thorndike."

Danielle blushed. Standing up, she said, "You're funny, Walt. I think I'll go see what Lily is up to."

Still sitting on the sofa, Walt watched Danielle leave the room. "Ahh, run away, Danielle," he whispered to himself. "I'm just a spirit, nothing to be afraid of." He let out another sigh and smiled wistfully.

ACROSS THE STREET, the sun disappeared behind the houses. Beyond the houses, the fiery ball sank into the Pacific Ocean. Lily watched from her place on the porch swing, using one foot to keep the swing gently swaying back and forth.

When she heard the front door open and close, she glanced over to see who was coming. It was Danielle.

"Hey, Lily, are you home for the night?" Danielle asked when she reached her.

Putting her foot down to pause the swing, Lily held it motionless for a moment, giving Danielle time to sit down next to her. Once she was seated, Lily pushed the toe of her shoe against the ground and sent the swing back in motion.

"Yeah. Ian had some work to finish up. I thought I'd come on home."

The two friends sat in silence for a few minutes, enjoying the motion of the swing while watching the last evidence of the sun disappear.

"Dani, I think I have a problem."

Danielle glanced to Lily. "What sort of problem?"

"I'm in love with Ian."

Danielle chuckled. "Well, duhh, like we all didn't know that already? So why is it a problem now?"

"He's been so sweet lately. Oh, he's always sweet. But I think…I have this gut feeling he's going to ask me to marry him."

"Are you saying you don't want to marry Ian?"

"No! I want to marry him. I can't imagine marrying anyone else."

"Have you been talking about marriage?"

"Not really. We sort of talk around it. I mean, we talk about what we want to do next year or the year after that. Like we both know we intend to stay together. But we've never actually talked marriage per se. Although, Ian did ask me a while back if I wanted kids, which led to a long conversation on how we wanted to raise our children."

Danielle smiled. "Sounds to me you've already been talking marriage. But I don't see what the problem is."

Lily put her foot down and stopped the swing. She turned to Danielle. "I need to tell Ian about Walt. About everything."

Danielle's eyes widened. "Really?"

"I don't know how we can have a future together if one of us is keeping secrets. And this is a huge secret."

Danielle let out a sigh. With her right foot, she put the swing back in motion. "I suppose I understand. I told Lucas for that very reason. Of course, my secret is that I can see ghosts. Yours is that we've been living with one for the last year."

"That and all the other ghosts who've showed up since we've moved in."

"How do you intend to tell him?" Danielle asked.

"That's the problem, I can't."

"Why can't you?"

"Because Ian doesn't believe in ghosts."

Danielle started to laugh. "Most people don't believe in the beginning. Look how long it took the chief to realize his grand-mother really had been talking to his grandfather's spirit."

"It's not like that, Dani. A while back Ian and I were watching a TV show about a medium. I figured it was a good opening to bring up the subject. But Ian went all ballistic."

Danielle frowned. "What do you mean ballistic?"

"He's done some articles on supposed hauntings and mediums."

Danielle arched her brow. "Supposed?"

"After he researched the stories, he discovered they were hoaxes. He's now convinced they're all frauds. He really has a thing about it."

"But he knows about my history—what happened when I was a child?" Danielle asked.

"Sure. We even talked about it that night. He's convinced what happened to you back then was nothing but a child's overactive imagination. In fact, he praised your parents for sending you to a psychologist back then. He said that's exactly what he would have done in their place."

"I suppose it's harder for some people to believe."

"But, Dani, what am I going to do?"

"I'm not sure. I understand why you don't want to continue to keep the secret. But at the same time, if you do tell him, you need to find some way to convince him. Maybe we can get Walt to help?"

"Maybe..." Lily leaned back in the swing. "But let's wait until after the open house, okay? You have enough on your mind right now. And frankly, I don't want to deal with this when Kelly is here."

"She's coming for the party?"

"Yeah. She'll be here Friday morning and is staying for the weekend."

"You're probably right. It would be best to tell Ian when he doesn't have his sister staying with him, and when we don't have a house full of people."

"It will also give me a few more days to figure out how I'm going to tell Ian. Or more accurately, how to convince him I'm not crazy."

"Don't be silly, Lily. We all know you're crazy," Danielle teased.

TWO

Moonlight lit up the darkened corridors of Marlow House. Inside, most of the occupants had already fallen asleep. Making his nightly rounds, Walt Marlow moved through the rooms on the lower floor before starting on the second floor, where most of the bedrooms were located. He paused by Danielle's room. He could see light coming from under the closed bedroom door.

Walt moved through the wall leading to Danielle's room. He found her sitting on the bed, her laptop computer propped open on her lap. By her clothes—plaid flannel pajama bottoms and a T-shirt —and the damp dark hair piled haphazardly atop her head—he could tell she had recently showered and washed her hair and was ready for bed.

Looking up to Walt, Danielle smiled. He wore a gray three-piece suit, sans the jacket and tie, the sleeves of his white shirt pushed casually to his elbows. "Evening, Walt," she said in a whisper.

"You appear to be the only one up. All the other rooms are dark."

"I couldn't sleep." Danielle scooted over to one side of the bed, making room for Walt. He accepted her silent invitation.

Once on the bed, Walt kicked off his shoes. They disappeared before reaching the floor. He rested against the pillows stacked in front of the headboard while Danielle sat next to him, working on her laptop.

She glanced from her computer to Walt. "Lily plans to tell Ian about you."

Walt arched his brow. "She does? That will be interesting."

"Or should I say, she wants to." Danielle then went on to recount her recent conversation with Lily.

"I suppose it would be better to wait until after the open house to broach that particular subject. Observing Ian this past year, I have no idea how he might react. And I tend to agree with Lily. I don't think he'll be as accepting of the information as she was." Walt glanced to the laptop. "So what are you doing on the computer?"

"I was reading that blog." Danielle shook her head in disgust.

"I assume you're talking about the Mystery of Marlow House?"

"I wish I could figure out who this clown is. It's bugging me."

"Anything in particular this time?"

"He's been blogging all week about the curse of the Missing Thorndike." In the telling, Danielle gave special emphasis to *the curse of the Missing Thorndike*, making it sound like a radio announcer promoting an upcoming horror flick.

"Obviously, he's going for the sensational."

"Or she. It could be a woman. But I agree with you, whoever it is, is trying to stir up controversy to attract fans to the webpage. And I bet whoever it is will show up on Saturday. I'd be surprised if the blogger wasn't there last year. The pictures taken then—the ones he posted online—I don't recognize them. They aren't photos we took. But they could have been taken by anyone."

"Don't let it bother you."

Danielle shrugged. "I suppose you're right. And if I was being honest, there was a time in my marketing career when I might actually promote something like this for the extra exposure."

Walt glanced over to the laptop screen. He could tell she had opened a new website. "What are you looking at now?"

"I thought I'd play around with my account on Ancestry.com."

Walt frowned. "Play around, how?"

"Ever since Aunt Brianna's DNA results, I've been getting more interested in genealogy. I've been working on my family tree, adding ancestors when I find them."

"So how do you do that?" Walt asked.

Danielle flashed him a smile, an idea popping into her head. "I know what we'll do. Let's see if we can find anything on you in here and then build your tree too."

"Me?" Walt smiled. "I doubt you'll find anything on me in there."

Her eyes on the laptop, Danielle said, "You'd be surprised. Okay, what was your middle name again?"

"Clint."

In Ancestry.com's search menu, Danielle typed in Walt's full name, along with the year of his birth and death, and then she clicked the search button.

"Wow, a lot of stuff came up!" Danielle announced.

Curious, Walt peered over her shoulder.

Danielle pointed to the left side of the screen. "Here's the list of categories to research. I like to start with family trees to see what might already be out there. Basically, we're checking other member's family trees, those who've set their trees to public."

"Are you suggesting I might already be included in a member's family tree?"

"It's possible."

Walt shook his head. "I seriously doubt you'll find me on anyone's family tree. My great-grandfather was the only Marlow in our family to come to America, and I was the last one in his line."

"That may be true…but look! There you are!" Danielle clicked the link. Walt's ancestor profile page flashed onto the display. "Look! It even has a picture of you!"

Walt leaned toward the laptop screen and frowned. "How in the world did someone get that photograph of me and put it on the computer?"

"I suspect one of your distant cousins uploaded it."

Cocking his head slightly, Walt studied the page with keen interest. "It must be. I remember that photograph. It was taken before Grandfather passed away. Now that I recall, he regularly exchanged photographs with his cousin in London."

"Let's see what cousins you might have out there."

Danielle began clicking through the pages, starting with Walt and moving back one generation at a time. "Okay, it says your parents were Alexander Oliver Marlow and Anna Elizabeth Holland."

Walt nodded. "Correct."

Reading Walt's parents' birth and death dates, Danielle frowned.

"Wow, you were pretty young when they died." She clicked several links. "Whoever put this tree together doesn't list anything for your mother, aside from her name and birth and death dates. But they have your father's parents down. But that doesn't surprise me. Whoever put this family tree together is obviously on the Marlow side of your family, since they call the tree *Marlow Family Tree*."

"There's no photo of my mother, but there is one of my father." Walt sounded disappointed.

"Wow, you looked a lot like your father."

"I've heard the Marlow men tend to bear a striking resemblance to each other."

Danielle glanced at Walt. "Do you have any family photos stored somewhere in the house? I've never seen any."

"Hmmm, now that you mention it…" Walt thoughtfully considered the question. "I can't recall seeing our photographs. Perhaps they were thrown out after I died?"

"Were there a lot of photographs?" Danielle asked.

"We obviously didn't take photographs as often as you do now. Lily is always taking a picture of something. Just the other day I saw her taking a picture of her breakfast, and then she posted it on Facebook." Walt shook his head and chuckled. "But I had a Brownie I made good use of, and Grandfather religiously saw to it we hired a photographer to take our annual portraits."

"I wonder where those pictures are now," Danielle mused.

"We kept them in photo albums in the library. But now that I think about it, I don't recall seeing them there."

"I wonder…I always heard Aunt Brianna's mother wouldn't come inside Marlow House after you died, so I doubt she went through any of your photographs. Aunt Brianna was just a small child then, but later, I know she had people taking care of the house. It's possible she had someone go through your personal effects—after all, your clothes were all gone—but knowing what I do about her, I don't see her throwing something like family photographs away. Perhaps they're down at the museum? They have some photos of your grandfather down there. Maybe Brianna donated your photo albums to the museum. I'll have to check that out."

"I would like to see them again. But if they're at the museum, I doubt that would be possible."

"Let me see if they have them first, and if they do, I'll work something out. And who knows, we haven't gone through all the old boxes in the attic and basement, so perhaps they're there."

Danielle turned her attention back to the computer and Walt's online family tree. "Your paternal grandparents were Frederick Wright Marlow and Sarah Ellen Oliver. Ahh, that's where your father got his middle name."

"It was the custom; when naming a child, parents often gave the mother's maiden name as the middle name."

"I rather like that custom. Your grandparents only had one child?"

Walt nodded. "From what I understand, my grandmother lost several babies before she had my father."

"That's sad." Danielle sighed, still looking at the computer. "Here is your grandfather's parents, Alexander Gabriel Marlow and Mary Ann Clint. Interesting, you got your great-grandmother's maiden name, not your mother's. Ahh, these were the first Marlows to come to America!"

"Yes." Walt nodded. "And an interesting fact, my great-grandfather was a twin—as was his wife. And it just so happened my great-grandmother's twin sister married my great-grandfather's twin brother."

"Seriously?" Danielle looked from the monitor to Walt.

"Yes."

"Double cousins," Danielle murmured. "I remember hearing once that if twins marry twins, like your great-grandparents did, their children, the cousins, are biologically siblings."

"I don't know about that." Walt shrugged. "But I got the feeling my grandfather was close to his cousin, even though they'd only met in person maybe twice in their lifetime. However, they did correspond regularly."

Danielle looked back on Walt's great-grandparents' pages. "It says here they had three children, but according to the dates, the only one who survived to adulthood was your grandfather. Is that correct? Maybe there were other children who just aren't listed."

Walt shook his head. "No, that information is correct. Grandfather had a brother and sister; they both died during childhood. As you can see, my Marlow line was not terribly prolific."

Looking back at the computer, Danielle said, "This tree only goes back as far as your great-great-grandfather Walter Broadwater Marlow. The only children listed for him are the twins, your ancestor, and his brother, Charles Gabriel Marlow, and his wife, Jane Ann Clint. Do you know if there were more children?"

"No. Their mother died giving birth to the twins. According to family legend, my great-great-grandfather was heartbroken. She was reportedly the love of his life and he never got over her death. He raised his sons with the help of a nanny.

"The twin who stayed in London, their son Thomas, was the one who grandfather mentioned in the will. His son, also named Thomas, is the one who I briefly mentioned in my will. Like our branch of the family, they were not prolific."

While listening to Walt, Danielle clicked through the family tree. "This is interesting. The cousin Thomas, the younger one who you briefly had in the will, his grandson moved to the United States. His name was Steven Giles Marlow; he was born in 1954. Looks like he died two years ago. Wow, look at these photos. That family resemblance is remarkable. You're right. The Marlow men definitely look like each other."

"I had a cousin who moved to America?" Walt grinned at the thought.

"It looks like he settled in California. According to this, he has a living son. But because the son's still alive, his profile is set to private. So I can't see his name or date of birth or any photographs that might have been added to his page."

"I'd love to know something about him," Walt said wistfully. "Such an odd feeling to realize I have living relatives in the United States."

"Tell me about it," Danielle grumbled under her breath. Since beginning her genealogical research, she hadn't located any living cousins.

"I wonder if he still lives in California, considering that's where his parents settled?" Walt mused.

"I just thought of something," Danielle said excitedly. "If he was born in California, I can search birth certificates. Since I know his father's name and his mother's maiden name, and I have a general idea of when he might have been born, I may be able to find something."

Walt silently watched as Danielle typed away on her keyboard and then used the trackpad to move through the search results.

"Holy cow!" Danielle said a little too loudly, considering her guests and Lily were sleeping.

"What?"

"The name of his son—Walter Clint Marlow. He has your name!"

"I'll be damned," Walt muttered. "What else can you tell about him?"

"Just that he's around thirty-five years old now. But that's all I can tell."

"Can't you do an online search; find out more about him?" he asked.

Danielle turned to Walt. "In effect, I already have. And nothing came up on him."

"What do you mean?" Walt frowned.

"When I was researching your death, I did a lot of searches for Walt Marlow and nothing came up on him." Danielle paused a moment and frowned.

"What is it?"

"I'm not sure I ever searched Walter, just Walt. And I know my searches never included your middle name."

Turning her attention back to the computer, Danielle closed the Ancestry.com page and opened a Google search. Typing "Walter Clint Marlow" in the search box, she then clicked the magnifying glass icon.

Danielle grinned. "I found something!"

After opening the webpage, Danielle and Walt stared at the monitor. It was a website for a California Realtor named Walter Clint Marlow. The website included a photograph.

"Holy crap, Walt," Danielle muttered. "He could be your twin!"

THREE

JULY 3, 2015

Ian normally didn't notice the monotonous ticking of the antique wall clock. Its persistent rhythm hammered dully, one beat after another, providing the only background sound aside from an occasional snore from the dog napping at his feet. The timepiece—along with the majority of the house's furnishings—belonged to the owner of the rental house, Marie Nichols.

After returning from Marlow House fifteen minutes earlier, Ian hadn't bothered to turn on the television or music. Sitting alone in his living room, with his golden retriever, Sadie, Ian studied the gold ring in his hand, its diamond glistening each time he turned it ever so slightly, capturing bits of light from the overhead fixture.

Settling back comfortably on the sofa, one leg casually propped over the opposing one, Ian let out a sigh and smiled, his focus still intent on the engagement ring.

"How do you think Lily will like this, Sadie?" Ian asked aloud.

Hearing her name, Sadie opened her eyes and lifted her head, looking up at her human, who continued to stare at the small object in his hand. Letting out a grunt, Sadie closed her eyes again and rested her chin back on her front paws.

Glancing down at the grunting dog, Ian let out a snort and shook his head. "I hope that's not a commentary on my choice." Looking back to the ring, a thought crossed his mind—*Maybe I'm doing this all wrong?*

Asking Lily to marry him while Fourth of July fireworks filled the night sky seemed like a romantic gesture to Ian Bartley. However, selecting a ring that Lily might not like—or one that didn't fit—might diminish the gesture. He wondered if he should have simply proposed and then gone with Lily to pick out the ring.

Headlights momentarily lit up the front window, distracting Ian. He looked up. *Did someone just pull into the driveway?* A few moments later the sound of a car door slamming confirmed his suspicions. Sadie, now fully awake, leapt up from her spot by Ian's feet and dashed to the front door, her tail wagging.

Hastily, Ian reached for the small ring box he had set on the coffee table ten minutes earlier. Carefully returning the ring to its velvet nest, he glanced around for someplace to stash the ring box. Before he settled on a hiding place, he heard the front door open. Without thought, he shoved the small box into his jeans' pocket, making it bulge. Grabbing one of the sofa's throw pillows, he tossed it across his right hip, concealing the pocket.

"I didn't expect to find you home," his sister, Kelly, said as she entered the living room and tossed her purse on an empty chair. Sadie trailed by her side, tail wagging. Kelly had arrived that morning from her home in Portland. Tomorrow was Marlow House's July Fourth party, which she planned to attend with her boyfriend, Joe Morelli.

Still sitting on the couch, Ian glanced over his sister's shoulder and asked, "Is Joe with you?"

"No. I had him drop me off. I have a blog post I need to finish. Why are you home so early?" Kelly kicked off her shoes and sat down on a chair facing Ian. Sadie stood by Kelly's side, persistently nosing her for attention. Absently, Kelly complied, scratching behind the dog's ear as she looked to her brother.

"After getting ready for the party, Lily was exhausted. She's probably already in bed."

Kelly glanced over to the front window. The curtains were open, but it was dark outside. Across the street was Marlow House, where Ian's girlfriend, Lily Miller, lived with Danielle Boatman. Together they ran a B and B.

She looked back to Ian and said, "I have a question for you." Repositioning herself on the chair to get comfortable, Kelly pulled her bare feet up into the chair, tucking them under her. Sadie plopped down on the floor, preparing to nap.

"What's that?" Ian rested his right arm over the throw pillow.

"Why didn't you ever tell me Marlow House is haunted?"

Taken aback by the unexpected question, Ian frowned at his sister. "What are you talking about?"

Kelly laughed. "Well, maybe not really haunted, but the fact so many strange things happen there some people think it is. Why haven't you ever mentioned it before?"

Ian shook his head. "I have no idea what you're talking about." He then reconsidered his words and asked, "Is this about that blog someone's doing on Marlow House?"

"No. This is about other strange things that have happened to people who've visited Marlow House since Danielle and Lily moved in. Although, I imagine the blogger would love the stories."

"I have no idea what you're talking about."

"Come on, Ian, seriously?" Kelly scoffed.

"Where is this coming from?"

"Joe and I went to Pier Café for dinner, and Brian Henderson was there. We asked him to join us. We started talking about the open house tomorrow, and one thing led to another, and they started telling me about all the strange stuff that's gone on at Marlow House. Of course, Joe thinks there's probably a logical explanation for everything that's happened, but I got the feeling Brian thinks the place is haunted."

With a snort, Ian said, "I find it a little difficult to imagine Brian Henderson believes in ghosts."

"Maybe not ghosts exactly. But considering the stuff that's happened over there…" Kelly shrugged.

"What kind of *stuff*?"

"Are you serious? Lily and you haven't discussed this before?"

"Discussed what? A lot has gone on since they moved in across the street, but as far as I know, ghosts have not been an issue." Ian chuckled at the thought.

"Wow. It's just that Lily—being Lily—I can't believe she hasn't discussed this with you."

"What is that supposed to mean? Lily being Lily?"

"Hey, you know I love her. But she isn't really someone to hold back."

"Wait a minute…" Ian frowned. "Joe told you what happened to Danielle when she was a kid, didn't he?" Ian then grumbled under his breath, "*Gossip*."

"What are you talking about? What does Danielle's childhood have to do with what's gone on over at Marlow House?" Kelly frowned. "So, what did happen to Danielle when she was a kid, anyway?"

"Are you saying Joe didn't tell you Danielle claimed to be able to see ghosts?"

Kelly bolted upright in her chair and placed her feet on the floor. "Danielle can see ghosts? And you never told me before?"

Ian groaned. "No. I'm saying when she was a child she claimed to see them. But that was a long time ago, when she was a kid with an active imagination. Please do not say anything. It's pretty embarrassing for her."

"Well..." Kelly shrugged and slumped back in the chair. "It's a little disappointing to know she can't see ghosts. That would put an entirely different spin on the story."

"On what story? What has Joe been telling you?"

"It's not just Joe, it's Brian too. I guess there've been a series of unexplained things happening at Marlow House. Like people feeling like they've been punched, and no one is there."

"What people?" Ian demanded.

"Brian for one. Joe too. But also, those two FBI agents." Kelly paused a minute and looked critically at her brother. "Are you seriously saying Lily has never mentioned any of this to you?"

"Maybe Lily doesn't know. Although, I suspect Joe and Brian are pulling your leg."

"No, they aren't," Kelly insisted. "Do you remember when Chuck Christiansen was arrested in Danielle's backyard?"

Ian frowned. "Of course."

"Did you know the gun mysteriously flew out of his hand and landed on the roof?" Kelly asked.

Ian rolled his eyes. "There was nothing mysterious about it. There was a scuffle between Christiansen and Bart Haston, and during the commotion, the gun flew out of his hand and landed on the roof."

Kelly shook her head. "No. According to Brian, Haston didn't touch him. And even Joe admits a number of officers witnessed it, and none of them can explain how the gun flew out of Christiansen's hand."

"That's ridiculous. Nothing mysterious about an overexcited person who moves too quickly, letting go of something he's holding and it goes flying. Hell, I suspect we've all done something like that one time or another. Sounds like Joe and Brian are just messing with you."

"No, they aren't. You weren't there. And how about when Joe and Danielle were in that home invasion? Joe doesn't remember getting the gun away from the guy."

"You think some ghost helped them out?" He snickered.

"I'm just saying he doesn't remember."

"That's because he was knocked out and lost his memory."

"Maybe." Reluctantly, Kelly added, "Actually, that's what Joe said too. But what about those books flying off the shelf in the Marlow House library?"

"Books flying off the shelf?" Ian chuckled. "Okay, tell me about it. This sounds good."

"One of Danielle's guests insisted the books started flying off the shelf in the library."

"What guest?" Ian asked.

"I don't know her name. But she told Joanne, and Joanne told Brian about it."

"I sure haven't heard about it."

"That is precisely my point!" Kelly insisted.

"You're losing me again, kid."

"Ian, don't you think it's strange Lily never mentioned it to you before? It doesn't matter if it actually happened; but according to Joanne, the woman made a big deal about Marlow House being haunted—she even told the other guests. I'd just think Lily would share the story with you, that's all."

"She probably didn't think it was a big deal," Ian suggested.

"And what about that cigar smell?" Kelly asked.

"Cigar smell? Are you talking about how it sometimes smells like someone's been smoking over there?"

Kelly nodded. "Yes. Haven't you and Lily ever discussed it?"

"We've talked about how old houses get odd smells. So what?"

"And what about Sadie?"

Ian glanced down at the golden retriever napping by his sister's feet. "What about Sadie?"

"Whenever I've seen Sadie at Marlow House, all that dog seems to want to do is go hang out in the attic. Doesn't Lily think that's strange? Her boyfriend's dog going up to the attic alone? Wasn't that where Walt Marlow was murdered?"

Ian chuckled. "Lily certainly has never mentioned a haunted attic. What are you suggesting, my dog sees ghosts? Did Joe and Brian tell you this too?"

"Umm…no. But when Joe was driving me home tonight, and I was thinking about what he and Brian had been telling me, I started remembering how strange Sadie acts over there. And I have heard animals are very sensitive to paranormal activities."

Ian started to laugh. "Okay, first you tell me Joe and Brian have witnessed some strange happenings at Marlow House, yet Joe thinks there's a logical explanation, and it's not really about ghosts. You just want to know what Lily has said about it. And now, you jump to there are ghosts, and my dog is communicating with them." Ian laughed harder.

Kelly stood up and let out a sigh. "I'm just saying, according to Joe, a lot of people have noticed strange—unexplained occurrences at Marlow House—lots of people. Yet you know nothing about it, and your girlfriend has never once mentioned it to you, and she lives there."

"Maybe she never mentioned it because there was nothing to the story."

Again, Kelly arched her brow and silently shook her head. Stepping to the chair next to the one she had been sitting on, she scooped up her purse and turned back to Ian. "You really are missing the point. It doesn't matter if there is a logical explanation for the number of things that have gone on over there, but I would have assumed Lily—being Lily—would have at least mentioned it to you. Even just to have a laugh over the cops' active imagination."

"I doubt Lily is even aware of the fact Brian imagined someone hit him."

"Not true. According to Brian, Lily was standing right there when it happened. In fact, he landed on the floor."

"That's what Brian says. You're sounding more and more like you think Marlow House is haunted."

Holding her purse, Kelly shrugged. "Frankly, I find the idea that Lily has never once discussed these things with you stranger than the possibility Marlow House may actually be haunted."

"And I find it strange that someone like Brian Henderson is discussing the possibility that some ghost knocked him down."

Kelly shrugged again and turned toward the door leading to the hallway. "I'm going to go take a shower and then write that blog post."

Ian watched his sister leave the living room. A few minutes later, he heard the door to the guest bedroom open and close. He glanced down at Sadie, who had just lifted her head and looked in his direction.

"What do you think, Sadie? You believe in ghosts?" Ian asked with a chuckle.

In response, Sadie cocked her head.

A memory flashed through Ian's mind. It was something that had happened one year earlier at Marlow House—last July Fourth. It was before all the guests had arrived for the open house. Danielle's cousin, Cheryl, had fallen to the floor—it looked as if she had been shoved, and she had insisted it was Danielle who had pushed her.

At the time, Ian was on his way to the kitchen and had only glimpsed the incident from the corner of his eye. He remembered it hadn't appeared as if Danielle had touched her cousin; however, something had pushed her. He had convinced himself it must have been Danielle.

Ian stood up from the sofa. Slipping his hand into the pocket holding the engagement ring, he clutched its box as he wandered to the living room window. The blinds had not yet been drawn. He looked out into the darkness and could see some of the lights in the windows, across the street at Marlow House.

FOUR

The residents of Marlow House were up early on Saturday morning. It was July Fourth, the day of the bed and breakfast's annual open house. The house and yard had been decorated for the festivities the previous day, with an abundance of red, white, and blue bunting, American flags, and sparkly stars. Last year the task of decorating fell primarily on Lily and Ian. But this year, neighbors Chris Johnson and Heather Donovan, along with several of the guests, helped with the decorations.

Danielle and Joanne had spent most of their time focusing on preparing baked goods. This year, Danielle decided on cupcakes. She also made a large batch of homemade potato salad. The rest of the food—hot dogs, watermelon, and potato chips—required less preparation.

Another change from last year, they were charging admission, which would include a tour of Marlow House. Proceeds were being donated to the local schools. Chris and Heather had volunteered to sell tickets at the back gate, while Lily, Danielle, and Ian would be giving the tours.

The vintage croquet set Lily had discovered in the attic the previous year was set up on the side lawn—as it had been during the first open house. Folding tables and chairs were strategically set up along the side and backyard of Marlow House, and several large metal tubs waited to be filled with ice, beer, and soda.

Chris, Heather, Ian, and Kelly had come over after breakfast and had helped set up the tables and chairs, but they had since returned home to get dressed for the party. Joanne, the housekeeper, was alone in the kitchen, slicing cold watermelon into wedges, while the guests of Marlow House sat around the dining room table, playing a board game.

Upstairs, Lily had just finished changing her clothes, while Danielle was in her bedroom with Walt, taking the Missing Thorndike out of the wall safe. When Lily stepped out of her room, she noticed the door to Danielle's room was ajar.

A few moments later, Lily stood in the open doorway of Danielle's bedroom and watched as the Missing Thorndike—an antique necklace bejeweled with diamonds and emeralds—seemingly floated across the room to where Danielle stood. What Lily couldn't see was Walt, who carried the necklace to Danielle. While Lily couldn't see him, she knew he was there.

Danielle looked into the mirror over her dresser and stifled a giggle as she watched the reflection of the necklace floating in midair in her direction. Fortunately, Joanne along with the guests currently staying at Marlow House were all downstairs, so there was no worry one of them might suddenly look into her room. If any of them headed up the stairs, Lily would surely hear them coming.

While Danielle couldn't see Walt in the mirror—a ghost did not have a reflection—if she turned toward the approaching necklace, she would see him. Instead of looking his way, she continued to stare into the mirror while she used her right hand to lift her braid out of the way. She waited for Walt to fasten the necklace around her neck. When she had worn the Missing Thorndike last year, her cousin, Cheryl, had broken its clasp. It had since been repaired.

Lily's gaze moved down from the necklace. With a sigh she said, "I love that dress."

Standing still, Danielle glanced down while Walt fastened the antique piece around her neck. "I wish I could have found a new dress to wear this year, but there just wasn't time."

"That dress is perfect," Lily insisted. It was the same vintage pale green dress Danielle had worn at last year's open house.

"Lily is correct," Walt said after he stepped back from Danielle to get a better look.

Danielle released hold of her fishtail braid. It fell back in place, hanging along the midsection of her back. Still facing the mirror, she gently touched the front of the necklace, gingerly running her fingertips over the priceless gems. Turning to Walt, she smiled. "It's lovely."

"So are you," Walt whispered.

"You look pretty lovely yourself," Lily said as she stepped into the room. She glanced down at her own outfit—white pedal pushers and a crisp red, white and blue blouse. Her dragon tattoo peeked out from under one of the blouse's short sleeves. "Although I feel underdressed."

Danielle laughed. "Hardly, considering we're serving hot dogs, potato salad, and watermelon on paper plates. I have to admit I feel a bit conspicuous dressed like this."

"Which is sort of the point," Lily reminded her. She glanced over to where she imagined Walt was standing. "What is Walt wearing today?"

Danielle looked over to Walt, a mischievous grin turning the corners of her mouth. "His gray pinstripe suit. And I must say, he looks rather dashing."

Walt flashed Danielle a grin.

"I have a feeling that's what he would have worn to a Fourth of July picnic back in his day." Lily smiled. "And I bet the women would be dressing more like you back then too. Well...except for the necklace, of course."

"While that's a lovely dress, tell Lily it's not a style worn back in the '20s," Walt said.

Danielle glanced down at her dress and then turned to look in the mirror. "This is more a style from the fifties."

"I just meant being dressed up in general. People are much more casual today." Lily glanced to the empty desk chair. "Is Walt sitting there?"

Danielle looked to the chair. "No, why?"

In response, Lily sat down on it. In turn, Walt took a seat on the end of the bed while Danielle remained standing, her back now to the dresser mirror.

"I wonder if our blogger is going to come to the open house?" Lily asked.

Absently fondling the necklace, Danielle took a seat on the end of the bed, next to Walt. "I was wondering that myself."

"According to our mystery blogger, he—or she—insists the Missing Thorndike is cursed," Lily said.

"I know." Danielle released hold of the necklace and folded her hands on her lap. "I guess we'll just have to prove him wrong."

"Or her," Lily interjected.

Danielle shrugged. "Whoever. But today is going to be fun and drama free."

"And I promise," Walt added, "this year I will not let you or the necklace out of my sight."

"Unless I go outside," Danielle reminded him.

"Don't go outside," Walt insisted.

"Maybe you shouldn't go outside," Lily suggested. "At least not while you have the necklace on."

Danielle chuckled. "You two crack me up."

Lily frowned. "Why?"

"You've no idea how often you say practically the same thing that Walt has just said."

"It's just because Lily and I are stating the obvious. It would be best if you stay inside for the party. It'll just make it easier for me to keep an eye on the necklace," Walt said.

"You both seem to forget people wear expensive jewelry all the time—out to dinner, to the theater—and nothing happens."

"And sometimes people get hit over the head for a pair of expensive jogging shoes. Anyway, that necklace is supposedly cursed. So why take a chance?" Lily asked.

"I'll be careful. But cursed? You really need to stop reading that blog," Danielle scoffed.

———

THE BLOGGER GLANCED at the clock and cursed. There wasn't much time. A post needed to be made before leaving for the open house. Sitting in front of the computer, the blogger began to type.

RUMOR HAS it Danielle Boatman will be wearing the cursed Missing Thorndike to Marlow House's Anniversary July Fourth Open House. Who will die this year? Because someone will. We don't have long to find out who this year's victim will be—the party starts in just a couple of hours. Will you be there?

Last year, Danielle Boatman's cousin fell victim to the curse. If you'll recall, she took off with the necklace and was murdered. Before she was murdered,

Samuel Hayman swapped the real diamond and emeralds for fakes. The curse caught up with him quickly, landing him in jail. When her killer took the necklace, he ended up dead before the year was out.

Walt Marlow took the necklace before it went to Danielle Boatman. He died young, at the end of a noose, in the attic of Marlow House.

The owner of the necklace before Marlow was Eva Thorndike. And like the others, she died young. Even the men who stole the gems from Eva suffered from the curse.

Danielle Boatman is luckier than the rest, because she is still alive. But she has suffered this last year. Just read some of my previous posts to see what she's been through since she found the Missing Thorndike at Marlow House.

And now she dares to bring out the Missing Thorndike, again tempting fate. And again, someone will die. Mark my words.

Someone will die at Marlow House today.

FIVE

Defeated, Joyce Pruitt plopped down on the recliner and whined, "Please, Mother, don't make me go."

"You're a grown woman, Joyce," Agatha snapped. "I certainly can't *make* you do anything."

"You know what I mean. Just go with Martha. She said you can go with her and Dennis. They have plenty of room in their car. Your wheelchair will fit in their trunk."

"I want us all to go as a family, and if you stay here, then it won't be the entire family, will it?"

"It's too embarrassing; you have to understand."

"What, that my only child is a thief?"

Joyce groaned. "I gave the coins back, Mother."

"No, you didn't. Danielle found them where you'd hid them. And why did you hide them anyway? You were hiding them from me, weren't you? Ungrateful child. After all that I've done for you!" To punctuate her point, Agatha slapped the side of her chair with a cane.

"I explained it to you; I was just surprised to find them in the safe deposit box, and I didn't know what to do."

"What, you couldn't come talk to your mother about it? What are mothers for?"

"I don't want to go over this again. Just go with Martha and enjoy yourself. I'm sure I'm the last person Danielle Boatman wants to see at her party."

"Don't be silly, it's open to the public. Anyone can go," Agatha insisted. "Anyway, I already called Danielle and asked her about you."

"You what?" Joyce closed her eyes and moaned. "Please tell me you didn't!"

"Why would I do that? Because I did call her. And she said you were perfectly welcome to come. She understands about the coins. Not that I understand about the coins. Especially the fact you hid them and didn't tell me until after you went to the police. And I wonder, if you thought your little part in all this would not have gone public, would you have told me? Or would you still be keeping your shameful little secret?"

Her eyes still closed, Joyce shook her head. "I'm so embarrassed."

"Then you should have thought of that before you took Danielle's property out of the bank. Or before you hid them from me. You know, had you brought them home, Danielle would never have found them."

Joyce opened her eyes and stared at her mother. "Are you saying you aren't mad at me for taking the coins, just for not telling you about finding them? And if I would have brought them home, would you have wanted me to keep them? Even after Danielle was arrested?"

"I don't believe Danielle would have been arrested had she not found them. So you see, no one would be hurt, and we could have kept the coins."

Joyce shook her head. "I can't believe you, Mother. You actually think I should have kept them?"

"Don't look at me that way. I'm not the one who walked out of the bank with Danielle Boatman's gold coins."

Joyce stood up and started to say something, but then changed her mind. Taking a deep breath to calm herself, she sat back down and looked at Agatha. "Mother, why do you even want to go to this open house? Just the other day you were saying how ridiculous it was that someone like Danielle Boatman, with all her money, was selling tickets for her barbecue."

"I do think it's ridiculous. If she wants to donate money to the local schools, she has enough money to do it herself. I don't know why she's trying to get us to donate our money. But I guess that's what rich people do."

"So why do you want to go if you feel that way?"

"Because I went last year, and I want to go this year. And I don't have that many years left. And I want my family with me. Is that really so much for an old woman to ask? Are you really so selfish you can't do this one little thing for me?"

———

DENNIS PULLED his car up in front of his mother-in-law's house and parked. Turning off the ignition, he made no attempt to get out of the vehicle. Instead, he looked over to the passenger seat, where his wife, Martha, sat.

"I wish we could have just met them over at Marlow House," Dennis said with a sigh.

"I know." Martha forced a smile. "But Mom's hoping Gran will go with us so she doesn't have to."

With a snort Dennis said, "Yeah, right. Like that's going to happen. Her Majesty is not about to attend the shindig without her court in attendance."

Stifling a giggle, Martha said, "You're probably right. If Gran wants Mom to go, she will. Frankly, I'm kind of glad we're going. It was fun last year. Well, at least it was fun until Danielle's cousin went missing with the necklace, but then it got kinda exciting." Martha reconsidered her words a moment and then let out a sigh. "I guess that sounds sort of shallow, considering her cousin ended up murdered."

"Just a little," Dennis said with a chuckle. "By the way, I don't mind going with you to this thing, but I just wish we didn't have to go with your whole damn family."

Martha unhooked her seatbelt and leaned toward her husband. She planted a kiss on his cheek and then sat back in her seat, still looking at him. "Okay, fess up. Last year, did you really have to work?"

Dennis laughed. "Yes, I really did." He leaned to Martha and kissed her nose.

"But did you *have* to?" She eyed him critically.

Dennis noticed the smile tugging on the corner of Martha's mouth in spite of her serious expression. He grinned. "Alright, I admit it. When the boss asked for volunteers to work the Fourth, I offered."

Martha let out a laugh and then playfully swatted his arm. "I knew it!"

"Hey, we needed the money!" he said mischievously.

"Yeah, right. Maybe we did, but I know the real reason you volunteered."

Noticing movement in the rearview mirror, Dennis turned and looked out the back window. "And here is one reason now."

Martha turned in the direction Dennis was looking. Her oldest brother, Larry, was parking behind them. She waved in his direction, but he didn't wave back. The next moment a second car pulled down the street and parked in front of Dennis's vehicle.

Turning back around in the seat, Dennis unhooked his seatbelt and muttered, "And there is the second reason." In the car ahead of them was Martha's younger brother, Shane.

"Oh, be nice." Martha giggled.

"Hey, I'm always nice." Dennis flashed Martha an exaggerated Cheshire cat grin. He opened his car door.

AT LAST, Larry was alone with his grandmother. He had been hoping to arrive at his mother's house before his siblings. As it turned out, his sister and brother-in-law were already parked in front of her house when he had pulled up, and then his youngest brother arrived. But now they were all in the kitchen with his mother. He figured this would be his last opportunity today to speak with Gran alone. His other brother, Henry, was sure to arrive at any minute, and when that happened, the kiss-up would probably not leave the old witch's side.

"Gran, I need to talk to you about something," Larry said as he sat down beside the elderly woman.

Pursing her lips, Agatha narrowed her eyes and studied her eldest grandson. "When are you going to cut off that ridiculous ponytail?"

Concealing his emotions, he forced a smile. "Actually, I've been thinking of doing that," he lied.

"I wish you would have done it before today," she snapped.

"Gran, I need to ask you about something."

"Go ahead. I'm not stopping you."

"I've been offered a job in Vancouver, at another water company."

"Vancouver?" Agatha frowned.

"It'll give me a chance to spend more time with Curt." Curt was Larry's young son, who a year earlier had moved to Vancouver with his mother after his parents' divorce.

"Are you asking for my permission to go? I told you to fight Cynthia when she wanted to move out of state with your son. But did you listen to me? No." With a grunt, her lips again pursed, Agatha shook her head.

"Gran, you know Cynthia's parents live in Vancouver. I understood why she wanted to be near them."

"And you have family in Frederickport!" Agatha snapped.

"I need to be closer to my son."

"You should have thought of that before you got a divorce." Agatha sat back in her chair and eyed her eldest grandson. "I suppose you'll do what you want. You always do."

"Gran, I'm not here to ask for your permission. I was hoping… that maybe you could give me a loan."

Widening her eyes, Agatha let out a snort. "A loan? What for?"

"It's expensive to move. I'll have to find a place to rent, and that means a down payment. And I have three more months on my current lease here, but if I want the job, I have to move in three weeks."

"You want money?"

"Just a loan. I promise. I'll pay you back as soon as I can."

"And how do you expect to do that? If you were responsible, you'd have something in savings and wouldn't have to come to me."

"It's been a rough year, Gran. With the divorce. Please. Just this once."

Stubbornly she shook her head. "No. Not a penny."

"Won't you even consider it? Don't you even want to know how much I need?" he pleaded.

"It doesn't matter if it's a dime or a million dollars. Like I said, not a penny. You have no business traipsing off to Vancouver, following that woman around. Your home is in Frederickport. And after I die, then I suppose your share of the inheritance will give you the freedom to move wherever you want. But for now, your place is in Frederickport."

"I GUESS I'M GOING," Joyce conceded. She sat at her kitchen table with her daughter and son-in-law, drinking coffee, while her youngest son, Shane, looked through her refrigerator.

"Mom, this is probably for the best." Martha reached across the table and patted the older woman's hand. "You can't avoid Danielle Boatman forever, and if you go today and get this awkward first confrontation out of the way, then you can move on. And Gran did say Danielle was fine with you going today. Seriously, Mom, you helped her out when you went to the police and told them what happened."

"Joyce, Martha is right," Dennis weighed in. "And the fact is, I bet most people would have kept what they found in their safe deposit box."

"I just wish Mother wouldn't have called Danielle." Joyce groaned.

Shane closed the refrigerator and looked over to the kitchen table. "So when are we leaving?"

Joyce glanced up at the wall clock. "We're just waiting until Henry gets here. Then we can go over there together. It's what Mother wants."

"Well, I'm going to use the john," Shane said as he headed for the doorway. Once in the hallway, he walked toward the bathroom, passing the doorway leading to the family room, where Larry sat with his grandmother. Shane paused a moment and listened. It sounded as if they were arguing. With a chuckle, he shook his head and continued down the hall.

He paused a moment at the coat rack, where a purse hung from one of its hooks. He knew it belonged to his mother. Looking down the empty hallway toward the doors leading to the kitchen and family room, he hastily turned his attention back to the handbag. Opening it, he pulled out his mother's wallet. Inside were two twenty-dollar bills. He removed the bills and then paused. Glancing back down the hall, he let out a sigh and then returned one of the twenties while shoving the other one in his pocket. Returning the wallet to his mother's purse, he smiled and continued to the bathroom.

Five minutes later, as Shane exited the bathroom, the front door opened and a male voice shouted, "Hey! Where is everyone?" It was the middle brother, Henry.

By the time Shane reached the doorway leading to the family room, Henry was already inside. Pausing by the doorway, Shane could hear his brother talking to their grandmother.

"Hello, beautiful!" Henry greeted her cheerfully.

"Oh, you scamp, you're always late!" Agatha chided, yet she didn't sound angry.

"I have to make an entrance. But there was no one to greet me," Henry said with faux disappointment. "Where is everyone?"

Standing outside the doorway, out of sight, Shane continued to eavesdrop. By the voices and conversation, he gathered Larry was no longer in the room with their grandmother.

"I imagine all in the kitchen. They just left me here all alone," Agatha said with a pout.

"I'm here now; you won't be alone."

"When we go to Marlow House, I really want to see the upstairs this year. I wasn't able to last year. But your mother insists it will be too dangerous for me to try the stairs."

"I tell you what, Gran, why don't you let me help you up the stairs. I'll bring up your wheelchair and give you the tour."

"You can carry the wheelchair up the stairs?"

"Sure, Gran. For you, anything."

SIX

Tucked into the right front pocket of Ian's tan slacks was a small velvet pouch holding the engagement ring. He had been tempted to leave the ring at home, but with Kelly staying with him for the weekend, he feared she might stumble across it. Ian wanted Lily to be the first one to see her ring, not his sister.

Standing on the front porch of Marlow House, Ian knocked on the door. The gesture was a mere formality; he didn't intend to wait for someone to answer. If unlocked, he would walk right in. Just as he reached for the door, it opened. Standing before him was the youngest of Police Chief MacDonald's sons, six-year-old Evan.

"Hey, Evan," Ian greeted as he walked inside the house.

"Where's Sadie?" Evan glanced around Ian.

Ian closed the door behind him. "I'm leaving her home today."

Evan's expression fell into a disappointed pout. "First Walt is busy and now Sadie's not coming," he grumbled under his breath.

"Walt is busy?" Ian asked with a frown.

Evan froze a moment and then looked up to Ian, his eyes wide. "I like Sadie," he stammered.

Cocking his head, Ian studied Evan. "What did you mean about Walt is busy?"

"Nothing. I didn't mean nothing." Evan shook his head. "Everyone is in the living room." Evan turned abruptly and ran down the hall, racing for the kitchen.

In the living room Ian found Danielle, Chris Johnson, Chief MacDonald and the chief's oldest son, Eddy. Who he didn't see was Walt, who lounged casually against the fireplace mantel, smoking a thin cigar.

"Hey, Ian. Lily's upstairs," Danielle greeted him when Ian walked in. She remained seated on the sofa. "She should be down in a minute. Where's your sister?"

Ian greeted both the chief and Chris with a quick handshake and then said, "She's across the street, waiting for Joe. She plans to come over with him."

The chief glanced to the doorway leading to the hallway. "I wonder where Evan took off to."

"Last I saw he was off to the kitchen. Probably to get one of those cupcakes," Ian said with a chuckle as he took a seat.

"Can I go see where he is, Dad?" Eddy asked.

MacDonald gently swatted his son's back. "Go ahead."

"When I was talking to Evan a minute ago, he said something about Walt being busy."

Eddy, who had dashed to the doorway, paused and looked back at Ian.

"What do you think he was talking about?" Ian asked.

Danielle and Chris exchanged glances while Walt listened intently.

"I bet he's talking about Walt Marlow's ghost," Eddy blurted out.

The adults in the room all turned to Eddy, who stood by the doorway, preparing to dash from the room.

"Ghost?" Ian asked.

"Enough, Eddy," MacDonald scolded.

"Well, he asked, Dad. And Evan thinks he can see Walt Marlow's ghost."

"You heard what I said, enough, Eddy," MacDonald repeated, his voice sterner.

With a shrug, Eddy dashed from the room.

"What was that about?" Ian asked.

MacDonald shook his head. "Just boys and their imagination."

"Where's Sadie?" Danielle asked abruptly.

"You knew Sadie wasn't coming over," Walt said with a chuckle. "Trying to change the subject?"

"That's what Evan asked," Ian said as he sat down. "I'm beginning to think people only like me for my dog."

"When I looked out the front window, I saw you crossing the street," Chris told Ian. "I said something about you being on your way here, and Evan ran out of the room to greet you at the door. But I suspect you're right, in this case, he was more interested in greeting Sadie." Chris chuckled.

Abruptly changing the subject, the chief said, "Hey, did you hear Alan Kissinger left town?"

"Left town? Isn't he still a person of interest for what happened at the bank?" Danielle asked. "Not to mention what his cousin did here."

"We know where he went. The bank transferred him to another branch. After what happened here, I guess they felt they needed to move him."

"Why not fire him?" Chris asked.

"I don't think they really have anything substantial to fire him on. Even the FBI hasn't been able to link what happened with the safe deposit boxes directly to Kissinger. But according to Susan, the new job is not a promotion. He's now an assistant manager," the chief explained.

"So that's who told you?" Danielle asked.

"Yes. She called me last night and let me know."

"Maybe he had nothing to do with the safe deposit boxes, but I still believe he's the one who sent his safe-cracking cousin after the Missing Thorndike."

"Ahh, you mean the cursed Missing Thorndike?" Chris teased.

"Oh hush," Danielle scolded.

"Well, if you think about it, if Kissinger was responsible for sending his cousin after the necklace, and he has since been demoted, perhaps there is something to that story about a curse," Chris suggested.

"I suspect the bad luck has more to do with people making poor choices and then having to deal with the consequences of those choices. What is that old saying, crime doesn't pay?" Ian countered.

Chris shrugged. "A curse sounds more interesting."

"I'm not sure what poor choice I made to get myself killed," Walt muttered. "I take that back—I married a gold digger."

Chris glanced at Walt and smiled.

Ian turned to Danielle and eyed the heirloom necklace. "The

Thorndike looks great on you, by the way. You should wear it all the time."

Danielle laughed. "Right."

MARLOW HOUSE'S July Fourth celebration was formally scheduled to begin in less than thirty minutes. Joanne was in the kitchen, completing some last-minute tasks, while Evan and Eddy helped her haul cans of sodas to the buckets of ice already set up outside. The guests staying at the bed and breakfast had finished their board game and had since taken off for a walk along the beach before the party. Unlike others attending the barbeque, they wouldn't have to pay for an admission ticket.

Lily still hadn't come downstairs, so Ian decided to see what was taking her so long. After he left the living room and Danielle was confident he was out of earshot, she looked at the chief and asked, "Does Eddy know about Walt?"

"Not exactly," the chief said in a low voice. His gaze flashed to the open doorway Ian had just exited through.

"I was wondering that myself," Walt said.

"Eddy overheard Evan and I discussing Walt. He asked me about it, which caught me by surprise. I had no idea he had heard us talking," the chief explained.

"When was this?" Chris asked.

"Just the other night. Earlier that evening, at dinner, I was talking to the boys about coming here this afternoon for the barbeque, and then later when I was alone talking with Evan, Eddy overheard."

"What did you say exactly?" Danielle asked.

"Enough for Eddy to get the gist of the conversation—that Marlow House has its own ghost."

"Why do they always have to say ghost?" Walt asked.

Chris glanced over to Walt and rolled his eyes. "Because that's what you are, Walt."

"Eddy knows?" Danielle groaned.

"Not exactly. I told Eddy he misunderstood the conversation. I told him that was what normally happens when you eavesdrop on someone. You think you know what they're talking about, when you really don't."

36

"And he believed that?" Chris asked.

MacDonald shrugged. "I thought he did. At least, until a few minutes ago."

IAN WAS on his way to the staircase leading to the second floor when he spied Evan stepping out from the kitchen, en route to the downstairs bathroom. Stopping in the middle of the hallway, he waited for the boy to reach him.

Noticing the chocolate frosting on the edge of Evan's mouth, Ian said with a grin, "You've been sampling the cupcakes, haven't you?" Ian pointed to the corner of his mouth.

The six-year-old stopped a few feet from Ian. His tongue swiped away the chocolate residue. "Joanne let us lick the frosting bowl."

"Lucky kid." Ian smiled. Just as the boy was preparing to take off, Ian impulsively crooked his finger at Evan, beckoning him to come closer. When the boy complied, Ian whispered, "It's okay, I know about you and Walt."

Evan's eyes widened. "You can see him too?"

Startled by Evan's response, Ian concealed his reaction and stammered, "Not exactly. But you can?"

"Lily told you, didn't she?" Evan whispered.

Lily? Resisting the urge to frown, Ian forced a smile and asked, "So you like Walt?"

"Oh yes! And you know, so does Sadie. She loves coming over here to play with him. But Walt has to guard Danielle and the necklace today, so I guess that's why Sadie couldn't come over, right?"

"Umm…yes, that's right."

"When Danielle puts the necklace back in the safe and Walt doesn't have to watch it, can Sadie come over then?"

"Ummm…sure…I guess so."

"Good!" Evan beamed. "I gotta go to the bathroom."

"Okay, but one thing, Evan. Can I ask you a favor?"

Evan blinked several times and nodded. "Sure, I guess. What?"

"I really don't want to get Lily in trouble for telling me. And then she'll get mad at me for saying something."

Evan grinned. "You don't want anyone to know you know about Walt, huh?"

"Something like that. But I don't want anyone to know I know

37

about you, either. Like I said, I don't want Lily mad at me for opening my big mouth."

Evan nodded solemnly. "I understand. They told me I need to keep the secret because people won't understand. I don't want Lily to be mad at you. I won't tell anyone. Promise."

"Thanks, Evan. I appreciate it."

Evan flashed Ian a wide smile and then turned and dashed to the downstairs bathroom.

Standing alone in the hallway, Ian stared dumbly at the now closed bathroom door, which Evan had just slammed shut behind him. Shaking his head in disbelief, Ian muttered, "What kind of game are they playing?"

SEVEN

"I think something's bothering Ian," Lily told Danielle later that afternoon. The two were alone in the kitchen. Alone if one didn't count Walt, who lingered nearby, keeping a close eye on the Missing Thorndike. Guests had been coming and going for several hours already, and Joanne was outside offering a tray of cupcakes to the people sitting in the side yard.

Danielle paused from her task of filling the pitcher with ice cubes and glanced over to Lily. "What do you mean?"

"I don't know, exactly." Lily narrowed her eyes, as if she hoped to see something that was just beyond her reach. "He just isn't acting himself. Did he say anything when he got here?"

Danielle dumped the ice in the pitcher and then turned to Lily and said, "There was just that thing about Walt."

"Walt?" Lily glanced briefly over to where she imagined Walt was standing—if one judged by the light scent of cigar smoke lingering in the air.

Danielle then went on to tell her about Ian's question when he arrived, along with Eddy's response.

"Hmm, that might explain why I found him staring at Walt's portrait earlier today, when he was giving someone a tour of the house," Lily muttered. She then looked at Danielle and asked, "Do you think he suspects Walt's ghost is here?"

"Spirit," Walt corrected. Unfortunately for Walt, Lily couldn't hear him.

Danielle laughed and poured tea into the pitcher. "I seriously doubt it. From Ian's perspective it was nothing but silly talk from a couple of boys. Trust me, when you start talking ghosts, people rarely take it seriously. If something's bothering him, I doubt it's that."

"I suppose you're right," Lily muttered, wandering over to the kitchen window and looking out to the side yard. She spied Ian standing by the barbecue in the outside kitchen, talking to Adam Nichols, who was roasting hot dogs. Beyond the outside kitchen she noticed Joyce Pruitt sitting at a table with her mother and two of her sons.

"I can't believe Joyce showed up," Lily said.

"I don't think she wanted to. I have to admit I feel sorry for her. She looked pretty uncomfortable when she got here."

Walt wandered over to the kitchen window and stood next to Lily. He looked outside.

"You think she asked her mother to call you, see if she could come?" Lily asked.

"No. My gut feeling, Agatha made that call on her own. I don't think Joyce wants to be here. Which is too bad, because I really don't have any hard feelings for her. Heck, Adam is out there roasting hot dogs for us, and if those gold coins ended up in his safe deposit box, we know what he'd do." Danielle laughed.

"You don't think he'd give them back?" Lily asked in a teasing voice.

"Only if his grandmother made him." Danielle snickered.

Lily grabbed the pitcher of tea Danielle had prepared. "I'll take this outside, since you're confined to the house."

A few minutes later, Danielle was alone in the kitchen with Walt. She stood with him by the window and looked outside.

"I think maybe I'm being a little silly staying inside. I really don't think someone's going to run up and grab the necklace off me."

Walt waved his right hand and his cigar vanished. He turned to Danielle. "You're probably right. But I must admit, I've been enjoying spending the day with you."

BEER IN HAND, Ian stood near the barbecue and watched as Lily walked from table to table, refilling ice tea glasses while chatting to the various guests. Beyond the tables, near the open gate leading from the side yard to the front street, Chris and Heather sat at a card table, selling tickets. Although, it had been over thirty minutes since anyone new had arrived.

He then noticed the chief at the other end of the yard, chatting with Joe Morelli, Brian Henderson, and his sister, Kelly. By the empty paper plates in their hands, he suspected they had just finished eating.

Ian had spent the last couple of hours giving tours of Marlow House, but now most everyone was outside, enjoying the food and pleasant weather. Should someone want a tour, Danielle was still inside.

"I haven't seen Melony today. I thought she'd be here," Ian asked Adam.

"She had to fly back to New York. It was kind of spur of the moment. Something to do with one of her past cases."

Ian nodded at Adam's answer and then glanced over at the house. "I'm surprised Danielle didn't arrange to have someone stay in the house with her."

"What do you mean?" Adam asked as he added more hot dogs to the grill.

"She's wearing the Missing Thorndike. I remember last year Joe kept an eye on her the entire time—and even then, Cheryl managed to get away with the necklace. I asked Lily what they planned to do about security this year, and she said the chief was going to be here, and Danielle planned to stay in the house and not go outside. For whatever reason, they felt she'd just be vulnerable outside. But she was inside last year when she lost the necklace."

"To be fair, she handed the necklace to her cousin. I don't think that's going to happen this year. And she probably feels safe with all those cameras," Adam suggested.

Ian took a swig of beer and then asked, "What cameras?"

"The security cameras she has installed all over the house." Adam poked the hot dogs with the end of a long barbeque fork, rolling them from one side to another.

"When did Danielle get security cameras?"

Adam shrugged. "She's had them forever. Of course, she's never come out and admitted it; I just figured you probably knew about them."

Ian shook his head. "No. This is the first I've heard about security cameras. And I've been all over the house. What makes you think she has security cameras set up?"

Glancing around to see who was within earshot, Adam moved closer to Ian and said under his breath, "I know you know about the time Bill and I...ummm..."

"Smashed the library window and broke into Marlow House?" Ian said with a chuckle.

"In all fairness, Bill broke the damn window. That wasn't part of the plan. And we did fix it. We didn't take anything. It was a stupid prank, I admit."

"But what does that have to do with security cameras?"

"How do you think Danielle knew it was us? Had to be security cameras, like the one I had in my office. Remember? That one caught Renton planting evidence."

"So you're saying Danielle knew you and Bill broke in because it was all captured by a security camera?"

"Had to have been it. After all, she even knew what shirt Bill was wearing that day. As far as I know, there were no eye witnesses. And when I've asked her about it, she's never denied it."

With a frown, Ian stared across the yard at Lily, who stood by a table, chatting cheerfully with Adam's grandmother, Marie Nichols, and the widow of Steve Klein, Beverly.

How is it possible Marlow House is rigged with security cameras, and I not know? Why wouldn't Lily have said something?

Absently, Ian shoved his free hand into his pocket holding the engagement ring. He squeezed the pouch briefly and could feel the hardness of the object inside. Since buying the engagement ring, he hadn't experienced a moment of doubt. At least, not until now.

IAN HELPED himself to one of the hot dogs. After filling his paper plate with a scoop of potato salad and a handful of chips, he walked to Lily, who was coming in his direction, carrying an empty pitcher.

"Have you had anything to eat yet?" he asked when they met.

"You mean aside from cupcakes?" Lily asked with a laugh. "No. But I'm not really hungry."

"You want to join me anyway?" Ian nodded toward one of the tables with some empty seats.

Standing on tiptoes, Lily kissed his cheek. "I'll be back out in a minute. I need to take this in the house. But start eating. Dani might make me do something when she sees me."

Smiling weakly, Ian nodded.

Instead of heading for the house, Lily paused a moment and studied Ian. "Hey, Ian, you okay? You seem a little...I don't know, distant today. Is something wrong?"

Ian considered her question a moment and then smiled. "No. I just have a lot on my mind lately."

"Maybe we can talk about it tonight at the fireworks display— just you and me. Okay?" Lily asked.

Ian smiled. "Yeah, that might be a good idea."

IAN ENDED up sitting alone with Brian Henderson. When he first arrived at the table, Kelly and Joe were sitting with Brian, but just as Ian sat down, Joe asked Kelly if she wanted to play croquet, a new game was about to start.

"They give you time off from playing tour guide?" Brian asked. He leaned back in the folding chair; the used paper plate sitting before him held only a crumpled paper napkin.

"Seems like everyone has moved outside. Did you take a tour with Danielle or Lily?" Ian picked up his hot dog and took a bite.

"I've seen the house. Anyway, I'd rather stay out here. That place always creeps me out."

Ian set his hot dog back on his paper plate. "Yeah, Kelly was telling me about that last night. Said you and Joe have experienced some strange things in Marlow House."

"Considering all the time you've spent over here, I imagine you've got some stories."

Ian shrugged. "Not really."

"Well, maybe Walt Marlow's ghost just likes you better," Brian said with a laugh.

"So that's who you think it is? Walt Marlow's ghost?" Ian asked.

Brian looked up at the house for a moment, his attention on the attic. He then glanced over to the side gate, where Chris sat with Heather at the folding table.

"In all seriousness? I have no idea what's really behind the strange things that have happened. But whatever it is, I'm not sure it's even about Marlow House per se."

Ian frowned. "What do you mean?"

Brian nodded toward Heather and Chris. "Take Heather Donovan, for example. She's an odd one. She's claimed she can see ghosts—and then later retracts her claims. And her ghosts aren't confined to Marlow House. Hell, maybe it's just something in the local drinking water." Brian picked up his can of beer and took a swig.

AGATHA PINE SAT with her family at one of the tables set up on the concrete patio portion of the side yard. A table on the lawn was not an option—not with Agatha's wheelchair.

She enjoyed the stream of guests, who while passing her way, stopped and chatted with her for a moment, inquiring on her overall health and remarking on how well she looked. They often commented on the fact she seemed to always be surrounded by her family—her daughter and grandchildren—which was of course a testimony to what a fine and grand woman she was.

"I'm sorry about having to borrow money from you," Agatha overheard Joyce say to Dennis.

"Don't worry about it," Dennis insisted. "I planned to pay for our own tickets anyway. You certainly didn't have to pay for all of us."

"I promise I'll pay you back," Joyce told him. "I swear I had forty dollars in my wallet."

"If you weren't so scatterbrained, Joyce, you wouldn't always be finding yourself in these embarrassing situations," Agatha snapped. Choosing not to reply, Joyce slumped down in her chair and took a sip of her soda.

A moment later, Evan MacDonald ran toward their table, en route to the croquet set on the far side of the yard. Just as he was about to pass Agatha, she reached out and snatched him by the arm, bringing him to an abrupt halt.

Startled, Evan, slightly out of breath, stood still and looked at the elderly woman through wide eyes.

"It's very rude to run, boy," Agatha snapped, her right hand still clutching his arm. Narrowing her eyes, she studied him. "You're the chief's youngest boy, aren't you?"

Evan silently nodded the affirmative.

Releasing his arm, she gave him a little shove and said, "You go tell your father to teach you some manners!"

When Evan didn't move, she gave him another shove. "Go, boy, do as I say!"

———

"WHAT'S WRONG, EVAN?" MacDonald asked his son when the boy appeared by his side, clutching his arm. The two stood under a tree near the croquet set.

Evan quickly told him what had just happened with the elderly woman. MacDonald looked over to the table where Agatha Pine sat with her family. She scowled in his direction, her lips pursed.

"Ahh, Agatha Pine. That explains it." MacDonald smiled and gently tousled his son's hair.

"Dad, why is she in that wheelchair?"

"Agatha has been in that wheelchair for about a year now. I suspect that's why she takes special offense to someone who can still use his legs."

"You mean she can't run anymore?"

"Or walk. From what I understand, the only way she can get around without that chair is if she holds onto someone's arm. Was a time she used a cane. But I don't think she can even do that anymore."

EIGHT

"I want to take that tour of the house," Agatha announced. "I want to see what's upstairs." She sat alone at the table with her daughter. Her grandchildren had all since wandered off, each saying they would return shortly.

"I told you, Mother, it's too dangerous. We can't get you upstairs in the wheelchair."

"You can help me walk up the stairs. You help me get around when we're at home."

"That's different. Helping you get into the bathroom is not the same thing as walking up an entire staircase."

"Two staircases. I want to see the attic. That's where Walt Marlow was killed. That's where Danielle found the Missing Thorndike."

"Now you're just being ridiculous."

"Don't be rude, Joyce. I can walk up the stairs if you help me."

"Even if I could help you up the stairs, you expect to hold onto me while you tour the entire second and third floor?"

"Henry said he could carry the wheelchair upstairs for me."

"Then I suppose you should talk to Henry about it when he gets back," Joyce suggested.

Fortunately for Joyce, Henry was one of the first of her children to return to the table. In his hand he carried a chocolate cupcake, which he set before his grandmother.

"Oh, Henry, how sweet!" Agatha gushed.

"That looks good," Joyce murmured, eyeing the cupcake. She looked up to her son, "Did you bring me one?"

Henry pointed across the patio to Joanne, who carried a platter of cupcakes. "Joanne's handing them out." He didn't offer to get his mother one.

"Henry, when I finish this, will you please take me on that tour you promised me? Your mother refuses."

"Sure, Gran." Henry leaned down and planted a kiss on her weathered cheek. "You enjoy your cupcake and let me run to the bathroom, and when I get back, I'll take you on the tour. No wheelchair is going to stop my gran!"

"Why can't you be more like Henry?" Agatha asked Joyce before shoving the cupcake into her mouth.

Twenty minutes later, Agatha had long since finished her cupcake, yet there was no sign of Henry. Joyce had retrieved a cupcake for herself and was just sitting down to eat it when Agatha said, "Wheel me into the house to find Henry."

"I'm going to eat this first, Mother," Joyce insisted.

"You could have eaten that when I had mine. I want to go now."

Joyce let out a sigh yet did not stand back up. Instead, she took a bite of the cupcake.

"If you must eat it, eat it while you wheel me into the house."

"You can just wait a few minutes. It's not going to kill you." Joyce leaned back in her chair and slowly nibbled the cupcake.

"You're just being insolent."

And you're just being demanding, as usual.

Before Joyce finished the cupcake, her eldest son showed up at the table.

"Where have you been?" Agatha snapped. "Why has everyone deserted me?"

"I'm still here," Joyce reminded as she dabbed the corners of her mouth with a napkin.

"I was checking out the house. I went upstairs to the attic. It's pretty interesting," Larry explained as he took a seat. "I didn't tour the house last year. They have some great antiques upstairs. I bet Henry is salivating over them. Although, nothing needs refinishing. They're in great shape."

"That's what I want to do. Did you see Henry? He promised he would take me!"

"No, I didn't see him. You want to go upstairs?" Larry asked.

"Your mother won't take me," she grumbled.

"Your grandmother seriously expects me to help her up the stairs and then carry the wheelchair up two flights so she can see the house. There is no way. I'd end up falling and killing myself."

"Henry said he'd take me," Agatha said stubbornly.

"Yeah, well, Henry is great at making promises. Not so great at carrying through," Larry muttered. He then looked at his grandmother and a thought popped into his head. "Ahh...Gran...you want me to help you?"

"You mean you'll help me up the stairs? Carry my wheelchair up?"

"Umm...sure. But like Mom says, it's a little dangerous. I don't want you to get hurt."

"I'm not going to get hurt," Agatha snapped.

"You sure you want to do this? Even if it's a little risky for you?"

"Don't be silly. It's not risky. Just a little inconvenient. Which is why your mother refuses to help me. God forbid I inconvenience her."

Joyce rolled her eyes, yet reserved comment. She watched as Larry wheeled her mother into the house. When they were no longer in sight, she stood up.

AFTER FINISHING A GAME OF CROQUET, Evan decided to go back into the house and see what Walt and Danielle were doing. In the kitchen he found Joanne and several other adults. They were sitting around the table, chatting.

From the kitchen he dashed to the library. A number of people were lingering there, some sitting, some looking over the impressive collection of leather-bound books, and others were discussing the massive portraits of Walt Marlow and his wife.

"Do you think that's what Walt Marlow really looked like?" one of them asked.

Evan wanted to say *yes!* But he withheld comment and took off to check the other rooms on the main floor. Just as he dashed out into the hallway, he almost ran headlong into an older woman who was walking in his direction. It was Agatha Pine. They both stopped and stared at each other.

"You're running again!" she snapped. "What did I tell you about running? Rude child."

Confused, Evan looked around yet didn't see what he was looking for. "You're walking," he stammered.

She cocked her head for a moment and looked down at her feet. "Oh. So I am."

"Where's your wheelchair?"

"My wheelchair?" She frowned and glanced around. "I don't know. It has to be around here somewhere."

"You're walking!" Evan exclaimed.

"Yes. And you're running. And running in the house is even worse than running outside. I'll have to have a talk with your father about this." She then turned and marched down the hall and into the kitchen.

"Oh crud, I'm going to get in trouble," Evan muttered, hanging his head and letting out a defeated sigh.

Evan's worries were put aside the next moment when a loud shout came bellowing down from the second floor.

"Help! Someone help! Quick!"

Following the shout, people ran out into the hallway from all the rooms—the library, kitchen, living room, parlor, and even the bathroom.

"What's wrong?" Danielle asked with a shout as she sprinted up the stairway leading to the second floor.

For Evan, he found the answer to one of his previous questions. There, sitting at the foot of the stairs leading to the second floor, was Agatha Pine's empty wheelchair.

***

WHEN DANIELLE AND THE OTHERS—THOSE who were in Marlow House and heard the cries—reached the second floor, they found Shane Pruitt kneeling by the crumpled body of Agatha Pine. At the foot of the stairway leading down from the attic, Agatha's motionless body lay sprawled on the second floor.

"Oh my god, I think she's dead!" Shane said in a panic as his hands moved from his grandmother's wrists to the base of her throat, searching for a pulse.

Kneeling by Agatha, Danielle rechecked the woman's pulse as Shane stood up, backing away from his grandmother. Still crouched on the floor by Agatha's side, Danielle looked up. "Someone call 911. We need to get the chief up here."

Taking a quick inventory of those now standing around her, gawking, Danielle spied Joyce standing toward the back of the crowd. She made no attempt to rush to her mother, but instead stood speechless, watching.

AGATHA PINE WAS DEAD. It appeared as if her neck was broken. But they would have to wait to see what the coroner had to say before determining the exact cause of death.

Everyone who had been in the house at the time they found Agatha's body was asked to wait in either the living room or library. While no one seemed anxious to leave—curious to find out what had happened—MacDonald instructed Brian to keep an eye on the people in the living room while Joe stayed with those in the library.

Chief MacDonald sat alone in the parlor with Shane Pruitt, listening to his account of the story.

"I was up in the attic, just checking it out. And then when I came back downstairs, I found Gran. She was just lying there." Combing his fingers through his hair, he shook his head and hunched over, as if he might get ill.

"Do you know how she got there?" the chief asked.

Shane shook his head. "I have no idea. Last time I saw Gran, she was outside with Mom, sitting at the table in her wheelchair. I don't even know how she got up those stairs. No way could she do it by herself."

"And you didn't help her up the stairs?" MacDonald asked.

"Me? No."

THE SECOND PERSON MacDonald interviewed in the parlor was Ben Smith. Ben, an elderly man who donated a good portion of his time to the local museum, was one of the first people Danielle had met when moving to Frederickport.

"I was using the upstairs bathroom," Ben explained. "I thought I heard something. Maybe someone slamming a door. My hearing is not great. When I stepped out into the hallway, I saw Agatha by the foot of the stairs and her grandson came running down from the attic and started shouting."

"I CAN'T BELIEVE this is happening," Joyce muttered when it was her turn to talk to the chief. She sat in one of the chairs facing the sofa, her hands nervously fidgeting with the straps of her purse.

"How do you think your mother got up those stairs by herself?" MacDonald asked.

Joyce looked up from her lap into MacDonald's eyes. "Well, she couldn't. Not by herself. I told her it was too dangerous. I warned her it was not a good idea. But Henry told her he would help her up the stairs. He even offered to carry up her wheelchair."

"Henry brought her upstairs? From what I understand, Henry was in the downstairs bathroom when his brother started shouting."

Joyce shrugged. "Well, Henry said he was going to the bathroom. He didn't come back to get Mother, so Larry took her."

"Larry took her upstairs?" the chief asked.

Joyce nodded. "Yes. What does Larry say happened?"

"From what I understand, Larry isn't here," MacDonald explained.

Joyce frowned. "What do you mean? Of course he's here. I just saw him not thirty minutes ago."

"According to your daughter, she saw her older brother drive off shortly before we found your mother."

"I DON'T BELIEVE THIS," Danielle groaned when she walked into the parlor with Evan. She closed the door behind them.

"Is Walt with you?" MacDonald asked.

"No. He's looking through the house, seeing if he can find any sign of Agatha." Danielle plopped down on the sofa.

The chief noticed Danielle was no longer wearing the Missing Thorndike.

"Did you put it back in the safe?" the chief asked, nodding toward Danielle.

Absently touching her throat where the necklace had been just minutes earlier, Danielle nodded. "I figured with all that's going on, it was foolish to deal with the Thorndike."

"Have you seen her?" MacDonald asked.

"I did, Dad," Evan piped up.

Danielle looked over to MacDonald. "When we were waiting for you to finish up in here, Evan found me and whispered what he thought he saw."

MacDonald looked at his son. "What he thought he saw?"

"I didn't know she was a ghost at the time," Evan explained.

"It must have been right after the fall," Danielle said.

Evan then went on to tell his father about his encounter with Agatha.

"She didn't happen to say what happened to her, did she?" he asked his son.

Evan shook his head. "I didn't even know she was dead."

"I just hope Walt doesn't find her and she has moved on. I don't mean to speak ill of the dead, but I really don't need a grouchy spirit like Agatha Pine hanging around Marlow House," Danielle said.

"Not so quick. It would help if you could talk to her before she moves on," the chief said.

"Why?" Danielle asked with a frown.

"Because I don't think this was an accident. I think Agatha was murdered."

NINE

W alt stood with Heather and Chris by the foot of the staircase on the first floor of Marlow House. Upstairs, the police had directed the curious observers to go downstairs, and now most of those had already been allowed to go home. By the commotion, Walt suspected they were preparing to bring Agatha's body down.

"So no sign of our recently departed?" Walt asked as he waved his hand for a cigar.

Heather shook her head, and Chris said, "Just Evan. And I suspect that was right after the fall."

"I hope that old witch doesn't end up at my house," Heather groaned. Twirling one of her jet-black braids between her fingers, she absently took its tip in her mouth and began to chew.

Chris turned to Heather and shook his head. "Pretty cold, Heather. The poor woman just died."

"Oh please," Heather scoffed. "She was a miserable woman in life, and I can't imagine death will rehabilitate her. If anything, it could embolden her to ramp up her bitchiness. Plus, she lived a long life. If she was my grandmother, I would have been tempted to shove her down some stairs a long time ago."

"Remind me not to piss you off," Chris muttered, and then he asked, "You think she was murdered?" Chris looked up the staircase.

"The chief seems to think that," Walt said. He then glanced

over at Heather, who continued to chomp on her braid. "I'm pretty sure there's plenty of food in the kitchen, if you're hungry."

Flashing Walt a scowl, Heather dropped the braid. It was no longer in her mouth. "Well, I know what I'm going to do."

"What's that?" Chris asked.

"As soon as I go home, I'm going to cleanse my house of spirits."

"Bringing out the oils?" Walt asked with a chuckle.

"Go ahead and laugh. It works. Just be grateful Danielle won't let me set them up here," Heather retorted. With a flounce, she turned from the pair and headed for the front door.

"How do you work with her all day?" Walt asked as he watched Heather disappear out the front door.

Chris shrugged. "She's not that bad. She's actually a pretty good employee."

"I thought she irritated the hell out of you."

"So do you. But I don't hold that against you." Chris grinned.

Rolling his eyes, Walt shook his head and looked back up the stairs again. He took a puff off his thin cigar. "So if it was murder, which one of her family bumped her off?"

"You didn't see anything, did you?" Chris asked.

"I told you. I was with Danielle in the living room, keeping an eye on the necklace."

"My gut says it's the grandson who found her. But supposedly the other grandson is the one who was bringing her upstairs, and he's missing." Chris noticed the chief walking toward them with Joyce by his side. When the pair reach them, Chris smiled sadly at Joyce and reached out, giving her arm a reassuring pat.

"Go on up. I'll be right there," the chief told Joyce. She gave him a nod and started up the stairs. MacDonald looked at Chris, and when Joyce was out of earshot, he said, "Please tell me the reason you look like you're talking to yourself is that Walt is standing with you."

"He is." Chris glanced around, now concerned someone else might have observed him seemingly talking to himself.

"Walt, I've told each family member they can see Agatha before they take her. Can you please get up there and listen to what they say?"

"Playing private dick? I can do that." Walt vanished.

With a snort, Chris said under his breath, "Oh brother, why

does he have to say something like that and then disappear before I have a chance to retort? What a waste." Chris chuckled.

"Is he still here?" the chief asked.

"He just left," Chris told him. "I suspect he went upstairs, playing *private dick*." Chris chuckled again.

"Private dick?"

"Nothing, just something Walt said." Chris chuckled again.

"I need to get up there to tell them to give Joyce some privacy." The chief dashed up the stairs.

———

"I DON'T KNOW if this day could get any stranger," Ian told Lily. He stood with her in the living room doorway, looking out into the hallway.

"So much for Dani's wish for a drama-free day," Lily said with a sigh.

"A few minutes ago I heard the chief telling Agatha's grandkids they could each go upstairs and have a few minutes alone with the body before they bring her down," Ian said.

"So?"

Ian shook his head. "That just seems odd. I wouldn't think they would want to see her like that, and normally those kinds of good-byes are saved for the viewing at the funeral home. But maybe he wants to see how they react."

"What do you mean, see how they react?" Lily asked with a frown.

"Maybe this wasn't just an accident."

"Yeah…I kind of got that drift myself," Lily muttered. "But to push your grandmother down the stairs, pretty cold."

"Or maybe your mother," Ian suggested.

"Joyce is really the only one of that bunch that I know, and I really don't see her doing something like that, but she did take Dani's coins."

"And did you notice Chris a few minutes ago? He was standing by the stairs, talking to himself."

Lily shrugged. "Chris often talks to himself."

Ian looked at Lily through narrowed eyes. "He does? I never noticed that before."

After a few moments of silence, Lily said, "So much for fireworks."

"You don't want to go?" Slipping his hand into his pocket, he touched the tip of the pouch holding the engagement ring.

"No. Not really in the mood." She turned to Ian. "Did you still want to go?"

Ian removed his hand from his pocket. "No…not really."

"I think I'll stay here and help Dani," Lily told him, thinking of the possibility Agatha's spirit might show up.

"I'll stay and help too," he offered.

"No," Lily said a little too abruptly. She then forced a smile and reached out, patting Ian's hand. "Why don't you go out to dinner with your sister and Joe? They asked us to go, and since Brian is going with them, it's not like you'll be a third wheel or anything."

"You want me to be Brian's date?" Ian asked dryly.

"Don't be silly." Standing on her tiptoes, Lily planted a kiss on his cheek.

Ian eyed her curiously. He made no attempt to return the kiss.

WALT WAS DYING FOR A CIGAR. *Not dying exactly*, Walt thought, *considering I'm already dead*. In spite of his urge, he resisted, worried that the smoke might distract Joyce, and considering his close proximity to her, there was no way she wouldn't notice.

The chief had come upstairs and asked all his people to go on downstairs, to allow each member of the family to see the body before it was removed. If anyone thought the request unusual, they kept it to themselves.

Joyce had been standing next to her mother's body for several minutes, simply looking down. So far, she hadn't said anything, and if she continued in her silence, Walt imagined the chief would be disappointed. But then, Joyce stepped closer to Agatha and leaned down to the lifeless body.

When Joyce reached for the dead woman's hand, Walt expected her to hold it. He hadn't expected her to take her mother's pulse and then drop the hand as if it were a piece of litter to be discarded.

"I just needed to be sure you're really dead. It would be just like you to get our hopes up and then you shout surprise and ruin everything," Joyce whispered to her mother. "God, I'm glad I came today." Flashing the corpse a look of contempt, Joyce stood and walked away.

"Touching," Walt muttered.

A few minutes later it was Agatha's youngest, Shane, who came to see the deceased. Walt guessed the young man was about eighteen years old. If he didn't know Shane no longer lived with his mother, he might assume the boy was a little younger. But since he had overheard someone saying Shane lived with several friends in a rental house, he assumed he was probably older than he looked.

Tall and slender, an average-looking boy with closely cropped dishwater blond hair and a pale complexion marred with acne, Walt thought him a forgettable-looking fellow.

"Hey, Gran." Shane knelt by the woman's side. Like his mother, he checked her pulse. "Yep, you're dead. Bet you never thought this day would happen." Still kneeling by her side, he stared at his grandmother for several minutes before saying, "I wondered if I would feel something. You know, maybe a little guilty? Maybe even a twinge of regret?" He stared at her for a few more moments and then said with a chuckle, "Nope. Nothing. By the way, Martha and Dennis declined the offer to come up here. Of course, Martha is making it look like she is so distraught—you know, doesn't want to see you like this. I just think she doesn't want to walk up the stairs." Flashing the dead body a grin, Shane stood.

"This is a loving family," Walt said aloud, watching Shane head to the stairs. A few minutes later, after Shane had gone downstairs, the middle brother, Henry, arrived at their grandmother's side.

"Not exactly like we planned it. But this will do," Henry said as he looked down at Agatha. When he knelt next to the dead woman, he picked up her hand.

"Don't tell me you're testing her pulse too?" Walt said in disgust. Just as he predicted, Henry felt for a pulse. When he couldn't find one, he didn't stop with the wrist.

Henry placed his fingers on her throat, and then he leaned closer and pressed an ear against her chest. When he was satisfied, he sat up and smiled down at Agatha.

"This is going to be an awesome summer!" Henry said in a whisper. "A new car first. I bet you'd want me to have a new car, wouldn't you? After all, I was your favorite." Henry grinned.

"This is quite touching how your family is reacting to your

grandmother's death," Walt told Henry—who of course could not hear him.

"You know, Gran, I don't mean to be greedy, but if it turns out you divided our inheritances equally, I'm going to be pissed. I expect to be repaid for the years of playing the dutiful grandson. Don't disappoint me, old girl." Henry turned from his grandmother and headed for the stairs.

Remembering what Shane had said about their sister, Walt decided to go downstairs and see if she and her husband were still in the house. Maybe Walt wouldn't be able to eavesdrop on whatever Martha might say to her grandmother's dead body, but she might say something while still at Marlow House that could be of help to the chief.

Walt found Martha and her husband, Dennis, standing together in the library with Joyce.

"Are you sure you don't want to go up there?" Dennis was asking Martha when Walt arrived.

"I don't want to see her like that!" Martha cringed. "I can see her one last time at the funeral home."

"I think it's ridiculous she's being buried," Joyce muttered.

"Mom, that was Gran's wishes. She already made the arrangements. She wants to be buried near her parents."

"It's going to cost a fortune," Joyce retorted. "I'd rather see if we can sell the plot and have her cremated. After all, I intend to be cremated."

"Fortunately, Gran's already paid for everything, so it won't cost you anything." Martha reached out and patted her mother's hand.

TEN

"I thought you were looking forward to taking Lily to the fireworks tonight," Kelly asked her brother. He sat in his dining room with Joe, having a beer, when she walked into the room. Kelly had just changed her clothes after returning from Marlow House.

"I was," Ian said before taking a swig of beer. "Murder has a way of screwing up your plans."

"You think she was murdered?" She sat down at the table. Grabbing Joe's beer, she helped herself to a sip.

"I don't know how she could have gotten upstairs by herself. And the grandson who took her up there is missing," Ian reminded her. "Looks to me like someone got her to climb up the stairs, and then when no one was around, gave her a little shove. With someone that age, even a broken hip could be lethal."

"Looks like it was her neck, not hip that was broken. But the unofficial word is a tragic accident," Joe said.

"We know why that is," Ian scoffed. "The chief is playing it close to the vest, doesn't want the family to know they're suspects."

Joe shrugged. "All I know, Marlow House seems to be cursed. Maybe that blogger is onto something—the Missing Thorndike is cursed."

Kelly looked at Joe and smiled. "I can't believe you of all people is saying that. What happened to *there is always a logical explanation?*"

Joe shrugged again and snatched his beer back from Kelly.

Before taking a sip, he said, "I'm beginning to think maybe some things defy logic."

"One thing, Joyce Pruitt's fortunes have taken a sudden change of direction," Ian said.

Kelly stood up from the table. She walked to the nearby kitchen and grabbed herself a beer. As she sat back down, she said, "I heard she was really rich."

"Her husband invented something. I can't remember what it was," Joe said. "But she's lived with her daughter for as long as I've known her. She's one of those rich people who doesn't like to spend their own money. Kind of a polar opposite from Danielle."

"Danielle, you think she'll get sued?" Kelly asked.

"That's what she has insurance for," Ian said. "Although, I'd be surprised if Joyce would press a suit against her, especially considering she took off with Danielle's coins, and Danielle has made it clear she didn't want any charges pressed."

"Of course, there is also the grandchildren. But I imagine they'll be busy spending grandma's money—or figuring out how to stay out of jail," Joe said.

"I just feel horrible for Danielle. She really does have the worst luck!" Kelly looked at her brother. "You sure you don't want to go with us to get something to eat? The restaurant has a great view of the fireworks."

Ian shook his head. "No. I think I might go back over to Marlow House in a little bit. I need to talk to Lily."

"THIS IS ABSOLUTELY the last July Fourth party I'm ever hosting!" Danielle said as she slammed the dishwasher shut and turned it on. Night had fallen in Frederickport, and the only people remaining at Marlow House were Danielle, Chris, Lily—and one spirit, Walt. The four gathered in the kitchen.

From the distance they heard a booming sound. Chris had just dumped some trash in the kitchen garbage can. He paused when he heard the boom, looking out the window. "Sounds like the fireworks have started."

"And once again I'm missing them," Danielle said as she poured herself a glass of wine. "Lily, Chris, you want a glass?"

Chris walked to the kitchen table and sat down. "Is it that good stuff?"

"Yep," Danielle said as she filled her glass to the brim.

"I thought you're only supposed to fill it halfway," Lily teased.

"To heck with protocol. You want some?" Danielle asked from where she stood at the counter.

"Sure," Lily and Chris said at the same time. They sat at the table, watching Danielle.

"Let me help you," Walt said after Danielle filled the three glasses. He picked up Chris's and Lily's glasses and carried them to the table while Danielle brought hers and sat down.

"What did you do with Ian?" Chris asked Lily.

"I didn't do anything with him," Lily said as she sipped the wine.

"I thought you were going to the fireworks show? In fact, from what I recall, when we were all discussing it, Ian made it clear you two were going alone."

Lily shrugged. "Yeah, I guess he found a new place to watch them from. He thought it would be kinda romantic if just the two of us went."

"So why are you sitting here with us?" Chris asked.

Lily looked up at Chris and rolled her eyes. "Might have something to do with one of our guests dying today."

Chris shrugged. "Not like you could do anything now. And let's be honest, it wasn't like Agatha Pine was someone you really knew —and from what I gather, if you knew her well, you probably wouldn't like her."

"But she did die here," Danielle said. "And I understand why Lily decided not to go." Danielle sipped her wine.

"I just figured I wanted to stick around in case we end up having another—" Lily looked across the table at where she imagined Walt sat. She was about to say ghost, but changed her mind. "—spirit around here. I'd like to know about it and not walk in on something I don't understand. Anyway, Ian went out to dinner with his sister and Joe."

———

NO ONE BOTHERED to turn on the kitchen's porch light. Nor had the exterior lighting along the side and backyard of Marlow House been turned on. Yet light was coming from the kitchen, the room brightly illuminated by the interior fixtures. Had those been turned off, Ian might have decided to walk to the front door instead of cutting through the side yard and entering through the kitchen. With the bright lights shining through the uncurtained kitchen windows, Ian easily made his way through the dark side yard. No one had bothered to lock the side gate.

He hadn't brought Sadie with him. She remained back at his house across the street. When he reached the kitchen door, he looked in the window and saw Lily sitting at the kitchen table with Chris while Danielle stood at the counter. It looked as if she was pouring herself a glass of wine.

Ian was preparing to knock on the door and walk in when motion from the counter by Danielle caught his eye. Standing in the darkness, looking into the house, Ian's eyes widened as two full glasses of wine floated up from the counter and then moved through the air to the kitchen table, where they landed—one in front of Chris and the second in front of Lily.

Unable to make himself move, Ian remained standing outside the window, looking into the house. He couldn't grasp what he had just seen.

The creak of the side gate opening broke his concentration. Without thought, he moved farther into the darkness, hiding in the bushes. Looking toward the sound, he didn't see anything, but he could hear footsteps making their way toward him in the darkness.

When the person reached the door, he was able to make out her identity—it was their neighbor Heather Donovan.

Standing on the kitchen porch, just a few feet from where Ian hid, Heather knocked on the door. A moment later, the door opened, and Heather entered the house.

Inching out from his hiding place, he peeked back inside through a window. Heather stood at the table and appeared to be talking to an empty chair. With a frown, Ian continued to watch. The chair appeared to move on its own, and then Heather sat down on it.

Motion from the counter caught Ian's attention again. But this time, it was the bottle of wine and an empty wineglass floating across the room. The people sitting at the table—Danielle, Lily, Chris, and Heather—continued to chat as if nothing unusual had happened. None even flinched when the bottle of wine tipped slightly, filling the empty glass sitting before Heather.

"What the hell is going on?" Ian muttered.

"WELL, LARRY ISN'T THERE," Dennis said as he drove away from the apartment his brother-in-law rented. His wife, Martha, sat in the passenger seat, and in the backseat was his mother-in-law, Joyce.

"You might as well take me home, Dennis. If Larry would answer his phone, we wouldn't be running around town, trying to find him. I guess he'll just have to wait until tomorrow to find out his grandmother died, or maybe he'll hear it on the radio," Joyce said.

"You really think that's what happened?" Martha asked her mother, referring to the possible scenario they had discussed, regarding Larry's sudden disappearance.

"I'm sure it is," Joyce said. "He probably helped Mother upstairs, and then they got into another argument. Like Shane told us, he heard them arguing earlier at my house. He probably left her upstairs, figured someone would help her, and he just took off. Larry was always impulsive like that."

Ten minutes later they were at Joyce's house.

"Are you sure you want to be alone?" Martha asked her mother. She stood at the front door of Joyce's house with Dennis, preparing to leave. "You could always spend the night at our house tonight."

Joyce shook her head and smiled. "Don't be silly. I'll be fine here."

"But you'll be all alone. Gran has always been here. Maybe you shouldn't be alone tonight," Martha said.

Joyce reached out and patted her daughter's hand reassuringly. "Yes, dear, she always has. But she isn't now. Mother lived a nice long life. Any of us should be so lucky. Don't worry about me, I'll be fine. You two go. In fact, I think you can probably make the fireworks show."

"Fireworks?" Martha gasped. "Mom, I can't go watch fireworks after Gran died today!"

"Gran is fine, dear. She has simply moved on to be with my father. I'm sure she's very happy."

"You're so strong!" Martha said before giving her mother a hug goodbye.

Ten minutes later, after Martha and Dennis drove away, Joyce walked into her mother's room, carrying several large trash bags. Turning on the overhead light, Joyce stood in the room, balled fists resting on her hips while still clutching the trash bags. She glanced around, surveying her mother's belongings.

"So here's the question, Mother. Do I bother fixing up this house, like I have always wanted to, or should I sell it and buy something better? Maybe a house right on the beach."

Tossing the trash bags on the bed, Joyce opened the closet door and began pulling her mother's clothes from their hangers and throwing them onto the floor in a pile. After she had removed all the clothes from the closet, she began opening the dresser drawers, emptying them. When she was finished, she picked up one of the trash bags, opened it, and began shoving the clothes she had piled on the floor into the bag.

ELEVEN

The blogger sat down at the computer and stared at the monitor. "People are going to think I'm clairvoyant." A moment later the blogger began typing.

The curse of the Missing Thorndike strikes again…

"I HOPE this guy isn't trying to make a living off his blog. He's a crappy writer," Kelly said when Ian walked into his living room on Sunday morning. Kelly sat cross-legged on his sofa, wearing yoga pants and a green T-shirt, her laptop computer turned on and propped on her lap. Sprawled out on the floor next to the sofa was Sadie, who lifted her head when her human entered the room.

Carrying a cup of coffee, his hair uncombed, Ian took a seat across from his sister and sipped his drink. Shirtless, all he wore was a pair of navy blue pajama bottoms. "What are you talking about?"

Kelly glanced up from the computer. "That anonymous blogger behind Mystery of Marlow House. He posted again last night." She glanced back down at the monitor. "He's not a very good writer, but I'm starting to wonder, he might be clairvoyant."

"Clairvoyant?" Ian leaned back in the recliner; its footrest popped up.

Looking back to her brother, she asked, "Have you read the blog lately?"

"No." Ian sipped his coffee.

"He made a post right before Danielle's party and predicted someone was going to get killed at Marlow House on the Fourth. And looked what happened. Someone did get killed."

Ian shook his head and mumbled, "I don't want to deal with this right now."

Kelly frowned at her brother. "Deal with what?"

"I just have a lot on my mind right now." Ian pushed the footrest down and set his feet back on the floor in front of his recliner.

"I thought you'd find this interesting."

"Like I said, I have a lot on my mind."

Closing her laptop, Kelly set it on the sofa next to her and eyed her brother. "Did you and Lily have a fight or something last night?"

"Fight? Why do you ask that?" Ian set his now empty mug on the side table and then leaned back in the chair.

Kelly shrugged. "I don't know. You said you were going over there last night, and now you say you have a lot on your mind. I just wondered if something happened between you and Lily."

"I didn't go over there last night," Ian lied.

"You didn't?"

"I changed my mind. Decided to turn in early."

Kelly glanced over to the window. "I wonder how they're doing over there today? Why don't we go see? I bet Danielle would be interested in this blog post."

"I imagine Danielle can find it on her own."

"Does that mean you don't want to go over there?" Kelly frowned.

Ian stood up. "I have some work I need to finish this morning. But first, I need to take a shower." He turned from Kelly. Just as he reached the doorway leading to the hall, his cellphone began to ring. Pausing a moment, he pulled his phone out of the pocket of his pajama bottoms and looked at it. Instead of answering it, he disconnected the call.

"Telemarketers?" Kelly asked playfully.

"Yeah, something like that," Ian muttered as he left the room.

Fifteen minutes later, Kelly headed for the guest room to get dressed. She paused at Ian's open bedroom door. She could hear his shower running in the master bath. She spied his cellphone sitting on his dresser. Curious, she entered the room and picked up his phone.

"I can't believe you're using that same password," she muttered under her breath as she logged into his phone. For a brief moment she glanced guiltily to the doorway leading to the bathroom, and then looked back at the phone, curious about the call he hadn't answered.

Wow, you didn't answer Lily's call. What is going on with you two?

Kelly went straight to the guest room and got dressed. When she came out, Ian's bedroom door was now closed, and she didn't hear the shower running. Hurrying to the front door before Ian came out of his room, she was greeted by Sadie.

"Sorry, girl," Kelly said as she gently pushed the dog away from the front door. "You have to stay here."

"HEY, KELLY," Lily greeted when she opened the front door. Glancing over Kelly's shoulder, she asked, "Isn't Ian with you?"

"He was taking a shower," Kelly explained when she stepped into the entry hall.

"Oh. I tried calling him a little while ago, and he didn't answer." Lily closed the front door.

"He was probably in the shower," Kelly said. "I came over to see how you're all doing, and if you'd read the Mystery of Marlow House blog today."

"I can't say I have. Dani's in the kitchen. Want some coffee and a cinnamon roll?"

"I'd love some." Kelly followed Lily down the hall toward the kitchen. "Where are your guests?"

"They checked out last night. Imagine that?" Lily said with a snort.

"Ahhh...because of what happened yesterday?"

Lily shrugged and led the way into the kitchen.

Danielle was sitting alone at the table with a cup of coffee and half-eaten cinnamon roll. "Morning, Kelly. Is Ian with you?"

"He's taking a shower," Lily answered for her and then pointed to the table, suggesting Kelly take a seat while she got her a cup of coffee and roll.

By the time Lily returned to the table, Kelly was already telling them about the blog post.

"That is strange," Danielle said after she finished.

"I'm going to tell Joe about it. After all, if that poor woman was murdered, then maybe the blogger had something to do with it," Kelly suggested.

"I can't believe we're even entertaining the idea Agatha's death was murder. But if there was no way for her to get where she was found without someone helping her get there, then something definitely isn't right," Lily observed.

"If someone did push Agatha down those stairs," Danielle said as she tore her remaining piece of cinnamon roll in two, "it was probably someone from her family—they had the motive. And if that's true, I seriously don't see one of them informing a blogger of their intentions."

"I suppose so. But it does seem suspicious," Kelly said with a sigh. Picking up her cinnamon roll, Kelly glanced over at Lily, watching as she drank her coffee and stared blankly at the back door. Setting her roll back down on its napkin, Kelly cleared her throat and said, "So Ian didn't come back over here last night?"

Startled back to the moment, Lily blinked and looked at Kelly. "Ian? No, he didn't. Didn't he go out to dinner with you guys last night?"

Kelly shook her head and then took a bite of her roll. After she swallowed, she said, "He told me he planned to come back here and see you."

Lily frowned. "Well, he didn't."

"I know. That's what he said this morning. Said something about going to bed early."

Lily let out a sigh. "It was an insane day yesterday. But I kind of figured he would have called me by now. Is he okay?"

Kelly swallowed nervously. She wasn't sure how to answer that question. After all, her brother had ignored Lily's phone call that morning. "Okay?"

"Yeah, he seemed a little…I don't know…distant yesterday."

"You mean after they found Agatha?" Kelly asked.

Lily shook her head. "No. Even before that. I swear, I kept catching him looking at me with the oddest expression."

"Love?" Kelly managed to squeak out, although she had a horrible feeling she was the cause of her brother's odd behavior, and she didn't think love had anything to do with it. Had the conversation she had instigated about Lily—raising questions on why Lily had avoided certain conversations—caused Ian to give the relationship a second thought?

"More like there was a Post-it note stuck to my forehead that said *idiot* and he was trying to figure out if he agreed with the note or should tell me to take it off."

Danielle let out a snort and popped the remaining piece of roll in her mouth.

"Why don't you go talk to him?" Kelly said impulsively. "With the kid sister staying with him this weekend, it is kind of hard to get some alone time. Why don't you go over now while I'm here?"

Ten minutes later, Danielle sat alone at the table with Kelly. Lily had taken the suggestion and left for Ian's house.

Danielle eyed Kelly critically as the younger woman finished her coffee. "Is something going on with your brother? Is there someone else?"

Startled, Kelly looked up at Danielle. "Someone else? You mean is Ian seeing someone else?"

"Well, I know Lily isn't. And Ian is the one who's acting distant. So yeah, I suppose that might be one conclusion."

Kelly shook her head, "No. It's not anything like that."

"Then what is it?"

"Trouble in paradise?" Walt asked when he appeared the next moment. "Sadie certainly has never mentioned another woman."

Danielle glanced briefly at Walt, who stood by the counter, unseen by Kelly.

"I'm afraid it might have been something I said," Kelly confessed.

"Something you said? Like what?"

"It's about the Marlow House stories—you know, how it's haunted," Kelly said guiltily.

"Is she suggesting people know about me?" Walt asked.

"Where did you hear that?" Danielle frowned.

"I'm not saying it's really haunted, just all the speculation about the strange things that people have experienced here."

"What kind of strange things?" Danielle asked.

"You know, like how Brian Henderson felt like someone hit him, and he landed on the floor."

Danielle frowned. "What does this have to do with Lily and Ian?"

"For one thing, Lily never mentioned it to him. He didn't know it happened. I just thought it was odd she wouldn't tell Ian something like that."

"Did Brian tell you that story?" Danielle asked.

"Yeah. And some other stuff, like that guest you had recently, she claimed the books went flying off the shelf in the library. Ian didn't know anything about that. I just thought it was odd Lily never mentioned it to him before."

"Good lord, Ian's little sister is certainly a chatty little thing, isn't she?" Walt scoffed.

When Kelly wasn't looking, Danielle flashed Walt a dirty look.

"Don't give me that face," Walt said defensively. "I'm not the one who knocked the books off the shelf in the library, and when I slugged Brian, he deserved it."

TWELVE

I an sat on the foot of his bed, staring at the engagement ring in his hand. If someone would have asked him last week what he would be doing on Sunday, it wouldn't be this—sitting alone in his room, looking at the ring he thought would be on Lily's left hand by now. He was no longer sure the ring would ever go on Lily's hand. He wasn't sure of anything anymore. Nothing made sense.

Ian's alter ego, Jon Altar, would normally be all over a story like this. Wineglasses floating through the air. Punchy ghosts who occasionally slugged an annoying trespasser. Books mysteriously flying off shelves. However, Jon Alter's angle wouldn't be some paranormal made-for-Halloween tale. His expertise was more exposé. Ian didn't believe in ghosts. Oh, he believed in conmen and hucksters who made people believe they were seeing things that weren't there, but ghosts? No way.

According to Adam Nichols, Danielle had installed security cameras. That would explain how she knew Adam and Bill had broken into the house. The fact Lily never mentioned the cameras troubled him.

While he had to admit, when he first saw those wineglasses floating through the air, it jarred his senses. Yet now that he had time to digest it, Ian was certain it had all been rigged. But why? Was this obviously fabricated ghost hoax just some prank, or was something else going on?

He refused to believe Lily—his Lily—could be involved in anything unethical. Whatever was going on, there had to be a good reason for it. He just didn't understand why she hadn't confided in him.

In the midst of his internal battle, Ian failed to notice his bedroom door open. It wasn't until he heard a soft feminine voice say, "Ian?" did he realize he was no longer alone.

Looking up at the doorway, he saw Lily standing there, staring curiously at him. It was then he realized he was still holding the engagement ring. Without thought, he released hold of the ring and snatched it in the grip of his palm, concealing it from view.

Tilting her head ever so slightly, Lily walked into the room. "What are you holding?"

"Nothing," he stammered. "Did Kelly tell you to come in?"

"Kelly? Kelly's over at Marlow House with Dani." Lily walked to the bed, standing over Ian.

As Ian looked up at Lily, he shoved his hand into his pocket, depositing the ring. "She is?"

"What did you put in your pocket?"

"Nothing," he lied.

"Don't be silly." Lily grinned. "You put something in there."

Ian stood up, his expression solemn. "Let's go out to the living room. We need to talk."

Curious, Lily nodded. Together they silently walked to the living room. Ian took a seat on the recliner while Lily sat on the sofa. Sadie, who was already in the living room, walked over to Ian and curled up by his feet.

"Okay, what's wrong, Ian? You've been acting a little strange the last couple of days. What's going on?"

"Why didn't you tell me Danielle installed security cameras throughout Marlow House?"

Lily frowned. "Security cameras?"

"Adam told me—"

Before Ian could finish his explanation, Lily began to laugh. "Oh, that! I remember Dani told me Adam was convinced she had security cameras in the house because she figured out he was the one who broke in."

"You mean there are no cameras?"

Lily giggled. "No. You're welcome to check for yourself. And just think about it, Ian, if there were security cameras in the house, I doubt the police chief would still be wondering how Agatha Pine got upstairs by herself. You don't think Danielle would be turning over that kind of video surveillance if she had it?"

"How did Danielle know what shirt Bill wore that day?"

Lily shrugged. "You'll have to ask Dani."

"What about the books flying off the shelf in Marlow House? Why didn't you ever tell me about that?"

Lily blinked several times. "Books?"

"Yes. In the library. A guest claimed books went flying off the shelf."

Lily shrugged. "Well, I never saw it."

"But she claimed it happened?" he asked.

"Yeah. So?" Lily frowned.

"Why didn't you ever tell me about it?" he asked.

Lily shrugged again. "I don't know. I…I guess I never thought about it."

"What about Brian Henderson getting slugged in the entry hall and flying across the room?"

"He didn't actually fly across the room," Lily scoffed.

"But you saw it?"

"He stumbled, yeah. Fell on the floor. Sorta like the time Cheryl did. You were there then. Remember?" Lily asked.

"And you didn't think it was odd? From what I understand, lots of strange things happen at Marlow House—like people imagining they're being pushed or punched, books flying off shelves, the scent of cigar smoke coming and going—and you've never mentioned it before."

Lily frowned. "Ian, what is this about? And we've talked about that cigar smell before. Some houses smell funny. That's not a big deal. What is going on?"

"Last night, I decided not to go out to dinner with my sister."

"I know. She told me. Said you wanted to go to bed early." Lily move restlessly in her seat.

"I lied to her. I didn't go to bed early. I went over to Marlow House."

"What do you mean you went to Marlow House? I was there. I didn't see you."

"I went to the back door. It was dark outside, but the kitchen was lit up. You were in there with Chris and Danielle."

"Why didn't you come in? I don't understand."

"I was going to." Ian stood up. He started pacing the room.

"What stopped you?"

Ian turned to Lily and stopped pacing. "I was about to come in when I saw something strange."

"Strange?"

"There were two wineglasses sitting on the counter and…they floated across the room. All by themselves. All the way to the table."

Lily swallowed nervously. "You saw that?"

"Yes. And then I heard someone come into the yard, so I hid in the bushes. It was Heather. I watched her go into the house. And then I saw something else. Now it was a wine bottle and a glass floating across the room. The trick got better. The bottle poured itself—just like someone invisible was holding it—filling up Heather's glass. She accepted the wine like it was the most natural thing in the world."

Lily groaned and leaned back on the sofa. "You saw all that?"

Ian nodded. "Tell me. What the hell is going on over there?"

Sitting back up on the sofa, Lily took a deep breath and licked her lips. She looked up at Ian and smiled weakly. "I've been wanting to tell you, but I figured you'd never believe me anyway, so I just kept it to myself. Actually, now that you've seen for yourself, it makes everything a lot easier. Kind of a relief, really, now that I think about it." Lily let out a sigh and sat back on the sofa and smiled.

"Are you going to tell me or just sit there?" Ian snapped.

"I'm sorry, I thought you probably figured it out already. Isn't it obvious? Marlow House is haunted."

Unsmiling, Ian stared at Lily. "Seriously? That's what you want to tell me?"

"Well, it's the truth," Lily insisted.

"Lily, I really am not in the mood for jokes. Just tell me what's really going on."

"I just did."

"Damn it, Lily, I'm not kidding. This isn't funny."

"I'm not trying to be funny. I'm telling you the truth."

Angry, Ian stood up and shook his head. "I thought we had something special. You obviously think it's all some joke. If you have such a difficult time with the truth, there is a real problem with our relationship."

Lily stood up abruptly. "Ian, what does Marlow House being

haunted have to do with you and me? Are you mad because I kept it from you? I'm sorry, but I didn't think you would believe me."

"Ya think?" he snapped.

"Then why are you mad?" she practically shouted.

"Come on, Lily, there are no such things as ghosts. I know something's going on over at Marlow House, I saw it with my own eyes. But it sure as hell is not a ghost. I don't know why you just don't tell me the truth."

"Ian, you admitted you saw the wineglasses float across the room. It was Walt. He carried the glasses to the table, but you couldn't see him. Only Danielle, Chris, and Heather can see him."

"Oh really? They can see ghosts, but you can't? I didn't see Walt —I am assuming you mean Walt Marlow—so I suppose I can't see ghosts either. Why is it they can? Explain it to me."

"I don't know!" Exasperated, Lily plopped down on the sofa again. "Why are you so angry? I don't know why they can see ghosts. Evan can see ghosts too."

Ian frowned. Turning from Lily for a moment, he muttered, "Evan…that's right. He said something about seeing Walt."

"See! I told you."

Turning to Lily again, he shouted, "Damn, Lily. Whatever you guys are up to, why drag a child into it?"

Lily stood back up again. "Just what do you think we're trying to do?"

"I have no idea. But the fact you keep lying to me doesn't make me feel better."

"I'm not lying to you!"

"Are you sticking to this ghost story?" Ian asked.

"It's the truth."

"Then I think you should leave."

Startled, Lily asked in a whisper, "Leave?"

"I've never made it a secret that women who play games are a major turnoff. That was one thing that attracted me to you. Your honesty. But now…" Ian shook his head wearily.

Tears filled Lily's eyes. "I am telling the truth."

"Just go, Lily."

Lily stepped toward Ian, but he put his hand out, stopping her.

"I'm not big on prolonging the agony. When something is over, it's over. I don't intend to tell my sister why we broke up—"

"You're breaking up with me?" Lily squeaked.

"Unless you can explain why you insist on lying, yes."

"But I'm telling the truth. Marlow House is haunted."

"Like I said, I don't intend to tell my sister why we broke up. It is no one's business."

"Ian, I can understand if you don't believe Marlow House is haunted. But I'm surprised you accuse me of lying. If I believe in something that you don't believe in, that is hardly the same thing as lying. An atheist might not believe in God, but he doesn't call a believer a liar."

"You forget what I saw in the kitchen last night," Ian reminded her.

Lily frowned. "You mean when Walt poured the wine?"

"Granted, it looked like the bottle was pouring itself from where I was standing outside. But I imagine from where you were sitting in the kitchen, you had to have been privy to whatever the trick was."

"Ian...that doesn't make sense..."

"You need to leave, Lily. Please. Now."

WALT HAD JUST STEPPED out of the kitchen when Lily came running through the front doorway, heading straight to the staircase. Curious, he followed her upstairs, where she ran into her bedroom, slammed the door shut, and threw herself onto her bed. Walt stood over Lily and watched as she broke into uncontrollable sobs.

The next moment, Walt was again standing in the kitchen with Danielle and Kelly, who sat at the table. Kelly was recounting a story Joe had told her, regarding the FBI agents.

Ignoring the fact Kelly was speaking, Walt leaned down to Danielle and said, "You need to get Kelly to go home. Lily needs you."

Danielle glanced over to Walt, frowning slightly in confusion.

"She just came in the front door, went to her room. At the moment she's crying. Something's wrong."

Danielle sat there a moment while Kelly prattled away. Finally, Danielle picked up her phone and looked at it. "Oh my, I almost forgot! I need to get going."

"I'm keeping you from something? Oh, I'm sorry."

Danielle stood up. "That's okay. I forgot all about it. But I need to change my clothes first."

As soon as Kelly left, Danielle dashed upstairs, Walt by her side. Like Walt had said, Lily lay sobbing on her bed.

Sitting on the side of the mattress, Danielle placed a hand on Lily's back and asked, "What's wrong, Lily?"

"It's over, Dani. Over." Still sobbing, Lily sat up and threw her arms around Danielle. "Ian broke up with me. I feel as if I'm dying inside."

THIRTEEN

"I should thrash Ian for making our Lily cry like this!" Walt fumed as he angrily paced the bedroom floor.

After calming Lily down, Danielle had tried to talk to Ian, but he wasn't answering his phone. When she went over to his house, she found his sister, who explained Ian was not at home and she had no idea where he had gone. Kelly explained that when she had returned from Marlow House earlier, both he and Sadie were gone, along with his car. He hadn't left a note.

SUNDAY WAS COMING TO AN END, and Lily had spent most of the day in her room, crying. She had finally fallen asleep. It didn't look as if Walt was going to let Danielle do the same—in spite of the last two days, both utterly exhausting and emotional. Yet even if Walt retreated to the attic, Danielle doubted she would be able to fall asleep.

The blinds to her bedroom window were open, revealing a dark night sky. Danielle sat cross-legged on the center of her bed and listened silently as Walt continued to rant.

"I'd like to give that palooka a good punch in the nose!"

"If he ever comes over here, you can do just that. I won't stop you," she promised.

Walt paused a moment and looked at Danielle. "If? Are you suggesting he might not come over here again?"

Danielle shrugged. "From what Lily said, when Ian calls it quits, he doesn't waste any time moving on. But I have to admit, this really surprises me about Ian."

Walt waved his hand and a cigar appeared. Just before he was about to take a puff, he realized where he was. In the next moment, the cigar vanished.

"Oh, go ahead. Considering the last couple of days, I think I can make an exception this one time. Have your cigar. But just be glad you aren't alive."

A smile curled on Walt's lips, yet he didn't summon another cigar. "Why is that exactly?"

"Because if you were alive, I wouldn't care what room you were in—or how crappy a day you had, I'd be snatching those cigars out of your hand before they ever touched your lips."

"Really? Why is that?"

Danielle flashed Walt a shy smile. "Why do you think?"

Walt grinned and then abruptly waved Danielle over to one side of the bed. "Move over."

The next moment, they lay side by side on the mattress, leaning back against the headboard.

"You sure are bossy," Danielle teased.

"Yet you're the one who threatens to rip cigars out of my hand."

"You have a point," Danielle said with a grin.

"So tell me, what did you mean a minute ago when you said Ian surprised you?"

"Since Lucas, I've come to the conclusion I really couldn't be with someone who didn't innately trust me. I really thought Lily had that with Ian. I'm just surprised he wouldn't even listen to her. Plus, he saw the proof with his own eyes."

"I've been thinking about that…" Walt muttered as he stared ahead, lost in his own thoughts. After a few moments of silence, he said, "As much as I want to thrash Ian, and as disappointed as you are right now in how he has reacted, perhaps we're not taking into account Ian's own experiences and how they've shaped his perception."

With her arms folded across her chest, Danielle glanced over to Walt. "What are you talking about?"

"Ian is more than just an author, he's an investigative reporter. I would assume to be good at that job, he'd have to be a skeptic—more skeptical than most people. I don't imagine a gullible person would make a credible investigative reporter."

Danielle shrugged. "Well, we know he's good at his job. Considering how well he's done."

"Although, I'm a little surprised Ian didn't take the stance that he believed Lily believed, and then proceeded to help her see the light," Walt mused.

"According to Lily, it was because he saw the wineglasses floating and was convinced it had to be rigged, and since she was sitting right there, she had to have been in on it."

"I suppose…" He sighed.

Danielle eyed Walt. "Just a few moments ago you wanted to punch his nose, and now you're making excuses for Ian."

Walt shrugged. "I still want to give the palooka a good punch."

"If he never steps foot in Marlow House again, that isn't happening. And if Lily is right about Ian, we should expect him to leave Frederickport. After all, Lily was the reason he stayed."

After a few moments of silence, Walt let out a shout. "No! Sadie!"

"Sadie?"

"He can't take Sadie with him!"

"I'm sorry, Walt, Sadie is his dog."

In the next moment, Walt stood by the bed. "Sadie is not just a dog. Sadie is…*Sadie!*"

Walt began to pace again. "Okay, we have to figure out some way to fix this. To bring Ian and Lily back together and keep Ian and Sadie in Frederickport."

Danielle sat up on the bed, her eyes on Walt.

"I can only think of one thing." Walt stopped pacing and stared at Danielle. "I'll have to talk some sense into Ian. Convince him Lily was telling the truth."

"Talk to him…how?" When Danielle suddenly realized what he probably meant, she started shaking her head. "Oh no…not a dream hop. No. That's not going to work. He'll just think he was dreaming. It won't prove anything."

"I have to try, Danielle, and I can be convincing."

"You did the dream hop once with Ian, when we were in Arizona. He didn't for a moment imagine it was anything but a dream when he woke up. I don't see how this will be any different."

"I have to try, Danielle."

"But let's see—" Before Danielle could finish her sentence, Walt vanished. She glanced around the room. He was nowhere in sight.

"Stubborn ghost," she muttered before letting out a sigh and leaning back against the headboard.

IAN OPENED HIS EYES. To his surprise, he was sitting in the library at Marlow House.

"What the—" Ian started to stand up.

Interrupting what Ian was about to say, Walt said, "Stay where you are. We need to talk."

Blinking his eyes in confusion, Ian looked across the room and saw Walt Marlow sitting on the sofa, looking at him. Instead of standing up, Ian settled back in the chair and silently studied Walt.

"Good," Walt said with a nod.

"Ahh, I get it." Ian laughed. "You're Walt Marlow. I recognize you. This must mean I'm dreaming."

"Do you always know when you're dreaming?" Walt asked.

Ian shrugged. "Not really. Sometimes, I guess."

Crossing one leg over the opposing knee, Ian glanced around the room. "I suppose I can understand why I'm dreaming about you."

"And why is that?" Walt asked.

"Probably because I just broke up with Lily, and you're the cause."

"Me?" Walt arched his brow. "So you do believe in…spirits."

"You mean ghosts?"

Not wanting to veer off course and get into a discussion of ghost versus spirit, Walt asked, "If you do believe in us, then why did you break up with Lily?"

"When did I say I believe in ghosts? Spirits maybe, not ghosts."

"I'm curious, what is the difference between ghosts and spirits? You say you might believe in one, yet not the other. Personally, I tend to see myself as a spirit." Walt waved his hand and summoned a cigar.

"I don't know what happens after we die, but I like to think our spirits—maybe it's our souls—move on. Not sure I buy the heaven and hell thing, but I've a gut feeling there is something more."

"That seems all fairly accurate," Walt said before taking a puff.

"Does it?" Ian said with a chuckle. He then sniffed. "There it is. That's the smell from Marlow House. It comes and goes."

"It's from my cigar. When I'm smoking, people nearby can normally smell it."

"Sure they do," Ian scoffed.

"You smell it now," Walt pointed out.

"But I'm dreaming."

"Do you always notice smells in your dreams?"

Ian shrugged. "Maybe. I don't remember."

"So tell me, you've explained your notion of spirit, what do you think a ghost is?"

"For one thing, it's no more than folklore."

"Folklore?" Walt arched his brow.

"Ghost jump out at people and say boo!"

Walt shook his head and muttered, "I can't remember ever doing that…well, maybe the boo part."

"Are you claiming to be a ghost?"

"As I said a moment ago, I prefer to think of myself as a spirit. But if we want to get technical about it, I suppose I am a ghost. As much as I loathe that term."

"When I looked into the kitchen window of this house, I saw wineglasses floating across the room. A moment later, it was a bottle of wine and a glass. Now, that is something I'd figure a ghost would do. I don't see a spirit doing something like that. It's much too…I don't know, earthy, materialistic. I don't see a spirit bothering with moving glasses around."

"Then you must believe in ghosts if you saw the glasses move."

"No. I believe in parlor tricks, in the art of prestidigitation. Over the years, I've witnessed some highly impressive magic acts. Watching those glasses floating across the kitchen was startling, yet nothing that makes me suddenly believe in ghosts."

"I'm sorry that you feel that way. You've hurt a very good woman, one who loves you. Trust me, finding that kind of love is rare and precious."

"And you don't think I'm hurting?" Ian snapped. "I was prepared to ask Lily to marry me. I even had the ring."

"You were going to propose?"

"Yes. At the fireworks after Danielle's party."

"Just like that, you have fallen out of love?"

Ian closed his eyes and let out a sigh. "Oh, I still love Lily—the woman I thought she was. This other one, the one who makes up elaborate tales, she's a stranger to me."

"She didn't lie."

Ian opened his eyes and looked at Walt. "Really?"

"Ian, does this feel like a regular dream?"

Ian considered the question a moment and then said, with a smile, "No it doesn't. But I've had dreams like this before. In fact, I had one once very similar to this, and you were in that one too."

Walt smiled. "That's because I was actually in that other dream."

"Didn't I just say that?"

"Ian, this is not a regular dream. I am the spirit of Walt Marlow, and I'm really here with you."

"Will I see the Ghost of Christmas Past tonight too?"

"Pay attention, Ian. I'm trying to explain it to you. This is what Danielle calls a dream hop."

"A dream what?"

With a sigh, Walt said wearily, "Perhaps it would be easier if I started at the beginning."

"Yes, the beginning. That's always a good idea," Ian said with amusement.

Walt's tale began with his own death, his lonely haunting of Marlow House, and then to when Danielle and Lily moved to Frederickport. He didn't elaborate on all the paranormal activities of the last year; he focused primarily on his haunting of Marlow House and his friendship with Lily and Danielle. When he was finished, he asked, "Well, what do you think?"

"I think I might have a career in fiction if I decide to change genres," Ian said dryly.

Walt frowned. "I don't understand?"

"I didn't realize I had such a vivid imagination."

"Are you suggesting everything I told you tonight came from your imagination?"

"I'm thinking getting over Lily is going to be more difficult than I imagined. My subconscious is obviously working overtime trying to create an alternate reality where I can accept Lily's explanation as the truth. To be honest, I would love to wake up in the morning believing everything Lily told me was true. That there are such things as ghosts. Yes, I wish this really was a dream hop. Because if it's not, when I wake up in the morning, it will be the same nightmare, one where the Lily I love is no longer in my life."

Ian disappeared.

"Where did he go?" Walt glanced around. "Damn, something must have woken him up."

Something had woken Ian up from the dream. It wasn't Sadie shoving her nose in Ian's face, telling him to wake up and take her out. It wasn't his sister returning home late after a date with Joe. What woke him were the tears running down his face.

FOURTEEN

W hen Kelly went out into the kitchen on Monday morning, she found her brother sitting at the table, drinking a cup of coffee and surfing through the browser on his cellphone.

"Morning. Did Danielle ever get ahold of you yesterday? Is everything alright?"

Still holding his cellphone in one hand, he looked up to Kelly. "Danielle?"

"Yeah. Yesterday she was trying to get ahold of you. You weren't answering your phone; she came over here. I left a note on the counter before I went out with Joe. Didn't you see it?"

Ian turned his attention back to the phone. "Yeah, I saw it."

"So did you talk to her?"

"I know what she wanted. It's okay."

Kelly studied Ian for a moment. "You seem kind of grouchy this morning. Did you sleep bad last night?"

"I slept fine aside from a bizarre dream I'd rather forget."

"Ahh, a nightmare. I hate those."

"Yeah, I guess it was a nightmare." Ian sipped his coffee and then set his cup down and looked back to his phone.

Frowning at her brother, whose attention was again focused on the phone's small display, Kelly poured herself a cup of coffee. When she sat down at the table a moment later, she said, "I'm going to take off in a few minutes. I need to head back to Portland. I have an early appointment, so I'm not going to have time to stop by Marlow House before I leave; would you tell Lily and Danielle bye for me?"

Ian set his phone on the table and looked at Kelly. "I need to tell you something. And I would appreciate it if you wouldn't start asking me a million questions. I really don't want to talk about it, and I would appreciate you respect my privacy."

Pausing mid-sip, Kelly frowned at her brother. "What's wrong?"

"Lily and I won't be seeing each other anymore."

Kelly's eyes widened. Unable to stop herself, she blurted, "What happened?"

"I said I don't want to talk about it." Ian took a drink of his coffee.

"But...um...okay...I guess..." She studied her brother a moment. "But when you want to talk, I'm here for you."

Ian nodded. "I know that."

Absently fiddling with her coffee cup, Kelly sat silently with her brother for a few minutes.

Ian broke the silence when he added, "You should probably know I'll be giving notice on this house."

Kelly frowned. "What do you mean, notice?"

"I'm not staying in Frederickport."

"Not staying in Frederickport? Are you serious? You love it here!"

"It's time for me to move on, Kelly."

"Ian, would you please not make any rash decisions. I have no idea what's going on with you and Lily, and I'll respect your privacy and not besiege you with questions—and trust me, that's not an easy thing for me to do. But as your sister, someone who loves you very much and wants what's best for you, I don't want to see you rush into anything. Please give yourself some time. Step back a moment and regroup. Please. Do it for yourself."

THE FIRST THING Lily did on Monday morning was take a shower. Afterwards, she dressed casually in yoga pants, an oversized T-shirt, and clipped her red hair atop her head in a messy bundle. Not bothering to slip shoes or slippers on her bare feet, she headed to the kitchen for coffee. There she found Danielle sitting at the table, drinking her second cup.

"Morning, Lily," Danielle said in a soft voice.

"No need to look at me like that," Lily said sharply as she poured herself a cup of coffee. "I did my tears yesterday, and now I am over it." Full cup in hand, Lily marched to the table and sat down.

Reserving comment, Danielle sipped her coffee and silently observed Lily, noting her red-rimmed eyes.

"Is Joanne coming in today?" Lily asked.

"No. She was here yesterday afternoon and got the rooms cleaned. I told her not to bother coming in until Thursday or Friday. Our next round of guests don't arrive until Friday."

"Hmm…I must have been in my room. I didn't even realize she was here." Lily slumped down in her chair. She had looked far more confident when she had walked into the kitchen a moment earlier.

"When she was here, I told her you were having one of your migraines and was lying down in your room."

Lily glanced around. "Is Walt here?"

Danielle shook her head. "I haven't seen him this morning."

"Has there been any news on Agatha?"

"I haven't talked to the chief today. I spoke to him on the phone last night. I don't think he sees this as just a tragic accident. He wants to find out who took Agatha up those stairs."

"I thought Larry did?" Lily absently fiddled with her coffee cup.

Danielle shrugged. "They still can't find him. At least they hadn't yesterday."

"I assume they went to his house?"

"Yes. And according to the neighbors, none of them remembers seeing him since Saturday morning before the party."

"Hmm…doesn't make Larry look good." Lily glanced from her cup to Danielle and asked, "Did you tell the chief about me and Ian?"

"Yeah. I hope you aren't upset. But I figured he needed to have a heads-up in case Ian goes to him. I hope you don't mind. I also talked to Chris."

"What about Heather?"

"Chris said he would talk to her this morning at work. But they agreed they would not butt in—that they wouldn't say anything to

Ian unless you wanted them to. But if he comes to them, they will tell him the truth."

"Thanks." Lily smiled sadly. "But I don't think he is going to go to any of you."

"Well, I did try calling him yesterday, and he wouldn't answer his phone."

Lily let out a weary sigh. "Because I was unable to offer an explanation he found plausible, he seems to have jumped to the conclusion that we're all keeping some big secret from him. And actually, we have been."

"I just think he's not able to wrap his head around all this. Maybe he'll come around," Danielle suggested. "Just give him time."

"I guess this makes him sort of like Joe. Unable to have faith in someone he supposedly cares about."

"I don't know, Lily. I think maybe it all happened so fast, Ian is just trying to put the pieces together in a way he understands. Are you going to try talking to him today?"

"No. After all those tears yesterday, I woke up kind of pissed."

Danielle arched her brow. "Pissed?"

"Yeah. The way he freaking ordered me out of his house. And the way he put his hand up, you know, *talk to the hand*. I mean, really, screw that." Lily stood up. "I still love Ian, but I'm not going to run after him and beg him to listen to me. And frankly, if I talked to him right now, I would probably punch him in the nose."

Danielle chuckled. "Now you sound like Walt."

"How so?" Lily carried her now empty mug to the counter and set it in the sink.

"Last night he said he wanted to punch Ian in the nose."

"I get first dibs," Lily grumbled. She turned to Danielle and leaned back against the counter, her arms crossed over her chest.

"Before you deck anyone, you need to keep your strength up. How about I make you some breakfast? Or we could go out to eat?"

Lily shook her head. "No, thanks. I'm not really hungry. And to be honest, I sorta want to be alone today and think. I'm not in the best of moods."

"I understand." Danielle glanced at the clock. "This morning, I'm going to run down to the bank and put the Missing Thorndike back in the safe deposit box, and I need to deposit that money from Saturday so I can send the check to the school district."

"Is the bank open today? I would expect it to be closed, because of the holiday," Lily asked.

"It's open today. I already checked."

"I imagine the bank is going to be surprised you've decided to put the Missing Thorndike back in their vault."

"I suppose. I feel a little guilty they got so much bad press, and it really wasn't their fault. It wasn't even Kissinger's fault—even though I'm pretty sure he was behind the attempt to steal the necklace."

"One thing I learned from that leprechaun wannabe, some ghosts can be a major pain in the butt," Lily snapped.

"I suppose we can be happy Agatha's spirit didn't stick around. From what I know of her, she wasn't that pleasant in life."

"I have to admit my patience is a bit thin right now. I know it's not Walt's fault Ian left me because he can't believe in ghosts. But I swear, if another ghost crosses my path, I'm likely to snap," Lily grumbled.

AFTER DANIELLE LEFT for the bank, Lily went up to the attic and peeked in on Walt. She knew he was sitting on the sofa—it was evident by the open book seemingly floating over it. He was obviously reading. She had no idea he had dream hopped with Ian the previous night. But she did know Walt had been concerned for her, and she wanted to let him know she appreciated his concern.

From the attic, Lily went down to the library to find her own book to read. When she walked into the room, she found Max dozing on the small sofa.

"Hey, Max," Lily said softly as she stopped by the sofa for a moment and ran her hand over his fur.

Lifting his head, Max opened his eyes and looked at Lily. He started to purr. Leaning down, she planted a kiss on his forehead. "You're a good cat, Max. I don't care what Sadie says." The moment she said Sadie, Lily felt her stomach drop. *Sadie—Ian*—she was going to miss them both.

Refusing to cry, Lily turned her attention to the bookshelf. As she did, she heard Max let out an unholy screech. Turning quickly to the sofa, Lily found Max standing, his back arched and his fur on end.

"What is it, Max?" Lily asked, glancing to where he seemed to be looking.

The cat jumped down from the sofa and crept toward the far wall, all the while emitting low gurgling sounds. When he was about three feet from the wall, he began to hiss, his right paw relentlessly batting the air before him.

With a frown, Lily stepped closer. "Max, what's wrong? Max, nothing's there…"

Lily froze. Instead of continuing her sentence, she focused on the space between Max and the wall. With narrowed eyes, Lily angrily planted her balled fists on her hips.

"It's you, Agatha Pine? Isn't it? You've come back."

Max stopped hissing. Instead, he sat down, his eyes still focused on the space in front of him while he made a low, growling sound, his tail twitching.

"I'm sorry you're dead. But we really don't need any more ghosts hanging around Marlow House. So please, follow the light, or whatever it is you ghosts are supposed to do, and freaking move on!"

FIFTEEN

The teller told Joyce to wait at Susan Mitchell's desk. She was the one who could help her. Joyce didn't want to set her new handbag on the floor of the bank. When she tried hanging it over the back of the chair, it kept falling off. It ended up on her lap. Fidgeting with its straps, she anxiously waited for Susan, her heart pounding and feet nervously tapping against the carpeted floor in anticipation.

"Morning, Joyce," Susan greeted when she reached her desk. "I'm so sorry about your mother," she said as she took a seat behind her desk.

"Mother lived a long life. I'm grateful for that." Joyce smiled weakly.

"What can I help you with today?"

"I understand I'm the beneficiary on my mother's bank account here," Joyce explained.

"Weren't you a signer on your mother's account?" Susan asked.

Joyce shook her head. "No. Mother liked to handle her own banking, and we always kept our bank accounts separate. But she told me I was listed as the beneficiary."

"It's just that many of our customers with elderly parents, especially if they live with them, normally are signers on the parent's account."

Joyce smiled. "Yes, I tried to get Mother to do that. But she was pretty stubborn."

"Your mother did have a mind of her own," Susan agreed, turning her attention to her computer. After clicking away on her keyboard and moving her mouse, she stared at the monitor. Finally, she said, "Yes, you're right. Your mother made you her beneficiary on the account."

Joyce broke into a wide grin. "So what now? Do you transfer it into my own account, or do I just use Mother's?"

Looking from the monitor to Joyce, Susan said, "I'm afraid, first you'll need a death certificate."

"A death certificate? Why?" Joyce frowned.

"That's just the rule."

"But you were there on Saturday. You know my mother is dead," Joyce reminded her.

"I'm sorry, Joyce, if it were just up to me, I'd let you have it now. But I really can't. I know the funeral home will help you order the death certificates. Normally you'll need a few to settle her estate."

Joyce let out a sigh. "I suppose I should have expected that." She glanced briefly at her purse and then looked back to Susan. "But can I ask you one favor?"

"What's that?"

"Can you at least tell me how much Mother has in the account? I have some things to settle for her estate, and I'd just like to see where she stands."

"Sure, that shouldn't be a problem." Susan looked back to the computer. After a few keystrokes she said, "She has a little over nine hundred."

"Nine hundred thousand? It should be more," Joyce said with a frown.

Susan looked nervously from the computer to Joyce. "Umm... no...nine hundred dollars."

"What? Only nine hundred dollars? What happened to my mother's money?" Joyce fairly shrieked, drawing attention from several customers standing in line in front of the teller windows.

"I don't know what to tell you, but according to this, your mother has never had more than a thousand dollars in her account." Susan turned her attention back to the computer and moved quickly through Agatha's online account.

Joyce shook her head. "That's impossible."

Susan looked back to Joyce, her expression sympathetic. "The only deposits she ever had were from Social Security." Susan paused a moment and then cringed before saying, "And I hate to say this, but I imagine most of the money that is currently in her account will probably be coming back out."

Joyce frowned. "I don't understand?"

"Her deposit from Social Security went into her account this morning. Until that deposit, she had less than fifty dollars in her account. Since it's the beginning of the month, they'll probably take the money back."

"Are you saying that on the day my mother died, she had less than fifty dollars in her account?"

"I'm afraid so."

"Then she must have another account here. Maybe a savings account?"

Susan shook her head. "I'm afraid not. This is the only bank account she has here. But I do remember her telling me, on more than one occasion, that she only used this account for her Social Security payments and that she kept her savings in another bank."

"I should have realized Mother—being Mother—wouldn't have kept her money here. That would make it too easy for her to actually spend it. This morning I made an appointment with her attorney in Portland. He has her will there. I imagine he also has the information on her other bank accounts."

WHEN DANIELLE PULLED up in front of the bank, she spied Joyce Pruitt coming out its front door. By the time Danielle parked and got out of the car, Joyce was no longer in sight.

"I can't believe you want to put the Missing Thorndike back in the safe deposit box," Susan told Danielle ten minutes later as she led her back to the vault room.

"I have a gut feeling whatever might have been a problem with the safe deposit boxes has since been resolved," Danielle said, thinking of the spirit who had moved the gold from her safe deposit box and who had since moved on.

"You mean Kissinger?" Susan said under her breath.

"Not saying a word," Danielle said with a grin. Considering she believed he had instigated the attempted robbery at Marlow House, she didn't feel guilty implicating him in the theft from her safe deposit box.

"I shouldn't be talking about it either." Susan stood in front of the safe deposit boxes while Danielle handed her a key. "But if people knew you had enough faith in the bank that you put the Missing Thorndike back in your safe deposit box, it would sure make my job easier."

"You have my permission to spread the word," Danielle told her.

"Gee, thanks, Danielle. I really appreciate it. I also wanted to say I think it was generous of you not to press charges against Joyce, and how you urged the bank not to pursue any charges. Like you said, most people couldn't resist that sort of temptation, and she eventually did the right thing."

"That's what I believe. By the way, I noticed Joyce coming out of the building when I pulled up." Danielle waited for Susan to open her box. "I still can't believe her mother fell down those stairs."

"That was horrible, but I can't imagine what Agatha was doing climbing those stairs in the first place." Susan handed Danielle the box.

"I don't need any privacy for this. Let me just put the necklace back inside the box, and you can lock it up."

Susan nodded and watched as Danielle pulled a pouch from her purse. She removed the necklace for a moment and showed it to Susan before returning it to the pouch and placing it in the safe deposit box.

"Gosh, that thing is gorgeous. Do you think it really is cursed?"

Danielle shrugged. "I'm beginning to wonder."

DENNIS PORTERFIELD TOOK a seat facing the chief's desk.

"I appreciate you coming in this morning," the chief said as he closed the office door.

Dennis let out a heavy sigh. "I still can't believe all this happened."

Taking a seat behind the desk, the chief asked, "Has anyone in the family heard from Larry yet?"

"No. We stopped by his house on our way home on Saturday.

He wasn't there. Martha has been trying to call him. But he hasn't answered the phone."

"I sent some officers over to his place, and his neighbors haven't seen him. Do you have any theories about what happened between him and his grandmother?"

"Joyce thinks Larry and Gran must have gotten into an argument after they got upstairs. Who knows, maybe once he helped her up the staircase he decided it'd be too difficult to haul the wheelchair up like she wanted. Gran could be pretty demanding. I could see them getting into an argument over that and then him just leaving her there, figuring someone else could deal with her."

"But if he helped her upstairs, and they argued over bringing the wheelchair up, I would have expected him to leave her standing there. She obviously made it over to the attic staircase."

Dennis shrugged. "Then someone must have helped her walk across the second floor. She couldn't do it by herself. Maybe Larry did, and they argued about something else when they started to go up to the attic, and he left her then."

"Does Larry have a habit of just taking off and not saying anything?"

"Actually, he does. Hate to say this, but all of Martha's brothers are a little flaky. But Larry is the one who keeps to himself the most. I think he had a hard time growing up in that house, more so than the rest of them. He has some resentment there—which is understandable, considering everything. His way of dealing is to shut people out. That's what he does. I think that's why his marriage fell apart."

"When I asked Joyce for Larry's ex-wife's phone number, she didn't have it. Do you?"

Dennis shook his head. "No. I just know she moved back to Vancouver."

"If Larry got into an argument with his grandmother before taking her up those stairs, could she have gotten up to the second floor by herself?"

"I suppose it's possible. If she held onto the rail and took one step at a time. She could do it."

"But once upstairs, on the second floor, would she have been able to walk to the attic staircase by herself?"

Dennis shook his head. "No. That would be impossible. Gran needed to hold onto something in order to move around. She stopped using a cane this last year because she said it wouldn't hold her up. To get around, she needed her wheelchair or something sturdy to hold onto. Whenever Joyce went somewhere, she either had one of us come over and stay with Gran or made sure she was in her wheelchair."

"Shane was in the attic when Agatha fell down the stairs. He insists he didn't know his grandmother was on the second floor until he started down the attic stairs and found her on the floor."

"That's what he told us too."

"Do you believe him?" the chief asked.

"The family all went over to Joyce's yesterday. All but Larry. Shane went on and on about how shocked he was to find Gran on the floor. As you know, Shane's history is a little sketchy. He's had his brushes with the law. But one thing about him, he's a horrible liar."

"Are you saying you believe him?"

"The way he kept going on and on, about how shocked he was to find her—he was so hyped up about it—it just didn't seem fake to me. Not knowing Shane like I do. Frankly, I'd be shocked if I found out he lied. Because that would mean he's become a good liar. Which, for someone as sketchy as Shane, is not a good thing."

"HOW DID IT GO?" Brian Henderson asked the chief after Dennis left the station.

"We need to find Larry. And I'd like to look a little closer at Shane."

Folding his arms across his chest, Brian leaned against the open doorway and watched as the chief gathered up papers from his desk, stacking them in a neat pile.

"Shane. That kid got into his share of trouble. I remember hauling him in for selling pot. And then there was that breaking and entering charge, and about a year ago the check fraud."

"The check fraud was his mother's account, and she got those charges dropped. Insisted it was all a mistake."

"Yeah, right," Brian said dryly. "So what's the deal? You think it really was something other than an accident?"

"After talking to Dennis and the coroner, I'm not convinced it was an innocent accident. It's very possible Agatha Pine was murdered."

SIXTEEN

"You're Walt Marlow," the raspy female voice accused.

Walt glanced up from the book he was reading. Standing in the doorway was Agatha Pine. Not Agatha in the flesh, but she looked just as she did when he had last seen her alive. Yet, unlike the living version, this Agatha didn't need a wheelchair to get around.

"Oh bother," Walt muttered with a sigh as he closed his book and tossed it on the sofa next to him.

"So this is the infamous attic?" As she entered the room, Agatha glanced around curiously.

"I had really hoped you had moved on."

"I've always wanted to see this room, but I didn't quite make it before." Standing in the middle of the attic, she looked up to the ceiling. "Is that where George Hemming found you hanging?"

"You're rather ghoulish."

"I'm a ghost, aren't I?" Agatha chuckled. "Aren't ghosts supposed to be ghoulish?"

"You really need to move on. I believe the proper protocol is follow the light. Have you seen the light yet?"

Turning to Walt, Agatha spied a folding chair next to the sofa. She walked to it and sat down. "I've heard people talk about the light. I was beginning to think it was nothing but a myth. You're here, so I have to assume you didn't see it."

"It's not a myth. And why I'm still here is not your concern."

"Did I ask why you're still here?" Agatha snapped. "I couldn't care less."

"You do understand you're dead, right?"

"Obviously. Although, I was a little confused at first. I ran into Chief MacDonald's boy, and he started talking to me. At that point, I was disoriented, and I assumed I was still alive. I ended up outside, but no one seemed to see me. I walked all the way home and waited for Joyce. And do you know what she did when she came home?"

"What's that?"

"At first, I thought she could see me too. After all, she was asking me questions. But then she started emptying my closet, throwing my clothes on the floor. I asked her what she thought she was doing and told her to stop."

"That was quick. She started getting rid of your things the day you died?"

"That was when I realized I had to be dead. Joyce would never dare go through my things when I was alive."

"Why did you come back here?" Walt asked.

Agatha frowned at the question. She sat in silence for a few moments before answering. "I'm not really sure. It was as if something was pulling me here. I didn't really have a choice. And then I ran into Lily Miller downstairs."

Agatha shifted slightly in her seat and looked directly at Walt. "How is it some living people can see me and some cannot?"

"You mean how was Evan MacDonald able to see you, yet Lily wasn't?"

Agatha shook her head. "No. I mean how are Evan and Lily able to see me, yet other people don't?"

"Are you saying Lily could see you?" Walt asked in surprise.

"She must have. Very rude young woman, if I do say so myself. Quite rude. After all, I've only recently departed, and one would think that would demand some respect from those who can see me."

"Are you sure Lily saw you?"

"She called me by name. What else am I supposed to think?"

"What did she say?"

"She told me to leave Marlow House."

"You obviously didn't listen to her," Walt smirked.

"I would have if I could," Agatha said primly, her back straight as she sat on the edge of the chair. "I'm not about to stick around where I'm not wanted. I endured enough of that during my life."

"You seem to have adjusted to the fact you're dead," Walt observed.

Agatha shrugged. "It's not as if I didn't know it was coming, considering my age. I just assumed I would die in my sleep. I never expected a violent death."

"You remember how you died?" Walt asked.

Agatha frowned at Walt. "Of course I do. I admit, things were a little fuzzy at first. When I left Marlow House, I didn't realize I was dead. Then I saw Joyce throwing my things on the floor, and when she didn't answer—obviously could not see or hear me, well, then I knew. After that, things became very clear."

"So clear that you remember how you happened to fall down those stairs?"

"Maybe that's why I came back," Agatha muttered, speaking more to herself. "I needed to walk up those stairs again—but this time, I wanted to make it all the way up."

"Who helped you upstairs the first time?" Walt asked.

Agatha started to say something, but then changed her mind and remained silent.

"What happened? Who took you up there and just left you?" he persisted. "How did you fall? Did someone…push you?"

"I…I don't want to talk about it."

"If someone pushed you, I think we should let the police know."

"How do you expect to do that?" Agatha laughed.

"I have my ways. But you need to tell me what happened that day."

"Didn't I just say I don't want to talk about this?"

Agatha vanished.

DANIELLE STOPPED by the police station on the way home. She wanted to talk to the chief, but the first person she ran into was Joe Morelli. Wearing his Frederickport Police Department uniform and holding his baseball-style department hat in one hand, Joe stood in the middle of the hallway. Danielle wondered if he was on his way in or heading out on police business.

"I talked to Kelly when she was on her way back to Portland this morning; she told me Ian and Lily broke up," Joe said.

"Wow, I guess this is really official if Ian is telling people,"

Danielle muttered. She glanced down the hallway at the closed door leading to the chief's office.

"So it's true?"

"Unfortunately, yes."

Joe shook his head. "I can't believe it. I thought Lily was crazy about Ian."

Danielle frowned. "She is. Ian broke up with her. She didn't break up with him."

"No way. Ian is nuts about Lily. He was going to ask her to marry him."

Danielle arched her brow. "What?"

"Damn," Joe muttered. "I wasn't supposed to say anything. I didn't even say anything to Kelly. Please, keep this between us. Especially now. Damn, I wonder what happened…"

"Why do you think he was going to ask her to marry him?" Danielle asked.

"Because, last week when I went to Portland to see Kelly, I stopped to pick up some wine, and next door to the wine shop was a jewelry store. Ian was inside. He was buying Lily's engagement ring. He asked me not to tell his sister. He told me he was planning to ask her during the fireworks show. That's why he didn't want to go with us when Kelly invited him."

"Oh my…" Danielle whispered.

"What happened, Danielle?"

She shook her head. "It's kind of complicated. Didn't Kelly tell you?"

"No. Kelly said she had no clue what happened. Her brother refused to talk about it. I just assumed Lily must have called it off. Maybe he asked her to marry him, and she turned him down?"

"No. In fact, Lily has no idea he intended to propose."

"I really thought they were a great couple. Considering everything they've gone through this last year, well, if anyone could make it, I would think it would have been Ian and Lily."

Danielle wondered briefly if Joe was thinking what she was. This same time last year, they had been dating several weeks when their relationship had fallen apart, unable to pass its first test.

"I WAS TALKING to Joe in the hall," Danielle told the chief when she entered his office a few minutes later. She closed the door behind her so they would have some privacy.

"He told me about Lily and Ian," the chief said.

"Did you say anything?" Danielle asked.

"I pretended I didn't know. But I can't believe Ian would just walk away from Lily over this."

"He obviously thinks she's blatantly lying, and we're all in on it. He won't even talk to me."

"If I didn't have a murder to investigate, I'd be tempted to shake some sense into that boy."

Danielle's eyes widened. "Murder?"

WALT WAS WAITING in the kitchen for Danielle when she got home. She found him sitting at the table, smoking a cigar.

"Hey, Walt. The Missing Thorndike is safe and sound in the safe deposit box at the bank, and as long as another klepto ghost doesn't come along, it should be fine." Danielle tossed her purse on the counter.

Walt's eyes followed Danielle as she went to the sink and washed her hands. "Agatha is here."

"Crap," Danielle muttered as she turned off the faucet and wiped her hands on a dishtowel. "Where?"

"She was in the attic, but when I asked her about the fall, she disappeared." Letting out a smoke ring, Walt watched as it drifted to the ceiling and dissolved.

"The chief is convinced she was murdered."

"Why does he think that?" Walt asked.

"It's how Agatha landed. According to the coroner, she must have fallen backwards. I guess they would have expected her to land differently had the fall been the result of her missing a step or stumbling."

"If it was murder, she doesn't seem overly concerned," Walt noted.

"But, does she know how she fell?"

"Yes. But she won't say who helped her get upstairs or if someone pushed her."

"You asked her if someone pushed her?" Danielle took a seat at the table.

"Yes. She didn't want to talk about it."

"And you're sure she remembers what happened?"

"Fairly certain. She has accepted the fact she's dead." Walt then muttered before taking another drag off the cigar, "Hell of a lot faster than I accepted my death."

"Well, dear, you have always been a little slow," Danielle teased, reaching over and patting his hand—which didn't particularly work out, as her hand moved through his, tapping the tabletop. With a frown she pulled her hand back.

Walt let out a dramatic sigh and asked, "Why do I take this abuse?"

"Because you love me?" Danielle teased.

Yes, I do, he silently thought.

"You're home," Lily announced when she walked into the kitchen a moment later.

"Hey, Lily. I'm sitting here with Walt. Have you had lunch yet?"

"No. But stop trying to feed me. I feel like I'm living with my mother again." Lily plopped down on one of the empty chairs.

"Another interesting development," Walt piped.

"What's that?" Danielle asked.

"Apparently, Lily can see Agatha."

Danielle turned to Lily and stared.

Noticing Danielle's peculiar expression, Lily frowned and said, "What?"

"Walt says you can see Agatha."

"Agatha? What do you mean?"

"Walt says Agatha's spirit was here earlier."

Slamming her fist on the table, Lily shouted, "I knew it!"

"So you did see her?" Danielle asked.

Lily rolled her eyes at Danielle. "Don't be silly. I didn't see her. But Max did. He was in the library, hissing up a storm, staring at the wall. And I've learned when Max or Sadie start acting as if something is there that I can't see, it's normally a freaking ghost. I just made a guess it was Agatha. What was the chance it was some other ghost?"

"What did you say to her?"

"She told me to leave, rude girl," Agatha said when she appeared a moment later.

SEVENTEEN

Danielle had to admit, death looked good on Agatha. She appeared to be about the same age as Agatha's last living version, yet she was no longer hunched over, nor did she seem to have a problem walking around. Of course, Danielle understood the body she was seeing was nothing but an illusion, so she wasn't surprised at the transformation. Although, in the past, Danielle had noticed new spirits typically displayed whatever handicap they had during life, and it was not until they fully adapted to death did they shed those illusions before moving on. Apparently, Agatha had adapted very quickly to her death, Danielle thought.

"Hello, Agatha," Danielle said calmly.

Eyeing Danielle curiously, a smile curled on Agatha's lips. "So you can see me too?"

"Oh dang, don't tell me she is here." Lily groaned. "I really can't deal with this." Without another word, Lily turned and marched from the room, and on her exit inadvertently walked through Agatha.

"Why! How rude!" Agatha looked down at her own body in dismay, startled by Lily's abrupt movement through it.

"You'll have to excuse Lily, she didn't realize you were there," Danielle explained after Lily left the room.

"What are you talking about? I know she can see me, so you can't use that excuse for her utter rudeness. She's made it perfectly clear she doesn't want me here. And frankly, I don't want to be here either!"

Danielle watched Agatha as she paced the kitchen. "No. Lily can't see spirits. She just guessed you were there earlier, because of how Max acted."

Coming to a stop, Agatha turned to Danielle. "Max? Who's that?"

"It's my cat."

"Another rude one! He also told me to leave!"

Danielle forced a smile. "Would you like to sit down? That way we can have a little talk without me getting dizzy watching you circle the room."

Agatha looked from Danielle to Walt, who sat at the table, quietly observing as he puffed on his cigar.

"I suppose you can see him too?" Agatha nodded toward Walt.

"Yes. Unlike Lily, I can see spirits."

"Like the chief's boy?"

"Yes." Danielle nodded. "Evan is able to see spirits."

"I've heard of people who can see ghosts, but I never quite believed it before."

Danielle glanced at Walt and thought, *Agatha doesn't seem to have a problem calling herself a ghost.*

"I'm not sure how proper it is, your sharing a house with Walt Marlow," Agatha said in a huff as she sat down.

Danielle joined them at the kitchen table. "I'm not sure what you mean."

Agatha eyed Walt critically. "He is an attractive young man. And you and Lily are both single women. Of course, with Lily's nasty disposition I doubt she has anything to worry about. However, you…" Agatha turned her attention to Danielle.

"Me?"

"It's rather scandalous, if you think about it." Agatha shuddered.

Walt flashed Danielle a grin.

"How about we talk about you," Danielle asked Agatha.

"What's there to talk about?"

"You said you didn't want to be here."

"I don't."

"Normally when a spirit is somewhere they don't want to be, it's because they have some unresolved issues to deal with," Danielle explained.

"Don't be ridiculous," Agatha snapped. "What unresolved issues do I have?"

"It could be the cause of your death that's keeping you here. You need to come to terms with it. Walt tells me you remember what happened, but you don't want to discuss it."

"I don't. There's nothing I can do about it now. So why dwell on the unpleasantness?"

"I understand your grandson Larry helped you upstairs."

"Helped me?" Agatha scoffed. "Is that what you call it now?"

Danielle was about to ask Agatha if Larry had pushed her down the stairs. But then she remembered what Walt had told her, that when pressed about the cause of her death, Agatha had vanished earlier. Danielle preferred to resolve whatever issues Agatha had in order to help her move on to the next level. She did not wish to play a perpetual game of peekaboo with a ghost who randomly appeared and disappeared, or worse yet, one who remained indefinitely at Marlow House.

Deciding to take a different approach, one that hopefully wouldn't cause Agatha to disappear, Danielle asked, "Can you tell me a little bit about your grandson Larry?"

"He's just like his father. Even has the same name. Looks like him too. That boy has been a constant disappointment."

"I was under the impression you were close to your grandchildren. Whenever I've seen them with you, they appear to be very attentive."

"Yes, they appear that way. Henry is the only one who ever cared about me. Darling boy. But Larry, his only interest is what he can get from me. When we came over here on Saturday, he was very angry with me."

"Why was he angry?"

"The same reason he always is. He wants money, and I won't give it to him. I'm not going to keep throwing good money after bad. The boy, just like his father, couldn't keep his marriage together. He expected me to bail him out. I told him he could just wait until I die to get my money." Agatha paused a moment and considered her words. She then broke into laughter.

"What's funny?" Danielle asked.

"I suppose he can try to get his money now." Agatha disappeared.

"She's gone again," Walt said as he flicked his cigar in the air. It, like Agatha, vanished.

"I suppose I need to call the chief, let him know she's here." Danielle stood up and walked to the counter where she had dropped her purse earlier. From it she removed her cellphone and made her call.

When Danielle got off the phone a few minutes later, she returned to the table with Walt.

"Agatha think's it's scandalous I'm living here with you," Walt said with a chuckle.

"I think Agatha has a dirty mind," Danielle scoffed.

Walt silently studied Danielle for a moment and then said in a low voice, "In some ways, Agatha would be disappointed. Our time together under this roof is fairly innocent. It's the dreams we share that seem to take us places we probably shouldn't go."

Danielle's gaze met Walt's. "Harmless kisses."

"Harmless?" Walt smiled. "Are they? If so, why is it we've never discussed them?"

Danielle absently fidgeted with the table's edge. "We are now. And they're just dreams. You can do anything in a dream."

Walt let out a harsh laugh. "Ahh, if that were the case, then Agatha would truly be scandalized."

"I didn't mean *that*," Danielle said with a blush.

Walt smiled softly.

Danielle glanced up to Walt. "I didn't tell you." She paused and looked at the doorway and then looked back to Walt. "According to Joe, Ian was going to ask Lily to marry him." She then went on to tell him about her recent encounter with Joe and their discussion at the police station.

When she finished recounting the exchange, Walt closed his eyes for a moment and let out a sigh. "I hope he comes to his senses. I hate seeing Lily so unhappy."

"And if he waits too long, she may be unable to forgive him. Lily can be pretty stubborn."

They were interrupted when a loud meow came from the doorway leading from the kitchen to the hallway.

Walt turned to Max, who sat just inside the kitchen, his tail twitching back and forth while his golden eyes peered into Walt.

"Yes, Max, that other spirit is still here." Walt stared at Max in silence for a few minutes and then said, "I understand."

"You understand what?" Danielle asked.

"Max doesn't like Agatha. I suppose she should not have been so open with her thoughts when her spirit-self first encountered Max."

Danielle frowned. "Why is that?"

"Apparently Agatha is not a pet-friendly person. She especially dislikes cats and is unashamed at what she's done to them over the years."

"Done to them?" Danielle gasped.

"She didn't brag about drowning kittens or anything," Walt began, only to have Max express his disdain for the comment by a low gurgling growl.

Danielle glanced to Max briefly. "I'm with you there, buddy. Anyone who hurts kittens is beyond contempt."

"As I was saying, while she didn't boast about hurting defenseless kittens, she admitted taking a cat Joyce had adopted to the pound, and then she lied to her daughter, claimed she hadn't seen it, and even offered to call down to the pound and see if someone had brought it in. Of course she never actually called."

"And you learned all this, how?"

"Like I said, when Agatha first met Max, she was pretty free with her thoughts. I don't think she was fully aware that Max could read them. In essence, she was telling Max that if she could do to him what she did to Joyce's cat, she would."

"Max just told you all this?" Danielle asked.

"Yes. In his own way."

"Ugh, we really need to get Agatha to move on."

Max stood up and strolled toward the table. He stopped before Walt and sat back down. Looking up to Walt, he let out a meow.

"Sadie?" Walt stared down at Max.

"What about Sadie?" Danielle asked, glancing from Max to Walt. Before Walt had a chance to answer, Max stood up and dashed to the kitchen door leading to the side yard. In a flash, he flew through the pet door and disappeared. Its door swung back and forth for a few moments before coming to a stop.

"What was that all about?" Danielle asked.

"Apparently, Max has noticed Sadie's absence. It seems those two care more about each other than they let on."

"What do you mean?" Danielle glanced over to the pet door.

"Max wanted to know why Sadie hasn't been over for a couple of days. I told him she wouldn't be coming over again, and I wouldn't be surprised if she was moving. He didn't take the news well." Under his breath, Walt added, "I can't say I blame him."

MAX HATED DOGS. At least, that was what he had told himself before moving in with Danielle. There was a time when the news of Sadie's departure would have satisfied his feline heart. Not so anymore. It actually surprised him how troubling he found the news. So troubling, he needed to find some way to prevent it from happening.

Climbing one of the trees in the backyard, he used it to make his way to the other side of the fence. Just as he was about to jump down onto the sidewalk, he paused and looked down the street toward Chris's house.

Could this mean I might actually come to like that annoying little puppy Chris has adopted? If a cat was capable of cringing at the thought, Max would have. Instead, he leapt down onto the sidewalk and made his way to the other side of the street, to Ian and Sadie's house.

IAN HAD JUST STEPPED out to the hallway when he heard Sadie barking at the front door. He hadn't heard the doorbell ring. When he reached the door, he looked through the peephole before opening it. No one was there. Sadie continued to bark.

"Get back, girl," Ian ordered as he eased open the front door and looked outside.

A loud meow greeted him. Just as he looked down, Sadie pushed by Ian's legs, her tail wagging.

Sitting on his welcome mat was Danielle's cat, Max. The moment Sadie went outside, Max stood up and began weaving around the dog, rubbing against her while purring loudly.

EIGHTEEN

R eception sucked along this stretch of highway. *Or maybe it's just my crappy car radio,* Larry thought. With one hand on the steering wheel and his eyes moving from the road ahead and back to the dashboard, he fidgeted with the controls. He was hoping to catch Paul's daily radio show. He couldn't remember when it was on exactly. Unfortunately, by the time he found the station, Paul was wrapping up the show.

"Before I sign off, I want to extend my condolences to the family of Frederickport native Agatha Pine, who passed away this last weekend. Her grandmother and father moved to Frederickport in the twenties. Services will be held Wednesday afternoon, at 2:00 p.m., at Frederickport Cemetery's Memorial Chapel. Mrs. Pine died when—" Larry's car radio lost the signal before Paul was able to finish his sentence."

"Hot damn!" Larry shouted, slapping his palm on the steering wheel. "Things are looking up!" Grinning ear to ear, Larry turned off the radio and began humming a tune. He was still smiling when he pulled up in front of his house on Monday afternoon. It wasn't until Brian Henderson pulled up behind his car and parked did the smile start to fade.

"WHAT HAS HE SAID?" the chief asked Brian as the two stood in the office adjacent to the interrogation room, looking through the two-way mirror, watching Larry Pruitt. He sat alone at the table, fidgeting with his wristwatch.

"I asked him if he knew his grandmother had died. He said yes. I told him we needed to talk to him and asked him to come in with me. He didn't seem to have a problem with it."

"I suspect he knew we would be showing up. I imagine he has his story already worked out," the chief said, turning from the mirror and heading to the door.

"AFTERNOON, LARRY," MacDonald greeted him when he walked into the interrogation room a few minutes later.

Larry turned to MacDonald, watching him approach. "When Brian said you needed to talk to me about my grandmother, I didn't think it would require questioning in here."

"I have some questions about how your grandmother died." MacDonald sat down across from Larry.

Larry flashed MacDonald a grin. "Just as long as she's really dead. That's all that I care about. I thought it would just be my luck if the old witch outlived us all. I bet my mother is over at her house celebrating."

MacDonald arched his brow. "You aren't even going to pretend to be sad?"

Larry laughed. "Are you serious? I'm glad she's dead, and I don't care who hears me say it. It's not like she can change her will now."

MacDonald frowned. Leaning back in the chair, he studied Larry. "I have to admit, your attitude surprises me."

"Why? Certainly you saw how she really was. A manipulative bitch who tried to control everyone in her family."

"Let me restate: I'm not surprised you're not sad over her death. I'm just surprised you're so freely expressing your opinion, considering how she died."

"What do you mean?" Larry asked with a frown. "What does how she died have to do with anything?"

"Considering she died under suspicious circumstances."

Still frowning, Larry repeated, "Suspicious circumstances?" He considered the chief's words for a moment. His frown turned to a smile, and he began to laugh.

Stunned at Larry's reaction, MacDonald asked, "What's so funny?"

"When you say *suspicious circumstances*, are you suggesting someone might have killed my grandmother?" he asked after suppressing his laughter.

"That's generally what it implies."

"So which one of them do you think did it? Frankly, I didn't think any of them had enough nerve." Larry leaned back against his chair and chuckled.

"You."

Larry's smile faded. "Me? I wasn't even here when the old battleax kicked off."

"You were the last one to see her alive."

No longer finding humor in the situation, Larry abruptly sat up straight in the chair. "Hey, I've been out of town all weekend. I wasn't even here. You can check with the Portland hospital. I've been there all weekend. Just got back to town less than an hour ago. Talk to the staff there; they'll back me up. I'll be happy to give you their names."

"You were here on Saturday when your grandmother died."

"Saturday? Are you saying she died on Saturday?"

"Right after you brought her in the house and took her upstairs. Did you just leave her there? What happened?"

Furiously shaking his head, Larry said, "I didn't even go upstairs with her. Yes, I took her in the house, but I didn't even make it up the stairs."

"Maybe you need to tell me exactly what happened after you wheeled your grandmother into the house the last time you saw her."

Taking a deep breath, Larry gave MacDonald a nod as he gathered his thoughts. "I wheeled her into the hallway, and just before we got to the stairs, my phone rang. The record of the call is still on it, you can check yourself."

"Who called, and what does it have to do with your grandmother's death?"

"It was my ex-wife. She was frantic, told me our son was in the hospital. It looked like a ruptured appendix. I told Gran I had to leave, asked her to tell Mom what was going on, and I just left her there. It's not like she isn't capable of getting around in the wheelchair; she does it at home all the time. She just wouldn't be able to get up the stairs by herself."

"So you just left?"

Larry nodded. "I drove straight to the hospital. Ended up staying there all weekend, taking turns with my wife, sitting with our son. He's doing better, so I just came home today to grab some things. I planned to go back this afternoon after I squared it with work."

"You haven't called them yet?"

Larry shook his head. "No. I had today off anyway because of the holiday. I planned to call my boss when I got back into town this afternoon, and see if I could get a few days off."

"Why didn't you answer your phone when your mother and sister tried to call you?"

Larry shrugged. "I told Gran if there was any news, I would call. I asked her to tell them not to call me."

Studying Larry's facial expressions, MacDonald asked, "Why would you do that?"

Larry let out a sigh. "Because Mom and Martha get all hovery when something like this happens. And frankly, I prefer they stay out of my private life."

"They are family," MacDonald reminded him.

"Yes, they are," Larry said coolly. "Which is precisely why I didn't answer their calls."

"I also left several messages on your phone to call me."

"I never answer a call from a number I don't recognize. Too many telemarketers calling cellphones now."

"I left a message," the chief said.

Larry shrugged. "Well, I was a little preoccupied with my son. I didn't bother checking my messages. I was at the hospital, and everyone I cared about was there."

"So you're saying your grandmother was alive when you last saw her on Saturday?" the chief asked.

Larry stood up for a moment and pulled his phone from his pocket. Leaning across the table, he handed it to the chief before sitting back down. "Yes. And you're welcome to check my phone. You'll see the incoming call from my wife right before I left Marlow House. And the text messages we exchanged about our son."

MacDonald looked at the phone briefly and then set it down on the table. He looked at Larry. "I'll do that in a minute. So tell me, do you think your grandmother could have gotten up those stairs by herself?"

"I would like to tell you she could. Maybe I'm not especially close to my siblings, but I really hate for one of them to go to jail for doing something that will make all of us happier."

"Is that a no?"

Larry considered the question, and then let out a sigh. He shook his head and said, "No way. Mom's house is a split-level; the only bedroom on the lower floor is the master. That was always Mom's room. But about a year ago, Gran said she could no longer get around without a wheelchair and insisted Mom switch rooms with her. Mom didn't want to do it at first, and she said she'd buy Gran a second wheelchair to leave on the upper level. There weren't that many stairs, and Mom insisted Gran could walk up them; after all, she is able to maneuver the shower with the grab rails. But Mom never bought the second wheelchair, and Gran got her room."

"What happened?"

"Gran could only maneuver up and down the stairs by holding onto the rail with one hand and having someone else hold her other arm. Mom realized the time she would be spending helping Gran up and down those stairs wasn't worth keeping the master bedroom. Plus, I think she suddenly realized it wouldn't be such a bad thing to have the upper floor to herself. Gran could no longer get up there by herself."

"Someone helped her up those stairs at Marlow House."

Larry shrugged. "Gran did say she was going to look for Henry to help her."

"Henry was supposedly in the downstairs bathroom when she was found."

"That boy must have been having a problem that day," Larry muttered.

"Why do you say that?"

"Because when we were sitting outside, Henry promised to take Gran to see the upper floors. He even offered to carry her wheelchair upstairs. But first, he said he wanted to use the bathroom. Promised he would be right back. But he didn't come back. He was gone for at least thirty minutes when I finally volunteered to take Gran. So was he in the bathroom that entire time?"

"What do you think?"

"I suspect he didn't go to the bathroom when he said he did. Henry was great at promising Gran things and not carrying through. But Gran had a soft spot for Henry, and she would ignore it when he did stuff like that." Larry shrugged.

"Do you think Henry could have taken her upstairs?"

"Sure. I mean, if she ran into him on the first floor, I don't think he could get out of it at that point. After all, he did offer to take her up there. You said she fell going up the attic stairs?"

"Yes. She was found at the bottom of the stairs on the second floor. Her neck was broken."

Larry cringed. "I can see him taking her up there. But if she fell, why didn't he admit he took her up there? I mean, it's not like he pushed her."

"Unless he did."

"So you think someone took her up the stairs—and then pushed her?"

MacDonald nodded. "It's possible. She didn't have her wheel-chair on the second floor. It was still downstairs. Somehow, she got up one flight of stairs, and then she crossed the second floor—without a wheelchair—and started up the attic stairs. If she couldn't walk without assistance, as you say, then someone had to have taken her up there. And if no one is coming forward to admit they helped her up the stairs, I have to wonder why."

"Maybe they left her because they were afraid. Not because they pushed her," Larry suggested.

"We know Shane was coming down from the attic when she fell."

"Shane? You didn't say anything about Shane being there."

"He's the one who found her. According to him, when he came down from the attic, he found her at the base of the stairs. He started shouting. That's when we found her."

"Shane..." Larry muttered. "I can't see him helping her up the stairs. But shoving her down the stairs? Yeah, I could see him doing that."

NINETEEN

Peeling back the foil wrapper, Adam was about to take his first bite of the breakfast burrito when he heard a soft knock at his door. He looked up and saw Ian Bartley standing in his office doorway.

"Hey, Ian," Adam greeted, rewrapping his burrito.

"I'm sorry; I'm interrupting your breakfast."

Adam shoved the now rewrapped burrito to the side of his desk. "No problem. What can I do for you?"

"Leslie wasn't in the front, so I hope it's okay I just walked on in." Ian took a seat facing Adam's desk.

"She's coming in late today. So what's up?"

"I need to talk to you about your grandmother's house."

"Is there a problem?"

"I need to move," Ian blurted.

"Move?" Adam sat up straighter in the chair. "Can't believe you found a better place in Frederickport, right on the water, for that price."

"No, I need to leave Frederickport."

"You're kidding me? Damn, I hate to see you go."

"I know I have another few months left on my lease. Of course I'll honor it. But I wanted to give you the heads-up. If you find someone who wants the house now, then they can have it, because I plan to move out by the end of the week."

"Where are you going?"

Ian didn't answer immediately. Finally, he said, "That's still up in the air."

"Is Lily going with you? If she is, I bet Danielle is going to miss her."

"Umm…no…Lily and I broke up."

Dumbfounded, Adam stared at Ian. "I'm sorry."

Ian shrugged. "It happens."

"Wow," Adam muttered, leaning back in the desk chair. He shook his head and let out a sigh. "Damn, I never thought I would feel this way."

Frowning in confusion, Ian asked, "What way?"

Adam shrugged. "I don't know. You and Lily just seemed so good together. Wow…" Adam shook his head and let out a sigh. "I hate to see you go."

"I've really enjoyed your grandmother's house. I can't imagine you'll have a problem re-renting it."

Sitting up straighter in the office chair, Adam looked at Ian. "Are you really sure about this?"

Ian nodded. "Yeah, it's for the best."

"Because I don't want to do anything rash if you and Lily get back together and you decide you want to stay. I mean, it happens all the time."

"No, it's really over, which is why I need to leave Frederickport and put all this behind me."

"Well, if you're sure. If you really plan to leave by the end of the week, I think I can let you out of the lease early, and you won't have to worry about paying August's rent."

"You have someone who wants to rent the house?"

"Actually, I have someone who wants to buy it. They've been bugging me for the last six months."

"Someone wants to buy it?" Ian said dully.

"Grandma has been considering selling the property for some time. When we first rented to you, it was only for the summer, so she figured it would give her a few months to get used to the idea. And then you wanted to extend the lease beyond the summer, and she liked you—actually she liked Lily," Adam added with a chuckle. "So she told me to go ahead and rent it to you for as long as you wanted, and that she'd think about selling when you decided to move out. I have a feeling though, she sort of hoped you would eventually want to buy the house."

IAN LEFT his car parked near Adam's office as he walked down to Lucy's Diner to have breakfast. He didn't see the need to drive his car such a short distance, plus parking was scarce downtown this time of year.

Walking down the street, he thought about his conversation with Adam. For some reason he couldn't fathom, it troubled him to think Marie was going to sell the house—*my house.*

No, it's not your house, Ian reminded himself. However, it was the first house since leaving his childhood home for college that actually felt like home. He had even entertained the idea of offering to purchase it from Marie after Lily agreed to marry him.

Walking away from Lily was proving to be even more difficult than he had imagined it would be. And he had never imagined it would be easy. A part of him wanted to believe Lily's outrageous story. But there was one thing the skeptic Ian could never believe in —*ghosts*. Over the years he had investigated a number of paranormal reports, and each one proved to be nothing more than a hoax.

It only took him less than ten minutes to reach Lucy's Diner. Once there, he grabbed the only empty booth, one located in the back corner. He had been served his coffee and was still looking over the menu, trying to decide what to order, when a female voice interrupted his concentration.

"Morning, Ian."

Looking up from the menu, he found Heather Donovan looking down at him. She wore a pink jersey T-shirt dress. Her coal black hair was pulled into two low braids, and her gray-blue eyes peered out at him from under straight-cut bangs.

"Morning, Heather," he said coolly, looking back at his menu.

"I guess you aren't going to ask me to join you," she said as she sat across from him in the booth. Tossing her purse on the bench seat next to her, she rested her elbows on the tabletop as she propped her chin on one balled fist. She stared at Ian.

Glancing up at Heather, Ian closed his menu and set it on the table. "I'd like to be alone."

"I'm not really supposed to talk to you," Heather announced, making no attempt to move.

"Why is that?"

"I know you broke up with Lily, and I know why. Chris told me we shouldn't butt in unless Lily asks us to. Which she hasn't. But if you come to us, Chris said we should be truthful."

"Did he now?" Ian asked skeptically.

The waitress interrupted their conversation when she came to take their order, coffee pot in hand. She set the full pot on the table and pulled out her order pad.

"I'll have bacon and eggs, scrambled with hash browns, and wheat toast. It's just me. Heather here was just leaving."

Heather smiled up at the waitress. "I was leaving, but that sounds good. I'll have the same thing. I'd like some coffee too."

"Why did you do that?" Ian grumbled after the waitress left.

"For one thing, I'm hungry." Heather picked up the cup of coffee the server had poured for her and took a sip.

Ian glanced around the diner, looking for somewhere else to sit, but all the tables and booths were full.

"Did you know I had a terrible crush on you when I first moved to town?"

"Can't say I did," Ian muttered as he picked up his coffee.

"I think Lily knew. Back then I wanted to be a writer like you." She sipped her coffee, her eyes still on him.

"I seem to remember something about you wanting to write."

"I was going to write about the ghost of Presley House. You know, the one who kept Danielle locked up in the basement right before the house burned down."

"I don't know anything about a ghost holding Danielle hostage."

Heather set her cup on the table and leaned back in the booth seat. "Oh, that's right. I think you were out of town at the time. I imagine Lily didn't tell you about it. She probably figured you wouldn't believe her, and then you'd walk out on her. Sort of like you're doing now."

"I don't know what you guys are up to, but I don't believe in ghosts."

"I used to think I gave up the idea of writing my book because without someone to back up my story, no one would believe me. I had sort of hoped that someone would be Danielle."

Ian glared at Heather. "Are you saying this is all about some book you're writing?"

Heather rolled her eyes and let out a sigh of exasperation. "You aren't paying attention, Ian. I just said I gave up on the idea of writing the book. You see, Danielle has been seeing ghosts her entire life, but she learned a long time ago that when you talk about it, people will just think you're crazy. So she prefers to keep it to herself."

"I know when Danielle was a child, she thought she could see ghosts. But she was just a kid at the time; she grew out of it," Ian explained.

"Did she now? She told you that?"

Picking up his cup, he took another sip and then shook his head. "No. It's just what I assume."

"I couldn't always see spirits." Heather paused a moment and chuckled. "I used to call them ghosts, but Walt has this thing about being called a ghost. He really doesn't like it."

"I don't care to hear about your make-believe ghosts," Ian snapped.

"I thought you would be curious. According to Chris, you saw Walt pour me a glass of wine the other night. By the way, I couldn't always see Walt. My sensitivity to spirits has increased since I moved to Frederickport. In fact, when I stayed at Marlow House, I only caught glimpses of Walt. Along with that damn cigar smell. Of course, everyone seems to notice that."

"So now you can see him?" Ian smirked.

"Yes. And I've seen a number of spirits since I've moved to town."

Ian set his mug back on the table, crossed his arms over his chest, and leaned back in his booth seat. He studied Heather. "So tell me, who all can see ghosts?"

"Chris is like Danielle. He's always been sensitive to spirits. Then of course there is Evan. He's more like Chris and Danielle. I'm a late bloomer."

Narrowing his eyes, he glared at Heather. "I don't know what you guys are up to, but dragging a kid into this?"

Leaning forward, Heather rested her elbows back on the table and met Ian's gaze. "You should be grateful for Evan. If it wasn't for that kid, you guys might have died in Arizona."

With a frown he asked, "What are you talking about?"

"That's something you should ask Lily about." Letting out a harsh laugh, she added, "Oh, that's right, you don't even want to hear the whole story. Chris told me you wouldn't even hear her out."

"I'd heard enough."

Again they were interrupted when the server brought their food. They spent the next five minutes in silence, each eating. Finally, Heather spoke.

"You know, everyone has the capability to see spirits. Some people are just more sensitive than others. I know Lily saw Darlene Gusarov at Pilgrim's Point."

Ian stopped eating for a moment and looked up at Heather. With a whisper he asked, "Pilgrim's Point?"

Heather eyed Ian with wry amusement as she slathered jam on her toast. "Yes. Of course, she's not the only one. Ever since I moved to town I've heard about Darlene, and then of course, she saved my life."

Ian stared blankly at Heather, who grinned back at him.

"You've heard the stories, haven't you?" she asked. "About Darlene Gusarov's ghost haunting Pilgrim's Point."

"Yes. I never thought much about it."

"I'm curious, did Lily ever mention her encounter with Darlene's ghost?"

Ian shook his head.

Before taking a large bite of her jam-covered slice of toast, Heather said, "I guess that doesn't surprise me. She probably thought you wouldn't believe her."

TWENTY

Ian felt Heather's eyes on him as he hastily made his way down the street, toward the offices of Frederickport Vacation Properties. When he was halfway down the street, he was tempted to turn around and see if she was still watching him. If he had, he would have found her standing near the newsstand in front of Lucy's Diner, hands on hips, shaking her head in disapproval. But then, he would have seen her turn away and walk in the opposite direction.

Just as Ian was about to pass the entrance of the rental office, Adam stepped out onto the sidewalk.

"Hey, Ian, did you forget something?" Adam greeted him.

Ian pointed to the parking lot. "No, I left my car down here while I walked up to Lucy's Diner."

"That's where I'm heading." Adam nodded toward the parking lot. "So how was breakfast?"

"It would have been fine if Heather Donovan hadn't decided to join me," Ian grumbled.

Adam chuckled. "Heather can be a little out there. But, she's nice looking, if you're into the Addams family look. I guess she's working for Chris now."

Ian paused a moment and looked at Adam. "Can I ask you something?"

No longer walking, Adam looked at Ian. "Sure, what?"

"Do you remember when Richard's car went over Pilgrim's Point?" Ian asked.

"Well, sure." Adam cringed. "I was the one who found him on the side of the road."

"I remember you told me a woman flagged you over."

Adam nodded. "Yeah, that was the weirdest thing."

"I also remember she took off before the police arrived."

"I guess you can say that," Adam muttered.

"You also told me you thought she looked like Darlene Gusarov."

Adam smiled. "Yeah. It was all pretty weird. I'd sure like to find that woman."

"Tell me again what happened," Ian urged.

"Why are you asking about this now?" Adam asked.

"It's just something Heather said."

"Oh, you mean how she saw her too?" Adam asked with a chuckle.

Ian frowned. "What are you talking about?"

"Heather claims it was Darlene's ghost who saved her when her car was hijacked. Said Darlene pulled her out of the car right before it went off the cliff. I suspect Heather jumped out. But being yanked out by a ghost is a lot more dramatic. Although, getting your car hijacked and managing to get out of it just before it flies off a cliff into the ocean is enough drama for me."

"That section of highway is deadly. Off the top of my head I can think of at least three people who've been killed along that stretch since I moved to town. Although Darlene's death wasn't from a car accident."

"It's always been a dangerous curve. As for Darlene's supposed ghost, I'm not sure how Heather would have recognized her, since I'm fairly certain Darlene was killed before Heather ever moved to town."

"How did Heather happen to tell you that story?"

"We were talking about how I found Richard along that stretch of highway. I told her a woman flagged me down, and after I checked on Richard, I turned around and she was gone. I mentioned the woman looked eerily like Darlene Gusarov, a woman who had been murdered at that spot."

"So she told you her story?"

"Yes." A thought crossed Adam's mind. Turning his head

slightly, he looked inquisitively at Ian. "When you asked me about the time Richard's car went over the cliff, and I asked what made you think of it, you said it was something Heather said. But if she didn't mention the carjacking, what made you think about Richard?"

"Not sure exactly how the conversation got started," Ian lied. "But Heather said something about Darlene's spirit haunting Pilgrim's Point. And when I saw you a few minutes ago, I remembered you telling me once about the woman who looked like Darlene."

Adam smiled. "Heather's right. I don't mean about Pilgrim's Point being haunted, but I've heard other people claim they've seen Darlene when they've driven down that section of highway."

"Active imaginations?" Ian asked.

Adam glanced around and then looked back to Ian. In a whisper, he said, "To be honest, I don't know. It was really strange that day. The woman looked exactly like Darlene. She was there one minute and gone the next. I've driven by that spot numerous times since that day, and I've never seen anything again. But still, it makes one wonder."

"You think it was her ghost?" Ian asked incredulously.

"The only thing I know, a woman flagged me over that day, and in the next instant she virtually disappeared. There wasn't another car nearby. I didn't see her walking down the highway. And a few minutes later the cops were climbing all over that hillside, and no one saw her. I've never been one to believe in ghosts, but after that day, I really don't know what I saw."

"Does this mean you believe Darlene pulled Heather out of her car?"

Adam laughed. "With Heather, I'd go more with the overactive imagination. To be honest, it's not the first time she's claimed to have seen a ghost."

Ian glanced at his watch. "I better get going. I have an article I need to wrap up."

"Okay. Oh, are you going to Agatha Pine's funeral? It's tomorrow."

"That's right." Ian let out a sigh. "Honestly, I don't know. I really didn't know the woman, but I was there when she died. I almost feel like I should. How about you?"

"Yes. Agatha's daughter, Joyce, works for me. I need to go," Adam told him.

"That's right, I forgot. Maybe I'll see you there tomorrow." Ian turned to his car.

"By the way, I called the prospective buyer. He still wants the house."

Turning back around, Ian looked at Adam. "Really?"

"He's coming to Frederickport this weekend, and we'd like to sign the papers then."

"This weekend?" Ian said dully.

"On Saturday. You still want to move?" Adam asked.

"Well…yeah. I guess, it's just happening so fast."

"You told me earlier you intended to move out this weekend. Remember, you have the house until the end of the month, so there really is no reason to move out sooner. This way, with the buyer, it gets you out of the lease."

Ian nodded. "Yeah…sounds good."

"I just have one favor," Adam asked.

"Sure, what's that?"

"Like I said, the buyer is coming into town on Saturday to sign the contract. But first, I need to have you come in and sign some papers to terminate the lease. He doesn't want to purchase the property if he's obligated to honor an existing lease with a tenant."

"He's not using the house as a rental property?"

Adam shook his head. "No. I guess he plans to live in the house. He wants to start remodeling it as soon as possible. That's why he doesn't want a renter."

"I guess I could sign that paper now, unless you need to go somewhere," Ian offered.

"That would be great. You might as well do it now, while you're here."

The two men turned from Ian's car and walked back to Adam's office together.

IAN COULDN'T HELP but wonder, what did Adam mean when he said the buyer intended to remodel his house? While it could stand to be updated, he loathed the thought of someone messing with the house's charm. It was one of the oldest houses on Beach Drive, with an outstanding ocean view. He wondered how much Adam was asking for the property. Not that he wanted to buy it—at least not now.

Ian drove up main street, his thoughts still on his rental house. As he passed Lucy's Diner, he began slowing down for the stop sign. On the corner to his right was the thrift store. As he pulled the car to a complete stop, he glanced over and noticed a woman loading large filled trash bags onto the ramp leading into the store. He took a second look. It was Joyce Pruitt.

———

ADAM NICHOLS PULLED up in front of his grandmother's house and parked. Marie was opening the front door by the time he was halfway up the walk.

"Did Ian tell you why he and Lily broke up?" Marie asked her grandson as she ushered him into her house.

"No. I didn't feel I could give him the third degree. I tell you, I sure didn't see that one coming." He followed his grandmother into the living room.

"So what is this about you selling my house?"

"We talked about this, Grandma." Adam sat down on the sofa after Marie took a seat on her rocking chair. "He's offering a good price, and he's paying cash. A quick escrow."

"I just can't get used to the idea those two young people broke up. I called Danielle after you called me."

Adam groaned. "You didn't, Grandma."

"I certainly did. Danielle wouldn't say what happened between them, but she did say she hopes they get back together. So we really can't sell Ian's house on him."

"Grandma, I hate to see Ian move too. But he sounded like it was over."

"Oh fiddle," Marie scoffed. "I'm sure it's just a little love spat."

"Well, if it makes you feel any better, we're not signing anything until this weekend. So if Ian and Lily get back together, and he wants to stay, I guess you don't have to sell."

"Not sure I want to," she huffed.

Adam almost rolled his eyes at his grandmother's words, but

caught himself in time. Instead, he decided to change the subject. "You'll never guess who called me on my way over here."

"Who?"

"Joyce Pruitt's youngest, Shane."

"She should have sold that boy to the gypsies when they passed through Frederickport."

"I suspect he is a little too old for them now," Adam said with a chuckle.

"So what did he want?"

"He wants me to find him a house on the beach."

"Certainly you aren't going to rent to him!" Marie gasped. "From what I remember, it cost Joyce a pretty penny when she had to pay for the repairs to that last house he and his roommates trashed. I was surprised he found someone willing to rent to him."

"He doesn't want to rent. He wants to buy a house. And he wants one right on the beach. If yours didn't have a buyer already, I would be tempted to sell it to him. But then Danielle would probably kill me when she met her new neighbor."

"Buy? He doesn't even have a job," Marie scoffed.

"According to Joyce, he sells things on eBay," Adam explained.

"What kind of things? Drugs?"

Adam chuckled. "I think he tried that once, as I recall. Landed him in jail. He used to work with his older brother Henry. They'd buy stuff at garage sales, fix them up. Henry refinishes old furniture."

"I still don't see how he could afford to buy a house. Especially one right on the beach."

"According to Shane, they're all coming into a significant inheritance, with Agatha gone."

Marie pushed her foot against the floor, sending her chair into rocking motion. "But doesn't that money go to Joyce?"

"According to Shane, it's to be divided equally between the grandchildren and Joyce."

Marie shook her head and uttered several *tsk-tsk-tsks*. "It really doesn't seem right. Joyce has been quite the devoted daughter, and the only one of her children worth a lick is Martha."

"Apparently there's enough to go around. According to Shane, his grandmother was worth millions."

"Yes. I always heard it had something to do with an invention of her husband's. I never really knew him. They moved shortly after they were married, and I didn't see Agatha again until she moved back to Frederickport with Joyce. By that time, she was a widow."

"Maybe I can sell them each a house," Adam said with a grin.

"I suppose this means Joyce isn't working for you anymore? Certainly she isn't going to keep cleaning houses."

"I assume she's going to quit. I haven't talked to her since her mother died. But I plan to go to Agatha's funeral. That's why I stopped over here, to see if you wanted to go with me."

Marie let out a weary sigh. "I suppose I should. I've known Agatha forever. Never particularly liked her, not even when she was a young woman. She always thought she was better than everyone else."

TWENTY-ONE

I an looked out the front window. It was dark outside. The windows across the street at Marlow House were lit up. He wondered what Lily was doing. He glanced down at Sadie. She had been restless all night, and each time he opened the front door, the dog tried slipping outside. But now she was sleeping, and he was hungry. There was no food in the house.

Thirty minutes later, Ian sat alone at the pizzeria, eating a slice of pepperoni pizza. He was about to take another bite when he looked up and noticed Chief MacDonald walk in with his two sons. He watched as the chief stood at the counter and placed his order, Eddy and Evan by his side.

When the chief turned around from the counter, his eyes met Ian's. Leaning down, the chief whispered something to his sons and pointed to an empty booth across the restaurant. The boys scampered to the table while the chief walked to Ian.

"Evening," the chief greeted him.

"Chief," Ian said with a nod.

"Can I sit down for a moment? We need to talk."

Ian glanced briefly to MacDonald's sons. "Please do. I've been meaning to talk to you too."

The chief sat down. "What about?"

Ian moved restlessly in the seat. "It's just something Evan said on Saturday. I thought you should be aware of it."

MacDonald cocked his brow. "Evan? What did he say?"

"Umm…remember when Eddy said something about Evan believing Walt Marlow's ghost was in the house?"

MacDonald smiled. "Yes. What about it?"

"I talked to Evan later that day, and he seemed convinced Walt Marlow's ghost is his friend, and it seems Lily is in on the game."

"Game?"

"I don't want to get Lily in trouble. But I thought you should know and maybe you'd want to talk to him."

"Ian, I'd like to tell you something off the record."

Ian eyed the chief. "What?"

"If you repeat what I tell you, I'll have to deny it."

"What are you talking about?"

"I know you broke up with Lily."

Ian let out a sigh. "I figured you did."

"And I know why."

Ian didn't respond.

"My son can see spirits. So can Danielle, Chris, and Heather."

Ian stood abruptly. "Please, Chief, not you too!"

"Would you sit down and listen to me."

"I feel like I'm living in that old movie *The Body Snatchers.*" Ian wadded up his paper napkin and tossed it on the table.

"Body snatchers?" The chief frowned.

"Everyone around me, people who I care about, have suddenly been replaced. They're talking about ghosts and haunted houses. Like it's the most natural thing in the world."

"Sit down, Ian."

"No. I'm getting out of here." Leaving his half-eaten pizza on the table, he headed for the door.

"What about your pizza?" the chief shouted after Ian.

Standing up, MacDonald watched as Ian left the restaurant. With a sigh, he turned and walked to Eddy and Evan. Before sitting down with them, he glanced to the door. It opened. But it wasn't Ian coming back into the pizzeria. It was Joyce Pruitt.

"WOW. You sure cleaned out Gran's closet quick," Martha muttered as she stared into the now empty closet in the downstairs master bedroom.

Joyce had followed Martha into the bedroom a moment earlier. She cursed herself for not closing the closet doors before her adult children arrived for dinner.

"Well, this was my bedroom." Joyce walked to the closet and closed the doors. "I just got rid of her clothes. There was no reason to keep them. And I plan to move back in my room." She turned to Martha.

"What did you do with her clothes?"

"I took them to the thrift store."

"Oh my, Gran would hate that. I remember how she used to put clothes she didn't want in the trash. Said she didn't want other people to wear her things."

"Well, Mother is not here anymore. And that's simply wasteful and selfish."

"I agree." Martha shrugged. "I'm just saying."

When Martha and Joyce returned to the kitchen, they found Martha's three brothers and her husband, Dennis, sitting at the table, eating the pizza Joyce had picked up for dinner.

"I hope you leave some for us," Joyce told them as she watched the slices of pizza quickly disappear.

"So what's the deal, Mom?" Henry asked. "Does the attorney send us each a check, or what?"

"I imagine it has to go through probate," Dennis said.

"What's probate?" Shane asked.

"It's a legal process the will goes through before the money is distributed," Dennis explained.

"I don't get it," Shane said. "If Gran has a will and she says it's divided between all of us, what business is it of the court's? Give us our freaking money!"

"It has to go through probate, Shane," Martha said as she took a seat at the breakfast bar. "They have to make sure the will is valid."

"Do all wills go through probate?" Shane asked. "When Stu's mom died, I don't think her will did. He got everything right away."

"From what I remember, Stu's mom didn't own much. I think small estates can avoid going through probate," Martha said.

"Well, we know Gran's will have to go through probate then," Henry said with a laugh. "Her estate isn't small."

Larry glared at Henry. "I wish Gran could hear you right now. Wouldn't she be shocked that you're practically wetting your pants. So excited to finally get your hands on her money."

"Don't be crude, Larry," Joyce scolded.

"You're one to talk!" Henry laughed. "At least I tried to be nice to her when she was alive. All you two did was fight."

"Please, boys, don't argue," Joyce pleaded.

"So how long does this probate take?" Shane asked.

"I think it can take months. Sometimes a year," Dennis said.

"Oh crap!" Shane groaned.

"You aren't serious?" Henry asked.

"We'll know more when I see the attorney on Thursday," Joyce said.

"I still think we should all go to the lawyer with you. After all, don't they normally read the will with everyone present?" Henry asked.

"You've been watching too much TV," Larry scoffed.

"He's doing me a favor, working me in. He already had a full schedule this week. He said it would be better if I came in alone."

"Why is that?" Shane asked.

"He probably figures the more people there, the longer the meeting will take," Dennis suggested. "And like your mother said, he's fitting her in."

"But why her?" Shane asked.

"According to what Gran always said, Mom is the executor," Martha reminded them.

"I don't want to go to the attorney's," Larry said. "But if we have to wait a year to get the money, that's going to suck."

"What about Gran's bank account here?" Martha asked. "I remember something about that not having to go through probate. Gran told me she had Mom down as the beneficiary, so the money in that account would bypass probate and go directly to Mom."

"That doesn't seem right," Shane whined. "I thought the estate was divided between all of us. Why does Mom get all of that money?"

"So where is it?" Henry demanded.

Joyce resisted her impulse to chastise her sons for their attitudes, and instead said, "It was the bank account where Mother deposited her Social Security checks. Most of the money that was in there is coming back out. Social Security is taking it."

"How can they do that?" Shane asked.

"Because when someone dies during the first of the month, their estate normally can't keep the money that was deposited that month," Dennis explained. "It happened to my grandfather."

"Well, that sucks," Henry said.

Dennis looked at Joyce. "What about the funeral?"

Joyce frowned. "What do you mean?"

"If it's going to take possibly months to settle your mother's estate, what about the funeral expenses?"

"Mom already took care of that. Basically she handled everything. She picked out her casket, chose what music she wanted, she even worked with someone to write her memorial. I admit I think it's an incredible waste of money, and I was tempted to see if there was some way to do something less expensive. But it is her money, and I suppose she has the right to decide if she wants to be buried or cremated. Plus, I have to admit I appreciate the fact she made all the arrangements, took care of everything, and I don't have to."

"So the estate doesn't have to pay for the funeral?" Dennis asked.

"No. She's already paid for everything."

"Yeah Gran!" Henry said with a shout as he grabbed another slice of pizza.

"You guys do know the cops think one of us might have killed Gran, don't you?" Larry asked.

Henry paused mid-bite and looked across the table at his brother. "What are you talking about?"

"You're just saying that because they dragged you into the station after you got back in town," Shane said. "Hell, we all wondered where you went."

"I told them what happened. Then they started quizzing me on if Gran was capable of getting upstairs on her own," Larry told them.

"That's ridiculous. None of us killed my mother."

"They questioned me too," Dennis said.

Joyce looked at her son-in-law. "You didn't tell me."

Dennis shrugged. "I just figured it was standard protocol. I think they're trying to figure out how Gran got up those stairs and why she was alone."

"Cops told me Shane was the one who found her," Larry said as he shoved the last bite of pizza into his mouth.

"So what? Ben Smith was there too. He came out of the upstairs bathroom just after I found her," Shane countered.

"Was that right after you pushed her?" Larry taunted.

"Larry!" Joyce snapped. "That's a horrible thing to say!"

"Of course, if Shane pushed poor Gran, that means we get to divide up his share," Henry added.

Narrowing his eyes, Shane glared at his brothers. "You guys are jerks."

"This isn't a joking matter," Martha interrupted. "Do you really think the police suspect one of us killed Gran?"

With a snort Henry said, "I doubt they think you did her in. You've always been such a goody-goody wimp."

Pursing her lips, Martha glared at Henry.

"Don't talk to my wife like that," Dennis snapped.

"She was my sister before she was your wife," Henry countered.

"Please stop!" Joyce shouted. "Enough. I don't believe anyone thinks any of us killed Mother. It was a tragic accident, nothing more."

"Speaking of that, I think we need to sue Danielle Boatman," Henry said. "That woman is worth a fortune. Maybe not as much as Gran. But she's got bucks."

"Getting greedy?" Dennis said under his breath.

"We are not suing Danielle," Joyce said.

"Why not? Gran fell at her house and got killed. I think it would be a slam-dunk lawsuit," Henry said.

"He's right," Shane agreed. "Anyway she probably has good insurance. Won't cost her anything."

"I am not suing Danielle Boatman," Joyce reiterated.

"It's the gold coins, isn't it, Mom?" Martha asked.

"Danielle Boatman was very gracious about those coins. Unless you want your mother to go to jail, you'll drop the idea of a lawsuit," Joyce told them.

"I still can't believe you actually took them out of the bank," Shane said with a laugh. "Of course, it would have been way cooler had you put them someplace where Boatman wouldn't have found them."

"You honestly think she's going to put you in jail for filing a legitimate lawsuit? Our grandmother died after falling down her stairs," Henry reminded them. "I bet she's expecting us to sue her."

"She could cause legal problems for your mother." Dennis spoke up. "If I was Joyce, I wouldn't want to test her either."

"Then Mom doesn't have to do it. We'll sue," Shane said.

"I don't think it works that way. The only one who can sue on behalf of your grandmother is her estate. Joyce is the executor of Gran's estate, and if she doesn't want to sue, then you can't," Dennis explained.

"Why not?" Larry asked.

"Because you wouldn't have any legal standing to sue. Only the estate would."

"But since we're the beneficiaries, aren't we the estate?" Henry asked.

Dennis considered the question a moment. "I don't know. I guess you would have to ask an attorney about that."

TWENTY-TWO

Ian sat in front of his laptop computer at the kitchen table. A week earlier he and Lily had been desk shopping. It was probably a good thing they hadn't found anything they liked.

His plan was to turn one of the spare bedrooms into a real office. After living in the rental house for a little over a year, he thought it was about time to create a more professional office space. Since graduating from college over a decade earlier, he had lived primarily in furnished rentals, never putting his personal stamp on his current abode. Being with Lily had changed how he looked at things. It had made him want to create a home. But now, he was single again.

The cellphone sitting next to the computer on the kitchen table began to ring. He picked it up and looked at it. His sister, Kelly, was calling.

"Hey, Kel, what's up?"

"I just called to see how you're doing. You sound tired."

"I didn't get much sleep last night," he told her.

"Thinking of Lily?" she asked.

"I told you I didn't want to talk about her. Anyway, I was up all night researching a new story."

"I thought you were done researching your article?"

"This is a new one."

"What's it about?" she asked.

"I'm not ready to talk about it. Not even sure I'll get around to writing it."

"That's funny, last week when I asked what your next story was, you said you didn't know."

"Well, that was last week," Ian retorted.

"Okay, so you don't want to talk about Lily; you don't want to talk about your new story."

"If you called to see how I am, Kelly, I'm fine."

"I called Lily," she blurted.

"You what?" he stood abruptly, holding the cellphone by his ear. He began to pace the kitchen.

"Now, don't be mad at me, Ian. But Lily is my friend too."

"I asked you to stay out of this."

"Just because you broke up with Lily doesn't mean I have to drop her as a friend."

"It might be best if you do," he told her.

"I can't believe you're saying that! It's so unlike you!"

"What did Lily say?"

"She just said you broke up with her. But she didn't say why, and I didn't ask her."

"So why did you call her?"

"I told you. Because I care about Lily; she is my friend. I just wanted to see if she's okay. I'd think you'd understand because you used to care about her too."

"Who says I don't care about her anymore?" he grumbled.

"I think you do still care, or you wouldn't be acting this way. She obviously did something that made you mad. That's why I told her she needed to talk to you."

"You what?"

Startled by Ian's outburst, Sadie, who had been napping nearby, lifted her head and looked at Ian.

"Lily told me that while she still loved you, if you wanted to talk to her, you would have to go to her. She said something about you no longer trusting her and that it wasn't her fault, it was your problem. She said if you didn't trust her, then there was no reason for her to talk to you. What happened, Ian, do you think she cheated on you? Is that why you no longer trust her?"

"Kelly, what part of *I don't want to discuss* this don't you understand?"

"It's just that you're my brother, and I love you. And I think you and Lily are terrific together. I'd never seen you so happy. But if you walk away from her over some stupid misunderstanding—"

"I have to go now." Ian disconnected the call.

ACROSS THE STREET at Marlow House, Lily carried Max through the rooms on the second floor. After inspecting each room, she gingerly made her way down the staircase, clutching the handrail with one hand while trying to keep hold of the furry bundle with the other hand.

Enjoying the ride, Max rested his front paws on Lily's left shoulder while looking back up the staircase. He let out a meow.

"That cat weighs a ton," Danielle said when she stepped out into the hallway and noticed Lily coming downstairs with Max.

"You're telling me," Lily said, slightly out of breath.

"Why are you carrying him?" Danielle asked when Lily reached the first-floor landing, still clutching the cat.

"Now that you're here, I guess I don't have to." Lily leaned down and released Max, who strolled away, heading to the parlor.

"I don't get it?"

"I've realized Max is an excellent ghost detector. Maybe I can't see spirits, but he does. And he does a great job of letting me know if we aren't alone," Lily explained. "Max and I checked the attic, along with every room on the second floor. Agatha is not up there." Lily glanced down the hall, first to the right and then the left. She looked back to Danielle. "Have you seen her down here?"

Danielle shook her head. "No. This morning, after I mentioned her funeral was today at two, she got all excited and left. I suspect I won't be seeing her again until the funeral."

Lily let out a sigh. "I wish you would have told me that before I carried that cat up one staircase and down two."

Danielle grinned. "Sorry."

"Where's Walt? I'm pretty sure he isn't in the attic."

"I believe he's in the parlor, watching television." Danielle glanced to the kitchen. "I was going to make myself a sandwich before I get ready for the funeral. Want one?"

"Sure." Lily followed Danielle to the kitchen. "If we're lucky, Agatha will decide to move on after her funeral."

"We can hope. Death really hasn't improved her disposition."

Once in the kitchen, Lily walked to the sink and washed her hands while Danielle removed a loaf of bread from the breadbox.

"Kelly called me this morning," Lily said while she dried her hands.

"Does she have any idea why her brother broke it off with you?"

"No. She said she called to see how I was, but I think she was trying to find out what happened." Lily tossed the dishtowel on the counter. "I got the impression she thinks I did something to make Ian break up, and was trying to get me to call him."

"Seriously?" Danielle reached into the refrigerator and retrieved a bowl of chicken salad.

"Yep. But that ain't happening."

Danielle shut the refrigerator door. "I understand how you feel. But maybe you should try talking to him again."

Lily shook her head stubbornly. "Absolutely not. He's hurt me, Dani. I would never have imagined Ian would be so unreasonable."

Leaning back against the counter for a moment, Danielle looked at Lily. "I didn't tell you earlier, but the chief called. He ran into Ian last night."

Opening the loaf of bread Danielle had set on the counter, Lily pulled out four slices and then asked, "And?"

"Ian wanted MacDonald to know Evan believes he can see ghosts."

Lily paused and looked at Danielle. "What did the chief say?"

"He told him Evan *can* see ghosts."

Lily's eyes widened. "Then what did Ian say to that?"

"Something about body snatchers."

IAN SLID OPEN the bedroom window, letting in the crisp ocean breeze. In other parts of the country, July's temperatures would be much warmer. He stood there a moment, drinking in the salty air while looking out at the ocean.

"Sadie, I'm going to miss this view," he muttered before turning toward his closet.

Hearing her name, Sadie lifted her head and looked over to Ian from where she had been napping on the bed. Her tail began to wag.

Sadie watched as Ian changed his clothes. When he picked his cellphone up from where he had tossed it on the bed earlier and slipped it in his pocket and headed for the door, Sadie knew he was ready to go out. Jumping down off the bed, her tail wagging, she followed Ian from the room, into the hallway.

Finally, they were going somewhere. Sadie was getting bored cooped up in the house the last few days. Ian had taken her for several walks on the beach, yet she wasn't used to staying home alone when he had to go somewhere without her. Then, he normally left her across the street with Walt.

Tail still wagging, she enthusiastically followed him to the front door. Before opening the door, he turned and faced her.

"Sorry, girl, you have to stay home. I'm going to a funeral and can't take you."

Not understanding what Ian was saying exactly, Sadie cocked her head, her tail still wagging. But when Ian said *sit* when she stood up, Sadie knew. He was leaving her.

Reluctantly sitting back down, Sadie let out a whimper.

Ian turned briefly to her as he opened the door. "Sorry, girl. I'll be back in a couple of hours."

When Ian opened the front door, a flash of black fur raced by his feet into the house.

"Max!" Ian said with a curse. Leaving the door open, he walked back into his house, where Sadie was now enthusiastically sniffing the cat and nudging him with her nose as the feline rubbed back and forth against her body, purring loudly.

"I don't know what's with you two," Ian said as he leaned down to pick up Max. "But I'm not leaving a cat in the house." Max let out a pitiful meow as Ian picked him up and tossed him back outside. "Go home, Max," Ian grumbled as he shoved Sadie—who was now halfway out the doorway, trying to follow Max—back into the house with his leg before closing the door behind him.

When Ian was backing out of the driveway a few minutes later, he didn't see Max anywhere in sight, and he assumed the cat had gone home. However, he did see Sadie, who was standing at the side window, her paws obviously resting on the windowsill as her nose pushed through the opening in the curtains to look outside. With the window down in his car, he could hear her barking.

Inside the house, Sadie watched as Ian backed into the street and then drove away, out of sight. Jumping down from the window, she cocked her head slightly when she heard something. Turning toward the sound, she raced through the house to Ian's bedroom.

When Sadie dashed into the room, she heard meowing coming from the open window. She recognized that meow. It was Max. Jumping up on the windowsill, resting her front paws on it, she looked outside. Max sat on the ground just outside the house, looking up at her, his black tail swishing back and forth.

Sadie let out a bark. Max moved away from the window. Sadie let out another bark and then lunged at the open window, knocking against the screen. She barked again, making a second lunge, this time pushing a corner of the screen from the window. Outside, Max stood several feet away, watching, while occasionally encouraging Sadie with a loud meow.

It took several lunges against the window screen before it finally fell outside onto the ground. Sadie didn't waste any time. With one graceful leap she flew through the window and joined Max outside. Together the pair made their way to the front of the property and then across the street to Marlow House.

Already on their way to the funeral, Danielle and Lily had left the driveway gate wide open. They saw no reason to close it, since they would be returning in a couple of hours. Plus, it wasn't as if Ian had left Sadie with them. Had that been the case, they would have shut the gate so the dog couldn't get out of the yard. But with the gate open, it was as easy for Sadie to get into the yard as it would have been for her to escape from it. And once in the yard, entering the house was simply a matter of slipping through the large pet door.

TWENTY-THREE

Agatha never understood why anyone would choose to be cremated. To her, it seemed somehow ironic that a person who denied him or herself certain pleasures in life, to avoid burning in a fiery hereafter, would willingly make plans to put one's body in a blazing furnace. After all, no one really knew the pain a dead body might experience. Agatha had not been willing to take that chance.

She had never been particularly claustrophobic, which was why the thought of being placed in a casket and then buried never bothered her in the same way as cremation had. Plus, as she got older, Agatha enjoyed sleeping.

What Agatha didn't enjoy was an uncomfortable bed, or the thought of being trapped for eternity in a tacky, cheap, uncomfortable casket. Now standing next to her open casket, her attention was not on the body that was once her, seemingly sleeping peacefully, it was instead on the luxurious interior of the casket, its plump satin cushioned padding inviting. If her body was not already occupying the space, she would have been tempted to crawl in and take a nap.

Running her hands over the glistening exterior of the highly polished casket, she imagined what it must feel like—had her hands not been only an illusion. It was a lovely shade of pale powder blue, her favorite color, and along its side was a custom painting of her family's crest. While she wasn't certain her family actually had a crest, she'd had Shane find her one online, which she later used when ordering her casket.

"AGATHA'S HERE," Danielle whispered to Lily when they entered the chapel.

"Where is she?" Lily asked as she and Danielle stepped away from the other mourners now entering.

"She's by her casket," Danielle said as they walked down the aisle, looking for somewhere to sit. She spied Joyce in the front row with her children and son-in-law. They were already seated.

"Oh gawd, it's an open casket." Lily groaned. "I hate those."

Halfway down the aisle, they paused and glanced around.

"I suppose we should first go up and pay our respects," Danielle said in a whisper.

"Shouldn't we do that after the service?" Lily asked.

"Actually, I meant to Agatha."

"Why? You just saw her this morning." Lily looked toward the front of the chapel. From her angle, she could barely see the profile of the woman inside the casket. "Wow, that's some coffin."

"No kidding. It must have cost a fortune," Danielle said.

"Such an incredible waste of money for something that's just going in the ground," Lily whispered. "I've never seen one quite like that before."

"I guess Agatha could afford it. She was worth millions," Danielle said with a shrug.

"I know, but still, why be a miser all your life and then spend a freaking fortune on your funeral? She's been living with Joyce for years, and have you seen the car Joyce drives? It's a piece of junk."

"Joyce's house isn't much better. But I guess now she can fix it up or sell it," Danielle said.

"But still, foolish woman. If she comes back to Marlow House, I just might tell her how I feel! Stupid woman," Lily snapped.

Danielle suppressed a giggle. "It's Agatha's funeral. You have to be nice to someone when it's their funeral."

Lily frowned at Danielle. "What? Are funerals like birthdays?"

"Never really thought about it before, but yeah, I guess they are." Danielle started toward the front of the chapel to pay her respects to Agatha, when Lily reached out and stopped her. Danielle turned back to Lily.

"You go on up. Dead bodies make me squeamish. Anyway, I think I better go to the bathroom before this thing starts. I shouldn't have had that Pepsi before we left home."

"Okay. I'll only be a minute. I'll find us a seat," Danielle told her.

With a nod, Lily released Danielle's arm and headed back toward the exit. The public restrooms were off the hallway leading from the chapel.

LILY DIDN'T NOTICE Ian when she stepped into the hallway. But he noticed her. He continued to watch her as she headed to the small alcove leading to the public restrooms. He followed her.

When Lily stepped out from the bathroom several minutes later, she found Ian waiting for her.

"Ian," she said in surprise.

"Lily, we need to talk," he told her.

Hands now on her hips, Lily looked Ian up and down. She reminded him of an angry pixy. "Here? At the funeral? I thought you didn't want to talk to me. As I recall, you ordered me out of your house."

"Lily, this all happened so fast. I'm trying to sort things out. I know we can't talk here. But I was hoping, after the funeral, maybe you could come over to my house, and we could talk."

"Does this mean you believe me now?" Removing her hands from her hips, she folded her arms over her chest and looked up into Ian's eyes.

Ian frowned. "Of course I don't believe it. But I still love you. And there has to be some rational reason why you're sticking to this story."

"You still think I'm a liar?"

Ian reached for Lily, but she took a step back, out of his reach.

"None of this makes any sense. Come on, Lily, we both know there is no such thing as ghosts. Is this some kind of practical joke that got out of hand. Or maybe it's some kind of test?"

"Test? What do you mean test?"

"I remember Danielle wouldn't date Joe again because he

believed she could have killed her cousin. He didn't have enough faith in her to simply take her at her word. Is this what this is about? Are you testing my faith in you?"

Lily gasped and abruptly stepped forward. She felt compelled to smack his arm but resisted the temptation. "How could you even ask that? Do you honestly think I'm so childish I would play such an idiotic game? I don't like games, Ian Bartley. I thought you knew me better than that."

Not waiting for his response, Lily turned from him and marched back into the chapel.

POLICE CHIEF MACDONALD sat at the far end of the back pew. Several minutes earlier, just before entering the chapel, he had received a text message from Brian Henderson. Brian was on his way there; he needed to tell the chief something.

As the chief waited for the services to begin—or for Brian to arrive—whichever was first, he spied Lily rushing into the chapel. He waved at her, but she didn't see him. She appeared to be preoccupied and in a hurry to get to her seat. When the door opened again, he saw what he believed was probably the reason for Lily's harried demeanor. It was Ian Bartley. He stood at the back of the room, looking forlorn, his eyes on Lily.

MacDonald didn't have long to ponder Lily and Ian's situation. The next moment, Brian entered. The chief waved to get his attention.

Brian immediately spied the chief and made his way over to him, sitting next to him on the pew.

"So what's up?" MacDonald asked in a whisper.

"We found our blogger," Brian said with a smile.

"It must be someone interesting or you wouldn't be here."

Brian removed a card from his shirt pocket. "Our blogger is here." He handed the chief the card.

MacDonald read it and then looked to Brian. "Are you sure?"

"If not the blogger, the one who owns the domain. Also the one who signed up for the affiliate ads that pop up on the page," Brian explained.

The chief studied the card for a few moments and then slipped it in his shirt pocket. "This really doesn't make any sense."

"I know. I was thinking about that. Is this person really stupid or what?"

"So you think this is the killer?" the chief asked.

"It looks that way, in spite of the fact it really doesn't make sense. Stupid thing to do, blog about who you intend to kill."

"Maybe. But look at all the stupid kids who brag about their crimes on social media. And then there are those who actually video record their crimes and post them," the chief reminded.

"I guess you're right. But this isn't a kid, yet definitely stupid. I guess I should stop trying to make sense out of these things. So what now?"

"Now we listen to Agatha's service, and then we give our condolences to the family."

CHRIS AND HEATHER didn't make it to Agatha's service. Chris had intended to go, but then something came up at the office; and he sent Danielle a text message telling her they would miss it. Since she assumed Joyce and her family barely knew who Chris or Heather were, she didn't imagine they would be missed.

Glancing over her shoulder, Danielle saw the chief and Brian sitting at the back of the chapel. On the other side of the room, also in the back row, she spied Ian. When Lily had returned from the bathroom earlier, she had told Danielle about her encounter with Ian.

Agatha's service was longer than Danielle had expected it would be. By the time it ended, everyone in the chapel—those who hadn't fallen asleep from boredom—knew every detail about Agatha's life, beginning with her remarkable childhood in Frederickport and her amazing marriage to an amazing man who did amazing things, and how she was an amazing mother.

"Who in the world wrote that?" Lily asked when they stood up to leave.

"It was pretty heavy on *Agatha the devoted mother and grandmother.* For some reason I can't believe her family wrote it."

"No kidding. It's not like they have to keep kissing up to her," Lily whispered.

Twenty minutes later, after giving her condolences to the family,

Danielle found herself outside, waiting for Lily, who was making one final stop at the restroom.

Leaning against the trunk of a large shade tree, lost in her thoughts, Danielle was startled back to the present when she heard a man say, "Danielle."

It was Ian.

Danielle stood up straight, no longer leaning against the tree.

"Where's Lily?" he asked.

"She went to the bathroom," Danielle said curtly.

"Danielle, maybe you can tell me what's really going on. I always considered you a good friend."

Cocking her head slightly, she studied Ian as a slight smile played on her lips.

"Walt explained it all, but you wouldn't listen to him. Why do I imagine you'll take my word for it?"

Ian frowned. "Walt? What do you mean?"

"The dream, Ian. The dream you had the other night. Walt Marlow was there. He explained everything."

Not waiting for a response, Danielle turned from Ian and walked away.

TWENTY-FOUR

There were more than a few people gathered around Agatha's grave site who found it somehow ironic that a woman with Agatha's disposition would be buried on a day with such perfect weather. Overhead the crystal blue sky showed only a smattering of pure white clouds, and there was just enough breeze to cool down the late afternoon sun, without threatening to send the women's hats flying.

A more fitting sky would be gray and drizzling, with the sun hiding behind threatening rain clouds. Fortunately for the mourners, the weather was splendid. However, calling them mourners might be an exaggeration. There wasn't a single damp eye in the crowd, aside from Ben Smith, and his was due to allergies.

It was a respectable crowd, close to fifty people, joining the Pruitt family at Agatha's grave site. Some attending were friends of the family, as opposed to friends of the deceased. However, the majority of people in attendance were there out of civic duty or basic morbid curiosity.

Weaving through the crowd, unseen by all but Danielle, was Agatha herself. She was eavesdropping on what her mourners had to say, and she was not happy.

"Agatha must have paid someone to write that memorial," Marie whispered to her grandson. Not wanting the people next to them to overhear, Adam smiled and looked ahead to the casket, now draped in flowers, as the minister said final words for the departed.

"And what's wrong with that?" Agatha snapped at Marie. "You're just jealous because your grandson will probably throw some silly words together when it's your time."

Agatha moved to Millie Samson, who stood about six feet from Adam and Marie.

"I was beginning to think I was at someone else's funeral," Millie told the woman standing next to her. "No way was that paragon the minister was talking about in the chapel the Agatha I knew!"

The woman nodded in agreement. "It was all I could do not to break out laughing."

Agatha gasped. "How dare you be so disrespectful! It's my funeral!"

Leaving Millie's side, Agatha continued to move through the crowd. Unfortunately for her, the opinions expressed about her did not improve. What was even worse, some in the crowd were not even thinking about her.

"I BET JOYCE IS CELEBRATING."

"That sermon was a joke."

"I should have gone to the beach today."

"You stopping at Joyce's after we leave here? I bet there will be food."

"Don't you think Chief MacDonald is hot?"

"Where do you want to go for dinner?"

"I bet Joyce has already quit her job."

"That casket must have cost a fortune. What a waste."

"Look at my forehead, is that a pimple?"

"THESE PEOPLE ARE HORRIBLE, JUST HORRIBLE!" Agatha told Danielle when she sidled up beside her.

Danielle looked askance at Agatha, but did not comment.

"I know you can't say anything," Agatha said. "People will think you're crazy, talking to yourself. But you know what? You shouldn't care. These people are mean. Mean nasty people!"

Lily leaned close to Danielle and whispered, "You see Agatha anywhere?"

"I swear you're getting clairvoyant these days." Danielle nodded to where Agatha stood. "She's right here."

Folding her arms across her chest, Agatha stared ahead, looking past her casket. "Well, that settles it. I'm not going to Joyce's for the wake after this. I refuse to listen to these horrible, horrible people."

"Maybe you should move on," Danielle whispered.

"Maybe I will. No one wants me here anyway."

Agatha vanished.

"She's gone," Danielle whispered.

Lily glanced around the cemetery, "I heard you tell her to move on. Do you think she did?"

"She said she wasn't going to the wake. I'm pretty sure she's been eavesdropping on what people have been saying about her."

Lily cringed. "I bet that wasn't pretty."

"I kinda feel sorry for her."

"Are you serious?"

Danielle shrugged. "She is dead. And like I said, you really should be nice to someone on the day of their funeral."

"I just hope she moved on."

Danielle cringed. "I hope the chief doesn't get mad at me if she did."

"What do you mean?"

"I know he wants her to tell me what happened before she died. But I don't think she's going to, and he isn't the one who has to deal with her if she sticks around indefinitely."

JOYCE STOOD at the door of the chapel and watched as her sons carried Agatha's flower arrangements out of the building to the parking lot. There had been so many floral arrangements, it hadn't been necessary to move the chapel flowers out to the grave site.

"Be careful," Joyce called out to Shane, who almost dropped an arrangement. "Don't lose the cards! I need to know who to send thank you cards too."

Just as Joyce's last son left the building, Mr. Pierce from the funeral home walked up to Joyce and touched her arm.

"It was a lovely service," Mr. Pierce told her. "I'm sure your mother would have been pleased."

Joyce smiled at Mr. Pierce. "You did a wonderful job. I will say I was shocked at how many flowers Mother received! I'm overwhelmed."

Confusion replaced his smile. "Umm…I thought you knew."

Joyce frowned. "Knew what?"

"The flowers, your mother ordered them. She picked out each arrangement."

"I don't understand. Surely she didn't order all the flowers."

"Not all of them. I do recall two arrangements that arrived. One was from Danielle Boatman and the other was from Adam Nichols and his grandmother."

"But the rest, Mother ordered?"

Mr. Pierce nodded. "You have to understand, when you get to be your mother's age, many of her friends have already passed. She just assumed there wouldn't be anyone left to send flowers, so she decided to do it."

"Oh…" Joyce glanced from the chapel to the parking lot, where her sons were now loading flowers into their vehicles.

"By the way, I tried calling you on Monday and Tuesday."

"I must have missed yesterday's call. But I did get your call on Monday, when you left a message asking if there were any changes to the funeral arrangements Mom made. I did call back. I left a message saying there were no changes. Didn't you get it?"

"Yes, I did. I just wanted to touch base with you and make sure you hadn't changed your mind about anything." He reached into his vest pocket.

"No." Joyce shook her head. "Mother was very particular about how she wanted her funeral. I figured since she already made all the arrangements, I wouldn't change anything. It didn't seem right."

"Good," he said with a smile as he handed Joyce an envelope.

She took the envelope and looked at it. "What's this?"

"It's the statement. I was hoping to get it to you sooner than this, but it didn't quite work out."

Joyce opened the envelope, removed the statement, and unfolded it. Her eyes widened. "Thirty-five thousand dollars? Mother's funeral cost thirty-five thousand dollars?"

"Actually, it was a little over forty, but that's the balance due."

Joyce looked up to Mr. Pierce, her expression blank. "I don't understand?"

He frowned. "The balance due for your mother's funeral. You do know she only paid a deposit. She made arrangements for the balance to come out of her estate."

Joyce swallowed nervously and glanced down at the statement. "But her estate has to go through probate first."

"Yes, I understand that. Your mother explained."

Joyce looked back at the bill and then showed it to Mr. Pierce, pointing to one of the lines. "Surely the casket didn't cost that much."

"Top of the line. Your mother loved it." He grinned.

"But that cost more than my car!"

"The craftsmanship in that casket is superb. It will easily outlast any casket on the market."

"Maybe, but it's going in the ground, and no one will ever see it again," Joyce squeaked. "It doesn't matter if it lasts a week or a hundred years."

"Oh, it mattered to your mother."

"Maybe we should rethink this," Joyce said as she refolded the statement and slipped it back in the envelope.

"Rethink what?"

"How about we cremate Mother? You can have the casket back. I'm sure you can resell it to someone else. And we'll sell the funeral plot. After all, she isn't buried yet."

"Mrs. Pruitt, it is not our policy to accept a casket back once it has been used."

"It's barely used. She's only been in it a couple of days."

"I'm sorry, we simply can't resell a used casket."

"What does it matter? Whoever buys it will be putting a dead person in it. What does the dead person care? The person won't even know. It's just going in the ground."

"Even if I could make an exception, you forget your mother had your family crest painted on the side of the casket. I don't believe anyone would be willing to spend that much on a casket that has someone else's family crest on it."

"Technically speaking, I don't really think it was our family crest. It could be anyone's."

"Ms. Pruitt, is there some problem with your mother's estate?"

Joyce let out a weary sigh and shoved the envelope with the

statement into her purse. "No. No problem. I see the attorney tomorrow. I'll give him the statement and tell him to send you a payment out of the estate."

Mr. Pierce smiled.

"YOU'VE GOT to be kidding? So you're telling me Gran's funeral is costing me seven thousand bucks?" Henry fumed.

Joyce had just told her sons what she had learned at the cemetery. They were crammed in her small kitchen while she and Martha hastily removed the casseroles from the refrigerator—dishes friends and neighbors had brought over earlier to serve at today's wake.

"Not so loud, Henry," Joyce scolded, glancing to the doorway leading to the hallway. Dennis was the only family member not in the kitchen. He was out in the living room, greeting the guests.

"Seven thousand bucks? That's a lot of money!" Shane groaned.

"It isn't costing you guys anything," Martha told her brothers. "The money is coming out of Gran's estate."

"Damn, you're simple, Martha. If we pay the funeral home thirty-five thousand dollars, that will be seven thousand dollars less we each get. So yeah, it is costing me."

"How much did you say that casket cost again?" Shane asked. When Joyce told them, both Shane and Henry groaned.

"Gran was worth millions," Larry reminded them. "At this point, who really cares how much the funeral cost? In the big scheme of things, it's just peanuts. We should just all be glad she's dead."

"Larry!" Joyce hissed, looking quickly to the open doorway to see if anyone overheard.

"You can be such a jerk," Martha muttered as she removed foil from a Jell-O salad.

"May be peanuts, but thems is a lot of peanuts!" Shane grumbled.

"That sucks that he won't let us return the damn casket," Henry grumbled. "If we could get the money back on that, at least it would be something."

"Maybe they won't take it back, but we could resell it," Shane suggested.

"What are you thinking?" Henry asked.

"Mom can call them up and tell them not to bury her. Cremate her. That has to be way cheaper. And then we can sell the plot like Mom wanted."

"It's not what I wanted!" Joyce snapped, glancing nervously to the doorway, afraid someone was going to overhear their conversation. "He just surprised me with that bill, and I was thinking off the top of my head."

"Well, I think it's a good idea," Henry said.

Larry began to laugh. "Seriously, Henry? What are you going to do, store Gran's casket in your garage after you kick her out of it and then try to sell it on eBay?"

Shane grabbed a bag of potato chips and ripped it open. Just before popping a chip in his mouth, he said, "Shipping costs might be a problem."

TWENTY-FIVE

Her hair looked like cotton candy, pink and frizzy. Ian didn't think the look suited her. He couldn't recall what Carla's natural hair color was. *Is she a blonde?* For months now it seemed her hair color changed on a regular basis, normally some pastel. He thought the burgundy had looked good on her, but pink wasn't her color. By the condition of her hair, he suspected the regular bleaching and dying was beginning to take a toll on it.

"Hey, Ian," Carla greeted him when she came to take his order. She glanced around. "You eating alone tonight?"

Picking up a menu off the counter, he opened it. "Just me."

Leaning toward Ian, Carla rested her elbows on the counter while revealing a hint of cleavage. "Is it true what I heard? You and Lily broke up?"

Ian looked up from the menu. "Where'd you hear that?"

Carla shrugged. "Around."

"I guess that's what happens when you live in a small town," Ian grumbled under his breath.

Reaching out with one hand, Carla ran her index finger down Ian's arm.

Startled at her touch, Ian's gaze flew to Carla's now smiling face.

"I get off in a couple of hours. Maybe you and I could get together. We could have some fun. You could show me your house. I heard it has a great view of the ocean."

Ian slammed his menu shut. "I'm kind of busy, Carla."

Standing up straight, removing her elbows from the counter, Carla shrugged. "Okay. But if you change your mind, let me know. I think we could have a good time."

"Like I said, I'm kind of busy."

Carla shrugged again and then opened up her order pad. "You know what you want?"

"The French dip. With a side of horseradish. But don't bother bringing the au jus, I never use it. It's a waste."

"And to drink?"

"Bud Light."

After writing down the order, Carla looked at Ian. "It's dead here tonight. I think everyone went to Agatha Pine's funeral, and I heard her daughter is having some sort of thing at her house with food."

"I went to the service, but I didn't go to the wake."

"I couldn't stand the woman. I sure wouldn't waste my time going to her funeral."

"And I wouldn't want you there, you tramp!" Agatha spat. She sat at the counter next to Ian. No one could see her.

"I'll put this order in and then get you that beer," Carla told Ian before she turned away.

"And you look ridiculous with pink hair!" Agatha called after her.

Without thought, Ian shook his head and rolled his eyes after Carla walked away. Still shaking his head, he picked up his phone and began checking his messages.

"Glad to see you didn't take her up on her offer," Agatha said aloud in spite of the fact no one was able to hear her.

HEATHER DONOVAN WAS on her way home from work when she decided to stop by Pier Café and grab a bite to eat. The moment she walked in the door, she spied Ian sitting at the counter, looking at his cellphone. Heather then turned her attention to the older woman sitting next to Ian, who appeared to be chatting away while he ignored her.

After taking a few steps in Ian's direction, Heather froze. *That's no regular woman!* Heather thought. *That's Agatha Pine!*

Heather stood there a moment, debating if she should go sit down in one of the booths or take the empty seat next to Ian and see what Agatha was yammering on about. Considering Ian's recent treatment of Lily, she decided tormenting Ian might be fun.

With a renewed spring in her step, Heather flounced over to the counter and plopped down in the seat next to Ian. "Hi, Ian."

Startled, Ian looked to Heather. "What are you doing, stalking me?"

Heather let out a snort. "Don't flatter yourself, bud."

Agatha leaned forward and looked down the counter at Heather. "Her hair is almost as bad as Pinkie's. Isn't she a little old for braids?"

Narrowing her eyes, Heather looked past Ian to Agatha and was tempted to tell the ghost to mind her own business. Instead, she picked up the menu and opened it.

Agatha looked Ian up and down. "My, you have all the ladies chasing you, don't you? If I remember correctly, you were dating that Lily Miller. If that waitress was correct, it must mean you've broken it off with her. Can't say I blame you. She's a snotty little thing. Was quite rude to me when I was at Marlow House. Told me to leave. Young people should have more respect for the dead."

Heather found it impossible to focus on the menu. Instead, she listened to Agatha.

"And you were smart to turn down Pinkie when she started with that, *oh, I'm off in a few hours; maybe we can go have fun.* Gracious, inviting herself to your house! Telling you she wants to see your great ocean view. But she didn't care about the view, not the way she was leaning over the counter, practically shoving her breasts in your face!"

Heather closed the menu and asked Ian, "So how was the funeral? Not a dry eye in the house?"

Before he could answer, Carla showed up with Ian's beer and then took Heather's order.

When Carla walked away, Heather asked again, "So, how was the funeral?"

Ian shrugged. "It was a funeral. Alright, I guess." He took a sip of the beer.

"I figure it must have been a really special funeral," Heather said with a smile.

Ian furrowed his brow. "Why is that?"

"It was a special funeral," Agatha said. "The flowers were beautiful. So many flowers."

"I just figured you got to take home a door prize. It must have been special." Heather grinned.

"Door prize? What are you talking about?"

"She's sitting right next to you," Heather said, looking across Ian to Agatha, who now looked at Heather with a confused expression.

"Who's sitting next to me?"

"Why, Agatha Pine."

Ian set his beer on the counter and turned to Heather. "That's not funny."

"You can see me?" Agatha gasped.

"Not trying to be funny. And I can prove she's sitting there."

Ian turned around in his chair and faced Heather. "Okay, this sounds good. Just how can you prove it?"

Peeking her head around Ian, Agatha said, "Yes, I'd like to know that too."

"Because Agatha was just yammering away about what happened right before I walked in the diner."

"I do not yammer!" Agatha huffed.

"Okay. I'm listening. Just tell me, what happened right before you arrived?"

Tilting her head slightly while lightly tapping the tip of her index finger against her chin, Heather said, "Carla leaned over the counter, gave you a good view of her cleavage, asked about Lily, and then suggested you two go out when she gets off work in a couple of hours, and apparently wanted to go to your house and see your great ocean view." Biting her lower lip, Heather tapped her chin again and asked, "Am I missing anything? Oh yes, I know. She said you'd have fun."

Speechless, Ian stared at Heather.

"I know! Tell him he ordered a French dip with horseradish. He told her not to bring the au jus," Agatha blurted. "Oh, this is fun!"

Heather leaned forward, flashing a grin to the helpful ghost. "Thanks, Agatha." She then looked back to Ian. "Agatha said you ordered a French dip with a side of horseradish and hold the au jus." She looked back to Agatha. "Is that everything?"

"How did you know that?" Ian stammered.

"Agatha told me. She's been sitting next to you since I walked in the diner."

Ian shook his head. "I don't know what's going on. But you guys are playing some weird game."

Heather rolled her eyes. "Please, Ian. Don't get all paranoid on me. I really had more faith in you. To think I once had a crush on you."

"So you aren't interested in him?" Agatha asked.

"Oh please," Heather scoffed.

Carla interrupted the conversation when she showed up with Ian's food. He stood up and took his wallet out of his pocket.

"Carla, would you please put it in a take-out bag. I've got to go," he said dully as he removed a twenty and tossed it on the counter.

A few minutes later, Heather and Agatha sat together at the counter and watched as Ian hurried out of the diner, his to-go bag in hand.

Heather reached for Ian's bottle of beer, still sitting on the counter. It was almost full.

"I think that boy's confused," Agatha muttered.

"Damn straight," Heather said before taking a long swig of beer.

IAN SAT IN HIS CAR, eating his French dip, trying to sort out what Heather had just said. The logical explanation, Heather had looked into the diner through the front window before entering and had seen Carla leaning over the counter in a suggestive manner. Had Heather seen the way Carla drew her finger down his arm, it wouldn't take much deductive reasoning to figure out Carla was hitting on him. The part about the beach house and view could have been a lucky guess. After all, that's how people who claim to be mediums often suck in their victims. He wasn't sure how Heather knew about the French dip and horseradish. Perhaps she'd read that off Carla's pad of paper when she was giving her order.

After Ian finished his sandwich, he shoved his trash into the to-go bag and crumpled it up. Tossing it on the passenger seat, he started up his engine.

When Ian pulled into his driveway a few minutes later, he was surprised Sadie wasn't waiting at the window. Normally when he came home, Sadie would hear his car pull in the driveway and would be looking out the window before he turned off the engine.

Unlocking the front door a few minutes later, he glanced to the nearby window and there was still no Sadie looking out. Pushing open the door, he expected to find her waiting. She wasn't there.

"Sadie!" Ian shouted. Assuming she had been sleeping, he expected her to immediately wake up and come running when she heard him call. Still no Sadie.

With a frown, Ian tossed the keys on a table and made his way through the house. It felt eerily vacant. Moving through the kitchen and then living room, panic began to set in. This didn't feel right. Sadie never failed to greet him when he came home.

Picking up his step, he moved first to his bedroom. Sadie like to sleep on his bed.

He didn't notice it at first. The window was open, and the breeze fluttered the curtain inwards. But he didn't notice the screen was missing until he was right at the window.

Panic renewed, he looked outside and glanced down. There on the ground just outside the window was its screen, broken and twisted. Ian dashed to the back door while calling Sadie's name. Hurrying to the rear yard, he expected to find Sadie waiting for him. But once again, his expectations were not met.

Ian ran the perimeter of the property, calling for his dog. But there was no sign of her—just the broken window screen lying on the ground. He ran down to the beach. There was still no sign of her.

Running from the beach back to his house, now out of breath, he made his way to the front yard. Stopping to catch his breath, he looked across the street at Marlow House.

Ian let out a sigh. "She's got to be there. That's probably where she went."

TWENTY-SIX

The only car parked next to Marlow House was Lily's. Danielle's Ford Flex was gone. From what Ian understood, they didn't have anyone staying at the bed and breakfast. He had been told the guests staying during the Fourth had checked out early, after Agatha's death. Apparently the police crime scene tape used to section off the area where Agatha had died didn't enhance the ambiance of Marlow House. While the tape had eventually been removed, it wasn't fast enough for those who had been staying for the holiday weekend.

Crossing the street to Marlow House, Ian noted the open driveway gate leading to the side yard. He suspected no one was home. Lily had gone with Danielle to Agatha's funeral, and he assumed they were still at the wake.

Once he got over to Danielle's side of the street, he called for Sadie. When she didn't appear, he entered the side yard through the open gate, heading to the kitchen door. While he had a key to the house, he didn't intend to use it. In fact, he needed to return it to Danielle. But he figured if Sadie had come over to Marlow House and had gone inside via the pet door, all he would need to do is call her name and she would come running.

When Ian arrived at the kitchen door, he looked inside and spied Max sitting on the kitchen table, looking at him, his black tail swishing.

"Sadie!" Ian cried as he knocked loudly on the door. Max didn't budge off the table. He continued to stare at Ian.

"If Danielle catches you on that table, you're in big trouble," Ian said aloud. If Max heard Ian's words through the closed door, he either didn't understand or he didn't care. He continued to sit on the table.

Ian stood at the back door for at least ten minutes, but when Sadie never appeared, he decided she wasn't in the house.

"Maybe she came over here and then took off when no one was home," Ian muttered to himself when he walked back toward the street. Taking the cellphone out of his pocket, he immediately called the local humane society to see if they had picked her up. While Sadie was wearing a collar and she was microchipped, it was possible the humane society had her but hadn't yet had time to contact him.

He was just crossing the street back to his house when they answered his call.

"Are you sure?" Ian asked after he was told they hadn't picked up a golden retriever.

"Sorry. But we did get a call about an hour ago about a golden lab running along the highway, about a mile south of Pilgrim's Point. We sent someone out there, but we couldn't find the dog. It's possible the caller got his breeds mixed up, and it was a retriever and not a lab."

"Okay, thanks. I'll go check. And you have my number. If anyone picks her up, please call me. It really isn't like her to take off like this."

After Ian returned to his side of the street, he walked to the back of his house and picked up the screen off the ground. He inspected it a moment, noting the gouges in the mesh.

"You did a number on the screen. This isn't like you, girl. What did you see out that window to make you take off like this?"

Before getting into his car to go search for Sadie, Ian went back into his house and closed his bedroom window. He intended to search the area along Pilgrim's Point first. If she had managed to run all that way, it was a dangerous stretch of highway, and the risk of her getting hit by a car was too great for him to ignore.

Ian was tempted to call Danielle and Lily and ask them to help look for Sadie. Despite all that had happened in the last couple of days, he had no doubt they sincerely loved his dog. But he knew they were both at the wake, and he felt a sense of urgency to check out where the dog had been sighted, especially considering the traffic along that stretch.

While driving, Ian watched for any sign of his dog. When he finally reached the highway, he experienced a wave of dread. The last thing he wanted to do was find his beloved golden retriever dead along the highway.

The sun was just starting to set. It hung low in the sky, hovering above the ocean, transforming the horizon into glistening orange and gold. Traffic along this section of the highway was moderate for a summer Wednesday. So far, there was no sight of any dog—retriever or lab.

Just as Ian approached the curve along the stretch leading to Pilgrim's Point, movement along the side of the road up ahead caught his attention. *Could it be a dog?* Slowing down, Ian turned off the side of the road and parked his car out of the way of oncoming traffic.

Exiting his vehicle, he slammed the door shut and shouted, "Sadie! Sadie!" Walking toward the area where he had spied motion, he continued to call her name.

He walked the area known as Pilgrim's Point. Located along the ocean side of the highway, its western border a sheer cliff overlooking the Pacific Ocean, it had been the site for several fatal car accidents during the past year—including one murder.

A car racing by him honked. Ian turned toward the highway and spied the rear of the vehicle as it disappeared down the road.

"Who is Sadie?" a female voice behind him asked.

Turning abruptly toward the unexpected voice, he found a woman standing between him and the cliff, the sun glaring brightly behind her, obscuring her features. Squinting, he used his right hand to shield his eyes from the sun.

"Where did you come from?" Ian asked. He glanced to his right and then left. He didn't see any other car parked along the highway aside from his own.

"Who is Sadie?" she asked again.

Ian looked back to the woman, who was no more than a silhouette, her features and form blurred by the glaring light of the setting sun. "She's my dog. Have you seen a golden retriever in this area?"

"You're the second person looking for a dog today. But hers was a Labrador. He went down to the ocean, that's where his owner eventually found him. You know labs, they love water."

"Oh damn," Ian muttered. "I guess it wasn't Sadie someone saw."

A branch from one of the trees growing along the edge of the cliff arched to Ian's right. When both Ian and the woman moved to his right, it placed the branch behind her, shielding the direct sunlight from Ian's view and allowing him to see the woman's features clearly.

It took Ian a moment for recognition to dawn. The woman was Darlene Gusarov's doppelganger. *No,* he told himself. *Doppelganger was someone who looked like a living person—Darlene has been dead for months.* He then remembered, in the original definition, doppelganger was the ghost of a living person. Either way, he couldn't wrap his brain around what he was seeing.

"Oh my, you look as if you've seen a ghost," she said with a laugh.

Dazed, Ian muttered, "You look exactly like Darlene Gusarov."

She cocked her head to one side and studied him for a moment. "Did we know each other? I can't remember?"

Ian blinked in response, unable to phrase a coherent thought. In the next instant the woman turned abruptly, moving effortless through the tree branch—not a single leaf rustled—and then she stepped from the cliff, disappearing from sight.

Letting out a shout in surprise, Ian raced to the edge of the cliff, first ducking under the branch. Looking down toward the ocean, he didn't see the woman anywhere. She had vanished.

Sitting in his car forty minutes later, Ian briefly considered calling the police and reporting what he had seen. But what would he tell them? That a woman jumped off the cliff and when he searched the area she was nowhere in sight. He had even driven down to that spot on the beach below the cliff, and he couldn't find her—or any evidence she had been there.

Closing his eyes, he tried visualizing what he had seen. Her face and figure was how he remembered Darlene. Of course, they had never been friends—and his memories of her were the few times he had seen her around town or the pictures that had appeared in the paper after her death.

He recalled Adam mentioning once that Darlene fancied herself a Marylyn Monroe double. While he couldn't see the resemblance,

BOBBI HOLMES

he suddenly realized the dress worn by the mystery woman looked exactly how he remembered the dress—the one worn by Monroe in her famous air vent scene.

It was now dark outside. He needed to get home. Hopefully Sadie would be there waiting for him.

"IAN'S NOT HOME," Lily noted sadly, when Danielle pulled the car into their driveway. "No lights are on in the house. I wonder if he went to Portland?"

Danielle parked the car behind Lily's. "I'm sorry, Lily. I wish I could help you."

"Ian is just one of those stubborn nonbelievers. And even when he sees glasses floating around in the kitchen, he can't for a moment consider it might actually be something paranormal."

"A lot of people are like that." Danielle turned off the ignition.

"But the problem is, in Ian's world, there isn't room for a believer. I guess if I can't agree with him that ghosts aren't real, then we can't have a relationship."

Danielle got out of the car. "In all fairness. You've also said you can't have a relationship with a nonbeliever."

"That's not entirely true," Lily argued as she got out of the car and slammed its door shut. "We've been going along fine this last year, Ian believing in nothing and me knowing the truth."

Together, Danielle and Lily walked toward the kitchen door.

"But you also wanted Ian to know about the spirits. You said it was important for your relationship to be honest with each other."

"I know. And I still mean that. I was the one who wanted to be totally honest in the relationship, and Ian wanted to be a jerk."

Lily entered the kitchen before Danielle. She wrinkled her nose and sniffed the air. "Is Walt here?"

"Hey, Walt," Danielle greeted him as she tossed her purse on the counter. "Yes, he's sitting at the table."

"Hi, Walt," Lily greeted him.

"How was the funeral?" Walt asked.

Danielle glanced around the kitchen. "Is Agatha here?"

"No. I haven't seen her since she left earlier." Walt took a puff off his cigar. "It's been just me and Max."

Danielle noticed black cat hair on the tabletop as she sat down.

164

With a frown, she brushed her hand over the table's surface, sending the cat hair to the floor. "That darn Max has been up here."

Walt shrugged and took another puff.

Danielle shook her head. "Now I have to sanitize the table. I really wish you would have a talk with him, Walt. Tell him to stay off the counters and tables!"

Walt nodded. "Will do."

"What did Walt say about Agatha?" Lily asked as she filled a glass with water at the sink.

"He hasn't seen her."

"How was the funeral?" Walt asked again.

Danielle shrugged. "The sermon was a little long. And I suspect it didn't paint an accurate picture of the deceased."

"You can say that again." Lily brought her water to the table and sat down.

"What I found uncomfortable was the wake," Danielle told Walt.

Lily nodded in agreement. "That was totally inappropriate."

"How so?" Walt asked.

"Whenever we've seen the Pruitts together, Joyce's kids always painted a picture of the doting grandkids. Even when Agatha was… umm…not the most pleasant woman, they would be all smiles and lovey to *Gran*. At the wake, they didn't even make an attempt to be sad."

"And then two of Joyce's sons, the youngest and middle one, had too much to drink and then started bragging about what they intended to buy with their grandmother's money," Lily said with disgust.

"I think you're exaggerating," Agatha said when she appeared the next moment.

TWENTY-SEVEN

I an drove down Beach Drive. Just before turning into his driveway, he looked over at Marlow House. While the upper portion of the house and the front windows weren't lit, there were lights coming from the side yard off the driveway. Danielle's car was also parked in the driveway, and the gate was still open. He assumed someone was in the kitchen or in the library.

Parking in his own driveway, Ian decided to check his house for Sadie first. If by chance Danielle or Lily had come across the dog, it was possible they had brought her over and put her in the house. Lily still had his house key. However, had Lily or Danielle found Sadie, he would also assume they would have called him by now.

Ian looked through his house. Sadie was not there. Panic surged. The only upside in worrying about his dog, it kept his mind off what he had seen at Pilgrim's Point. Although he couldn't forget it, and he hadn't found a rational explanation for the experience, he pushed it to the back of his mind.

When crossing the street, Ian didn't consider going to the front door. He went straight to the kitchen entrance, where the lights were on. If he spied stemware floating in midair this time, he wasn't sure what he was going to do.

Through the side window into the kitchen, he spied Danielle and Lily sitting at the kitchen table, with the overhead light on and the room brightly illuminated. Taking a deep breath, he knocked on the door. Both Lily and Danielle stopped talking and looked in his direction. Lily stood up and walked to the door.

"Hello, Ian," Lily coolly greeted him when she opened the door. Standing just inside the doorway, her hand still on the doorknob, she made no attempt to move to one side and invite him into the kitchen.

"By any chance is Sadie here?" Ian asked.

Lily frowned. "Sadie?"

"When I got home this afternoon, the bedroom screen had been knocked out and Sadie was gone," he explained.

Lily gasped. "Someone broke into your house and stole Sadie?"

Ian groaned. "Damn. I guess that means she's not here."

Stepping aside, Lily opened the door wider and motioned for Ian to enter.

Danielle stood up and looked at him. "What's this about Sadie?"

"Someone stole Sadie!" Lily shut the door and looked anxiously at Ian.

"I don't think anyone took her. It looks like she jumped out the bedroom window."

Lily frowned. "Jumped out the window? I can't imagine her doing something like that."

"The screen had been pushed out. When I got home, it was on the ground outside. I forgot to close the bedroom window when I left for the funeral. Someone from the inside would've had to have pushed it out. And by the tears in the screen, it looks like it was from Sadie's claws."

"Maybe she was barking at someone outside and she jumped at the window, and they took her," Lily suggested.

Ian shook his head. "I don't even want to consider that possibility. She's been acting a little restless the last few days. I don't think she was happy when I left without her."

"She's not used to being left alone," Lily said.

"When I first realized she was missing, I came over here and knocked on the kitchen door. I knew you weren't home, but I figured with the gate open, this would be the first place she'd go. But she didn't answer when I knocked on the door."

"Where else have you looked?" Lily asked.

"Walked along the beach, drove around town. I called the humane society. They told me about a dog that was sighted along…" Ian paused a moment before finishing his sentence. "Pilgrim's Point. But it wasn't her."

Danielle glanced over to Walt, who sat silently at the table, leisurely smoking his cigar. She frowned at his seeming lack of concern over Sadie's disappearance.

Agatha, who had been sitting quietly at the table, listening to what Ian had to say, finally spoke up. "I never understood why people keep dogs as pets. Useless things. Putting their noses in places they aren't wanted. Defecating all over the yard, and god forbid, sometimes in the house. And the hair! Sticks to everything and they make your house smell. Ugh." She cringed. "If he was smart, he wouldn't look for the dog. It did him a favor by running away. Good riddance, I say."

Walt turned to Agatha, his eyes narrowed. In a slow and even voice he said, "A person who doesn't care for dogs and cats doesn't have a soul. You might want to rethink that before you move on." Walt took another puff of his cigar.

"Rubbish, they're just animals," Agatha sniped.

Walt arched his brow. "When we were alive, we were also animals."

"Don't be ridiculous. While technically in the animal kingdom, you can hardly compare a human to a dog!" Agatha scoffed.

"So true in your case." Walt took a puff off his cigar. "A dog gives unconditional love, loyalty, and companionship. A dog will protect your home, give his life for his human family. Tell me, Agatha, when you were alive, did you ever do any of those things?"

In response, Agatha vanished.

Danielle's attention was divided between Walt and Agatha's exchange, which only she could hear, and Ian and Lily, who continued to discuss Sadie and what steps needed to be taken to bring her home.

Agatha's sudden departure allowed her to turn her attention back to Lily and Ian, yet she needed to talk to Walt.

"If you both want to go look for her, I can stay here, and if she comes home, I'll call you. I can even check Ian's house periodically while you're gone. But if we leave the side gate open and the light on, I'm sure she'll come here anyway," Danielle suggested.

A few minutes later, Ian and Lily left on foot to go look for Sadie. As they headed out the door, Lily called both Chris and

Heather to see if they had seen the dog in the neighborhood. Neither of them had.

When Danielle was finally alone with Walt, she turned to him, her movement slow and deliberate. Arms folded across her chest, her gaze wary, she asked, "Okay, Walt, what's going on? Where is Sadie?"

Assuming an innocent pose, yet failing miserably, he responded, "What? Me? I have no idea what you mean."

Rolling her eyes, Danielle dropped her arms to her sides, pulled out a kitchen chair, and sat down. Scooting up to the table, she leaned forward, resting her elbows on the tabletop while she gazed at Walt, who fiddled with his cigar, his eyes refusing to meet hers.

"Come on. There is no way in the world you would sit there so calmly while Sadie is missing. Where is she?"

Reluctantly meeting her gaze, Walt shrugged and took a puff off his cigar.

"Where is she?" Danielle persisted.

Letting out a sigh, Walt waved his hand. The cigar vanished. "She's in the attic."

"Why is she in the attic?"

"Because she doesn't want to leave Frederickport."

"Are you saying Sadie has really run away from home?"

"In a matter of speaking. Although technically, I know she would have happily gone running to Ian when he came looking for her when you were gone. The way she was whimpering, her tail beating the hell out of the sofa, it was killing her to stay put. I imagine it's been just as hard on her this time too. No doubt she heard Ian's voice when he came into the house."

"It's pretty clear you did something to make her stay put and hide. But why?"

Walt pointed to the kitchen door. "It worked, didn't it?"

With a frown, Danielle glanced to the door. "What worked?"

"Lily and Ian are together. They have a common goal, find Sadie. Think of it as a husband and wife who get into a spat and then something happens with their child, and suddenly things are put into perspective."

Danielle cocked her brow. "And Sadie is that child?"

Walt shrugged. "In a manner of speaking."

Before Danielle could respond, Chris entered the house through the kitchen door. "What's this about Sadie gone missing?"

"How did you know?" Danielle asked.

"Lily called me a few minutes ago, asked if I'd seen her." Chris took a seat at the table and nodded at Walt. "Hey, Walt."

"Where's Hunny?" Walt asked.

"I left her at home."

"Aren't you afraid she's going to chew up something again?" Danielle asked.

"I put her in her crate." Chris looked from Walt to Danielle.

"She hates that crate," Walt told him.

"She does not," Chris countered.

"She told me she did," Walt insisted.

Exasperated, Chris said, "Forget about Hunny. What is this about Sadie? Lily said something about her getting out the window? I'd think she'd just come over here."

"She did." Danielle flashed Walt an accusatory glare. "Sadie is up in the attic."

"Then why are Lily and Ian out looking for her?" Chris asked.

Danielle spent the next few minutes filling Chris in on what she knew about Sadie.

Chris looked at Walt and shook his head. "This might actually make things worse for Lily."

"Why?" Walt asked.

"You don't think Ian is going to be pissed when he realizes Lily knew Sadie was safe and sound, yet let him continue to worry? I know I'd be pissed if it was me."

"Lily doesn't know Sadie's in the attic," Walt told him.

"That's not the point. He's going to think she does. In a normal world, if a dog like Sadie has snuck into your house through the doggie door, Lily would know the minute she and Danielle came home. Sadie would be all over them."

Walt frowned. "Normal world?"

"One without a resident spirit who has the ability to conspire with the neighbor's dog," Chris said.

"Chris has a point," Danielle agreed.

"No, he doesn't. There's no reason for Ian to ever know Sadie was here. Once those two work it out, Sadie will mysteriously show up, and that will be that," Walt insisted.

"The only way that will work," Danielle said, "is if we don't let Lily know Sadie is here. I don't think she could keep something like that a secret, and this entire rift between them is about secrets and the fact Lily no longer wants to keep them from Ian. This could complicate the matter."

"Fine." Walt shrugged. "We won't tell Lily Sadie is upstairs. I'll let Sadie know she needs to stay hidden from Lily." In the next moment, Walt vanished.

"I think you need to restrict Walt's TV time," Chris said after he was confident Walt was no longer in earshot.

"Why do you say that?" Danielle asked.

"This thing with Sadie to get Ian and Lily back together reminds me of some overused sitcom plot."

"Walt just hates seeing Lily so unhappy. I think he wants to fix it. He tried a dream hop to talk sense into Ian, but that didn't work."

"I don't doubt Walt's good intentions. But the problem with Ian, he refuses to believe in the paranormal world. If Ian ever learns Sadie was here, I really don't see how you'll ever be able to convince him Lily wasn't in on it. To do that, you'd have to get him to believe in Walt."

TWENTY-EIGHT

Getting up early on Thursday morning to drive to Portland for the appointment with Agatha's attorney proved more difficult for Joyce than she had expected. She was exhausted. The previous day had been draining, beginning with her mother's service. The shock of discovering Agatha hadn't already paid for her funeral was followed by Shane and Henry's embarrassing behavior at the wake, when they both got drunk.

The only thing that kept Joyce from calling the attorney and trying to set up a later appointment was that she desperately wanted to get Agatha's estate settled. After that was done, she could leave Frederickport forever.

Leaving Frederickport was something she had been thinking about since finding those damn gold coins in her safe deposit box. Of course, she initially wanted to leave town so she could run away with the treasure without anyone knowing she had it. Yet now, she wanted to escape a town where everyone knew she had taken the coins. While no one had said anything to her about it—aside from her own children and mother—she could feel people looking at her, judging her.

She loved her children; however, the idea of putting some miles between her and her sons appealed to her. She would miss living close to Martha, but perhaps Martha and Dennis would consider leaving Frederickport with her. After all, they could afford to move and start a new life after the estate was settled.

She wouldn't miss cleaning houses. While she didn't mind the job—especially the fact she was able to work by herself without some employer hovering over her shoulder, she looked forward to hiring someone else to clean her house for a change.

Joyce arrived in Portland just in time to make her 11:00 a.m. appointment with her mother's attorney, Randall Hoover Jr. His father, Randall Hoover Sr., had represented Agatha and Agatha's husband decades earlier. However, Joyce had met neither Hoover.

At first, Joyce wondered if she had the wrong address. She had expected her mother's attorney to have an office in an impressive downtown business building. The Hoover Law Firm kept office in what had once been a residential Craftsman house. Joyce suspected the street had once been lined with residential houses, yet over the years the neighborhood had been rezoned, and the houses to the right and left of the law office had been taken down and replaced by office buildings.

"So nice to meet you, Ms. Pruitt. I'm just sorry for the circumstances," Randall Hoover Jr. greeted Joyce after she was brought into his office by his receptionist. He motioned to a chair. She sat down.

"Thank you for fitting me in. But as I told you on the phone, I don't have a copy of Mother's will. She always told me when her time came I was to contact her attorney, that he would have the will."

"As I'm sure you know, I never actually met your mother, but we'd spoken on the phone a few times over the years."

Joyce looked confused. "I didn't realize that. I assumed you and her kept in regular contact. At least, that's the impression Mother gave me. Considering the demands of her estate."

"Demands? My father was her attorney, but after he passed away, I took over his clients. Of course, he prepared the will, and there has never been a need to make any changes."

"I knew your father had been her attorney originally, but I just assumed…well, I'm just surprised you didn't have regular contact. I would think that with an estate like hers, it would have been necessary."

Hoover picked up a file from the corner of his desk and opened it. Glancing briefly at what was in the file, he looked up at Joyce.

"Your mother's estate is fairly straightforward. She, of course, left everything to you."

Joyce bolted upright in her chair. "To me? Everything?"

Startled by her reaction, he paused a moment and looked at her. "Why yes? Did you expect something different? I assumed you knew."

"I-I-I was always told the estate was divided equally between me and my children."

"That would have involved making changes to the will. Considering the date it was written, I doubt your children were even born back then."

"So what now? My son-in-law says probate can sometimes take up to a year."

"This is not really going to involve a probate like that." Hoover smiled kindly.

Joyce frowned. "I don't understand?"

"Well, the property isn't worth more than maybe fifty thousand dollars. That's, of course, if you get a buyer to pay that price."

"Property? What property?"

"Your mother's real estate in California."

"I still don't understand why this wouldn't involve probate."

"Considering the estate's value, it really doesn't warrant a lengthy probate process."

"What about my mother's money?"

He glanced down at the papers. "From what I have here, your mother had you listed as the beneficiary on her checking account in Frederickport. All you'll need is a death certificate to access that; you really don't need my help on that one, it's fairly easy. You just need to—"

"I meant her other money," Joyce interrupted. "I've already taken care of her Frederickport bank account."

He set the folder back on his desk. "Your parents set up a small interest-bearing account to help pay for any legal fees when settling the estate. Unless there are some unforeseen expenses, I estimate you'll be getting about two thousand dollars back."

"Where is her other money?" Joyce demanded.

"Other money? I'm sorry, there seems to be some sort of misunderstanding. Aside from that account I just mentioned, the only thing in your mother's estate is a piece of real estate in California and whatever personal property she had at home—and her bank account in Frederickport."

"If that's true, then it must be worth more than fifty thousand dollars." Joyce took a deep breath and told herself to calm down. "It's probably beach property or something, that can be worth a fortune. That sounds like Mother, investing her money in real estate."

Glancing down at the open file, he shook his head. "No, it's desert property located pretty much in the middle of nowhere. There are no roads or improvements, and when I looked it up on Google Maps, not close to any town. Your mother spoke of leasing it to wind farmers, but she never did."

Joyce shook her head in denial. "That can't be true. My father invented a self-watering system. It made them a fortune!"

"I'm aware of your father's invention. I was reading the notes on your mother's estate. Your father sold his patent for just under thirty thousand dollars and half of that was used to purchase the property in California."

"So you're telling me the only thing in my mother's estate is a piece of California desert that might be worth fifty thousand dollars?"

"DENNIS, PLEASE STOP!" Martha begged. "Mom's going to hear you!"

"I—I—can't help it," Dennis choked out, making a halfhearted attempt to suppress his laughter.

"This isn't funny!" Martha looked nervously to the closed door leading to the hallway. Joyce had showed up at their house twenty minutes earlier, coming straight from the attorney's office in Portland. She was now sitting in Martha's living room while Martha was in her bedroom, catching Dennis up on the new development.

"I knew it all along! Didn't I tell you your grandmother didn't have any money?"

"You always said she was probably broke, but technically speaking, she did own some property in Southern California worth fifty thousand. So you aren't as right as you think."

"Well, good luck on actually selling that land for fifty K. And when your brothers find out, they are going to have a fit!"

"Serves them right. They were all acting like jerks," Martha scoffed.

Dennis smiled and pulled Martha into his arms. He kissed her nose. "I love you, Martha Porterfield."

Wrapping her arms around Dennis's waist, she looked up into his eyes and smiled. "What was that for?"

"I'm just glad you aren't anything like your brothers."

"I suspect you wouldn't have married me, then," Martha said with a giggle. Looking up at her husband, she asked, "So you aren't terribly disappointed we aren't millionaires now?"

Dennis smiled. "I never for a moment believed your grandmother had the money she claimed. Frankly, if it had turned out she really was rich, the shock would have probably killed me."

"Hmm...then I would have been a rich widow..." Martha mused mischievously.

Dennis laughed, released Martha, and then gave her a playful swat on the backside. She turned to the door, prepared to go back to her mother, when a thought crossed her mind. She abruptly turned back to Dennis, her smile gone. "What about the funeral?"

Dennis groaned. "Damn. I forgot about that. It's going to be a mess. Your mom's going to have to sell the property and then pay off the funeral home. Who knows how long that's going to take."

"You think she'll be responsible for it?" Martha asked.

Dennis considered the question and cringed. "I don't see how she could personally be responsible, not unless she signed something she's not aware of. And with your gran, who knows what she got your mother to do."

Martha shook her head. "No, Mother can't afford to pay for the funeral. She can't even afford to keep her house up."

"Chances are your mother won't be personally responsible, but the estate probably will be. That means before she takes any money, she'll need to pay off Gran's debts."

"And what if she doesn't get what the attorney says the land might be worth?"

"Plus, there will be real estate fees when she does sell," Dennis added.

"Damn, what was Gran thinking?" Martha fumed.

"What your grandmother always thought about. Herself."

JOE MORELLI WAS SITTING at the table, talking on his cell-phone, when Brian Henderson walked into the lunchroom on Thursday afternoon. Just as Brian finished pouring himself a cup of coffee, Joe got off the phone.

"That was Kelly," Joe told Brian. "Ian's dog, Sadie, ran away."

"You're kidding me? I always thought that dog was well trained. Surprised it would run off." Brian took a seat at the table with Joe and sipped his coffee.

"Kelly wants me to keep an eye out for it when we're driving around town. I guess Ian is broken up about this."

Brian frowned. "Isn't that a job for animal control?"

"She didn't ask me to go looking for the dog, just to keep an eye out."

Brian shrugged. "I guess we can do that."

"I just hope someone didn't steal her like before."

Brian sipped his coffee and then set the cup on the table. "That's right. I forgot about that. The guy was into dog fighting. From what I recall, he got sent away for a pretty long time. It'll be a number of years before we have to worry about him again."

"Brian, Joe," Chief MacDonald greeted them when he walked into the lunchroom the next moment.

"Chief," Joe and Brian said in unison.

"I have some interesting information about the Agatha Pine case," MacDonald said as he poured himself a cup of coffee.

"What's that?" Joe asked.

The chief walked to the table and sat down. "While we still have a motive for our possible killer, it may be harder to prove in court."

"Why's that?" Brian asked.

"It seems Agatha Pine was a fraud. She wasn't wealthy like she led everyone—even her family—to believe. The only thing of value in her estate is a piece of property located in the California desert with an estimated worth of maybe fifty thousand dollars. And that was left to her daughter. She didn't leave anything to her grand-children."

TWENTY-NINE

L ily stood at the kitchen window, gazing out into the side yard. The afternoon breeze brushed the tips of the trees growing along the perimeter of the property. Leaves fluttered, reminding Lily of countless tiny hands waving furiously. It was a whimsical thought for someone with such a heavy heart.

"I imagine Walt is having a difficult time knowing Sadie is missing and unable to do anything," Lily told Danielle, who stood at the counter, preparing a chicken salad for their dinner.

Danielle glanced briefly at Lily—whose back was to her—and cringed. The last time she had lied to Lily like this was when she had failed to tell her about Walt's existence.

"I know how much Sadie means to him," Lily said with a sigh, still looking out the window as if she hoped Sadie would come bouncing into the yard at any moment.

"So you really didn't talk to Ian much when you were looking for Sadie?" Danielle asked as she divided the salad between two plates.

Lily shook her head. "No. We thought it would be best if we split up and each looked in opposite directions. I have a bad feeling about this."

"Bad feeling?" Danielle set the plates on the table.

Lily turned from the window and took a seat in front of one of the salads. "The last time Sadie went missing, someone did take her.

I can't imagine Sadie running away. She's too well trained. She loves both Ian and Walt too much. Someone has to have her."

"Well, I have a gut feeling this is all going to work out." Danielle speared a piece of chicken with her fork.

"Your gut feelings tend to be more spot on than mine, so I'll happily go with yours." Lily picked up her fork.

"I know you and Ian have spoken on the phone several times today. Any progress in your relationship?"

"We don't have a relationship." Lily stabbed her salad with the fork.

"You know what I mean. You two are just in a rough spot. I thought perhaps now that you're actually talking again, you might be able to work through this."

Lily frowned at Danielle. "Just because we're both worried about Sadie doesn't mean he's going to start believing in ghosts."

"I guess my great plan didn't work," Walt said when he appeared in the kitchen. Danielle glanced his way but did not make any attempt to acknowledge his presence.

Leaning back against the kitchen counter, his arms folded across his chest, Walt listened to the conversation. Not wanting Lily to be aware of his presence, he resisted the temptation to summon a cigar. If Lily started gushing to him about her concern over his feelings regarding the missing dog, it would be too difficult for Danielle to continue the charade. He decided in that moment that as soon as it was dark, he would have Sadie slip outside and return home.

"That's true. But now that he's at least talking to you, you have an opportunity to convince him," Danielle insisted.

Lily frowned at Danielle. "I can't believe you're saying that. It's like you actually want me to go groveling after Ian."

"It's not groveling. Ian is a good guy. He just doesn't understand."

"Dani, if you'll remember, you're the one who keeps saying you don't have room in your life for a guy who doesn't trust you. Why should I have room for a guy who doesn't believe me?"

"This isn't the same thing," Danielle argued.

"Anyway, you have your own relationship issues to worry about."

Danielle looked up from her salad and frowned. "What is that supposed to mean?"

"You and Chris. What's the deal with you two? One minute

you're taking off for the weekend with him, and the next you two act like old platonic pals."

"If you recall, that weekend didn't work out terrific for any of us."

"You know what I mean," Lily scoffed.

Danielle glanced warily to Walt, who continued to eavesdrop.

"You want to know what I think it is?" Lily asked.

About to take a bite of her salad, Danielle paused and looked at Lily. "What what is?"

"The problem with your relationship with Chris."

"Umm…not really." Danielle lifted her fork back to her mouth and took the bite.

"It's Walt."

Chewing her salad, Danielle shook her head and mumbled, "I really don't want to talk about this."

"Why? You don't have a problem discussing me and Ian. And if you're worried Walt might pop in, just say *hi, Walt,* and I'll know to stop talking."

"Maybe we should just change the subject? If you don't want to discuss Ian and your relationship, I understand. I'll respect your privacy." Danielle refused to glance over to see Walt's reaction to what Lily was saying.

"Oh, I don't really mind talking about me and Ian. But frankly, there really is nothing much to say at this point. We've pretty much come to a block wall. But you and Walt, that's another matter."

Danielle opened her mouth to say something, but Lily started talking again before Danielle could utter another word.

"I've a theory. I think Walt's the reason you can't move forward with Chris in any sort of non-platonic relationship. I know from personal experience that when you have strong feelings for someone, it's impossible to pursue a personal relationship with another guy. Which is why, if I don't get over these feelings for Ian, I'll probably stay single for the rest of my life. As for you, not sure you're ever going to get into a serious relationship with anyone as long as you have these strong feelings for Walt."

"Oh, hi, Walt!" Danielle blurted.

IAN FELT PHYSICALLY ILL. In less than a week his relationship with Lily had fallen apart, and his dog had run away. He felt as if his life was a poorly written dark comedy. After all, it included floating stemware and a mystery woman who disappeared off cliffs —one who looked eerily like a dead woman.

Flopping down in his living room recliner, Ian leaned back, closed his eyes, and ran the events from the last week through his head. Less than a week earlier Agatha Pine had fallen to her death across the street. He had watched them remove her lifeless body from the house. However, he had given the poor woman little thought, aside from attending her funeral. Instead, his thoughts kept going back to the unexplained things he had witnessed, trying to find a logical explanation for it all, while trying to find his beloved Sadie, not to mention dealing with his heartache over Lily.

Opening his eyes, he stood up and wandered over to the front window. Resting his hands against the windowsill, he looked outside and across the street to Marlow House. His gaze moved to the attic window. He often wondered if this was where George Hemming had been standing when he first spied Walt's lifeless body hanging in the attic.

Ian was just about to move away when movement from the lower section of the attic window caught his eye. Leaning forward, closer to the window, he blinked, unable to fathom what he was seeing.

"Sadie? Sadie is in the attic at Marlow House?"

Sadie, her front paws resting on the sill in the attic, stood at the window and looked outside. Her tongue hung out at a goofy angle as she glanced around.

LILY HAD JUST SAID HELLO to Walt—believing he had just made an appearance—when Ian came storming through the kitchen door without knocking.

"What the hell is going on, Lily?" Ian demanded.

Lily stood up and looked at Ian while Walt and Danielle exchanged quick glances.

"What are you talking about?" Lily asked.

"Has Sadie been here the entire time?" he demanded.

"Sadie isn't here," Lily snapped, now defiantly propping her balled fists on her hips.

"Don't give me that. I saw her in the window."

"Then you're seeing things! I would certainly know if Sadie came into the house since I've been sitting in the kitchen for the last hour, and the only way she could get in is the doggy door," Lily shouted.

"You wonder why I have a problem believing your outrageous tales when you've obviously been lying to me all this time!" Ian shouted.

Lily stomped her foot. "Lying, how?"

"Keeping Sadie here while I'm out looking for her, worried sick!"

"Sadie is not here!" Lily shouted at the top of her lungs.

In the next moment, Sadie ran into the kitchen, her tail wagging. She jumped up on Ian, licking his face.

"Damn," Walt muttered under his breath.

Wide-eyed, Lily stared at Sadie. "Where did she come from?"

"Oh please," Ian snapped. "Come on, Sadie, let's get out of here."

"I didn't know she was here, honest," Lily insisted. She turned to Danielle, looking for answers.

Danielle stood up. Just as Ian reached the door, she said, "Ian, wait. Lily really did not know Sadie was here."

"You knew?" Lily asked with a whisper.

"It was Walt's idea," Danielle began.

"Sure, blame me," Walt muttered.

"Please, don't bring *Walt* into this." Ian turned abruptly to the door and tried opening it. It refused to budge.

After letting out a sigh, Walt said, "Sit down, Ian, we need to get this cleared up."

"Why won't this door open?" Ian grumbled as he continued to twist the doorknob.

"What do you mean Walt's idea?" Lily asked Danielle.

"I think you need to sit down so I can explain." Danielle pointed to the chair Lily had been sitting on. Reluctantly she sat down.

Ian let go of the door. "Forget it, I'll go out the front door." Without looking at either Lily or Danielle, Ian called Sadie and marched to the door leading to the hallway. Just before he reached it, the door abruptly slammed shut.

Startled by the unexpected closure, Ian froze. He glanced back and saw Danielle and Lily sitting calmly at the table, while Sadie—who was not following him—sat next to Lily, watching him.

"Must have been some wind," he grumbled.

"In the house?" Danielle asked.

"Sadie, come!" Ian snapped. Sadie stood up and then looked to one of the empty chairs at the table. She then sat down again, giving a little whimper.

"Sadie, I said come!" Ian shouted.

Sadie lay down on the floor, resting her chin on her front paws. She peeked up to Ian, her canine expression conveying an undeniable expression of guilt.

Ian shook his head and walked to the kitchen door, intending to open it before retrieving his dog. But like the back door, it refused to budge.

Now fuming, Ian turned to Lily and Danielle. "What the hell is going on here?"

With supreme calm, Danielle pointed to an empty chair and said, "Please sit down, Ian. Let me explain, please."

Ian stared at them a moment, saying nothing. He then glanced down to Sadie, who made no sign she was prepared to go with him. Finally, he walked to the table and reluctantly took a seat.

"Thank you, Ian. I know Lily has told you about Walt," Danielle began. "We wanted—"

"How did you know about the dream?" Ian blurted.

Danielle arched her brow. "Dream?"

"You mentioned it at the funeral. How did you know I had a dream about Walt Marlow?"

"Because he told me," Danielle explained. "It's the only way he can communicate with people like you—people who can't see spirits. I call it a dream hop."

Sitting rigid in the chair, looking a bit like he might be in shock, Ian stared at Danielle, his expression blank. He remembered what Walt had said in the dream—that Danielle called it a dream hop. "I saw Darlene Gusarov yesterday at Pilgrim's Point. It was when I was looking for Sadie."

A smile curled the corner of Danielle's mouth. "Really?" She glanced to Lily and then back to Ian. "You aren't the only one who doesn't normally see spirits, but has been able to see Darlene."

"I've seen her," Lily said. She looked at Ian. "If you saw her yesterday, why didn't you tell me?"

Ian shook his head. "I just can't believe any of this."

"So you're saying you really didn't see Darlene yesterday? Or you imagined it? What, some sort of shared hallucination?" Danielle asked.

"Why didn't you tell me Sadie was here?" Ian asked Danielle.

"When you came over here looking for Sadie yesterday, Lily and I had no idea she was in the attic. I didn't find out until you both went looking for her. But I had a good idea Walt knew where she was, considering he didn't seem upset she was missing."

"Why didn't Walt say something?" Lily asked.

Danielle shrugged. "It was Walt's bright idea to get you two together to talk."

Waving a hand, Walt summoned a cigar. "Wasn't such a bad idea after all. They are talking." He took a puff.

Danielle rolled her eyes at Walt, but continued. "I guess when Sadie jumped out the window, she came straight over here to see Walt. When we were at the wake and Ian came over looking for her, Sadie wanted to come downstairs when Ian called for her. But Walt convinced her to keep quiet and stayed put, hoping it would eventually get you two to talk and get back together." Danielle looked to Ian. "Sadie doesn't want to leave Frederickport. She loves you, but she also loves Walt."

Ian shook his head, not able to comprehend what Danielle was saying. "How does a spirit communicate with a dog like that?"

Danielle smiled. "Apparently some animals—I'm not sure all—can see spirits. Both Max and Sadie, and even Hunny and Heather's cat have the ability. And spirits are able to communicate with animals. It's not that they actually talk, it's more of a mental telepathy communication thing."

Ian stood up, his expression blank. In a low voice he said, "I would like to go home and think about this."

The kitchen door leading to the backyard suddenly flew open. Startled, Ian stared at it.

"I guess that's Walt's way of telling you it's okay for you to leave. I suppose you do have a lot to think about," Danielle said.

Without a word, Ian walked to the open door. He paused and looked back at his dog. "Sadie, come."

Once again, Sadie did not budge. Confused, Ian looked to Danielle.

"Tell Ian Sadie will go with him, but first, I want to give him additional proof this is all real."

Danielle glanced nervously from Walt to Ian. "Ian, Walt says Sadie will go with you, but first he wants to give you some additional proof that all of this is real."

"What do you mean?" Ian asked dully.

Danielle shook her head. "I have absolutely no idea."

The next moment the pad of paper and pen sitting on the counter next to the telephone floated to Ian. Speechless, Ian grabbed them both, then looked back to Danielle, who only shrugged. His guess was as good as hers.

"Tell Ian to write down a command for Sadie. Something like roll over or run around in a circle. Whatever he wants. I'll read the paper and give Sadie the command. After she does it, he'll know there is no way you set this all up." Walt then added with a chuckle, "I'm fairly certain Sadie can't read."

After Danielle conveyed Walt's message, Ian numbly scribbled *run in a circle* onto the piece of paper. He looked down at Sadie. In the next moment she ran in a circle.

"Did you write run in a circle?" Lily asked.

Numb, Ian nodded. "I tried teaching her to do that once, and she never learned."

THIRTY

Martha stood at her mother's kitchen counter, making sandwiches, when Henry charged into the room.

"What did you do with the money?" Henry demanded. They stood alone in Joyce's kitchen as the rest of the family remained in the living room, discussing the recent turn of events.

Martha frowned. "What are you talking about?"

"You're the closest one to Mom. I don't see her doing this with Shane or Larry. And she certainly couldn't have done it by herself. Hell, a fortune in gold coins fell into her lap and she couldn't keep ahold of it."

Setting down the butter knife on the counter, Martha wiped her hands on the sides of her jeans and turned to face her brother. "I still don't know what you're talking about."

"Gran's money has to be somewhere. I can't believe you don't know where Mom put it."

"You think Mom's trying to cheat all of us and keep Gran's money?"

Henry shrugged. "I don't think she's trying to cheat you. Just her sons. She always favored you."

"If that's true—about her favoring me—it's probably because all any of you do is ask Mom for things. But if you think Mom somehow is trying to cheat you, you're nuts. You saw the will."

"Yeah. I saw a will. It doesn't mean it's actually the right one."

"Then contact the attorney, and ask for your own copy." Martha turned back to the counter and resumed preparing the sandwiches. "But you can make your own damn sandwich. I sure as hell am not making one for someone who thinks I'm trying to steal from the family!" Angry, Martha tossed the sandwiches onto a plate and turned away from Henry. She headed for the living room, leaving Henry alone in the kitchen.

———

"I SURE THOUGHT I would be getting more than ten thousand," Shane grumbled as he snatched a sandwich off the plate Martha had just carried into the room.

Joyce sat alone on the sofa, one hand cradling her forehead as she wrestled with a headache. After telling her sons about the visit with the attorney, they had done nothing but rant and rave. That was over an hour ago. She hadn't spoken another word since that time. She figured none of her sons would have given her a chance to speak had she had something to say.

"Who says you're getting ten thousand?" Dennis asked from where he sat on the hearth.

About to take a bite of the sandwich, Shane paused and looked over at Dennis. "What, you math challenged, Dennis? Fifty thousand five ways is ten thousand each."

"That property was left to your mother, not anyone else," Dennis reminded him.

"Stay out of this; you aren't family," Henry said when he entered the room.

"Yes, he is. And even if Gran had left it to all of us, it still would not be ten thousand each," Martha said as she offered a sandwich to her mother. Joyce silently took one from the plate and then smiled up at her daughter.

"You math challenged too?" Shane asked his sister.

"Shane," Dennis began, "first of all, there is no guarantee your mother will be able to sell that property for that much. The attorney said it *might* be worth up to that amount. But even if she was able to, you still have real estate fees, which could be five thousand bucks."

"Five thousand?" Shane shrieked. "What for?"

"I think Dennis is talking about a Realtor's commission." Larry spoke up.

"Then don't use a Realtor; we can sell it ourselves," Shane said. "What do you think, Henry?"

Henry plopped down on a chair and glared across the room at his mother. "I think we need to find out what happened to Gran's money."

Ignoring Henry, Dennis added, "And don't forget, there is Gran's funeral bill. That has to be paid out of her estate."

"I don't want to pay for that!" Shane whined. "We shouldn't have to. It's their fault they didn't get paid up front."

"It doesn't work like that," Martha said. "Gran signed papers saying the balance was to come out of her estate. The fact is, when Mom gets the estate settled, she'll be lucky to walk away with a few thousand dollars. I think you guys need to stop talking about how you intend to spend *her* money."

"But that's not what Gran said," Larry argued. "She said her estate was to be divided between all of us. Equally. And she said it was worth millions."

"Then she lied," Shane snapped as he sat down next to Henry.

"Or someone took the money and changed Gran's will," Henry added.

"I know what happened to Mother's money," Joyce announced. All heads in the room turned in her direction.

"What, Mother?" Martha asked. She now sat next to Dennis on the hearth. Teetering on her lap was the plate holding what remained of the sandwiches.

"The attorney said Father was paid almost thirty thousand dollars for his patent. Back then, Mother would have considered that a fortune. They used part of the money to invest in property. If it's worth fifty thousand now, it has increased in value. In Mother's mind, she probably thought she was rich. After all, Mother always thought anything she had was better than anyone else's."

"That's a big leap from fifty K to millions," Larry snapped.

Joyce shrugged. "I can't say what was in Mother's mind. Maybe over the years, when she told the story of what they had made from Father's invention, it grew. Sort of like a fish story. Each telling, the fish gets bigger and bigger. Until one day, the bluegill the fisherman pulled in becomes whale size."

"That doesn't explain why Gran said we were all in her will," Larry said.

"That was an obvious lie. But I also understand why she did it,"

Joyce said wearily.

"Why was that?" Henry asked.

"So we wouldn't leave her. She loved us. She wanted to keep us close." With those words, Joyce stood up and silently left the room. A few minutes later they could hear the door to her bedroom close.

"That is a load of crap," Larry scoffed. "Gran was a manipulative, mean-spirited old woman. She didn't give a damn about any of us. She obviously didn't have enough money to live on her own, so she figured out a way to sponge off Mom all these years while playing all of us."

"I have to agree with you," Dennis said. "But no matter what, Agatha was Joyce's mother. I don't know what purpose it will serve to point out to your mother just how bad the woman was. All it would do is make your mother resent the years Agatha lived with her—more than she already does. This way, she can find solace in the illusion it was all from misguided love."

"Bull crap," Larry snapped.

Martha let out a sigh. "I'm not sure Mom actually believes what she just said."

"There is only one thing left to do," Shane said as he stood up. They all looked at him.

"What's that?" Larry asked.

"Sue Danielle Boatman. Maybe Gran didn't leave us anything, but the poor dear old woman—that woman who loved us so much she lied to keep us close—tragically fell to her death at Marlow House. This one is a slam dunk, guys. Maybe it won't be as much as we imagined we'd be getting, but I don't see how we can't get at least five million."

Martha looked at her younger brother. "Shane, there is no way Mom is going to sue Danielle Boatman."

"And now that your grandmother left her estate to Joyce, you can't sue without her. She's the only one who can sue on behalf of the estate," Dennis reminded him.

"Then we have to get Mom to do it," Shane said stubbornly.

"Mom won't," Martha insisted.

Larry stood up. "Yes, she will. We'll make her."

Martha stood up, the plate falling off her lap, landing on the floor, scattering the sandwiches. "You can't bully Mother!"

"Martha, you can either be with us on this, or get out of the way. If you know what's good for you," Larry threatened.

THIRTY-ONE

Lily hadn't shut her bedroom door. When there were guests in the house, both Lily and Danielle kept their bedroom doors closed and locked. Since the next reservation wasn't arriving until tomorrow, Lily didn't bother closing her door.

She was just climbing into bed when she heard Danielle say from the doorway, "I'm surprised you didn't go over to Ian's."

Standing by the side of her bed, wearing a nightgown, Lily looked over to Danielle. "Why would I go over there?"

"You love the guy, don't you?"

"Yes. But what does that have to do with anything?"

"He obviously understands you were telling the truth."

Lily let out a grunt and climbed into bed. "The ball's in his court, Dani. He owes me an apology."

Danielle walked into the room and sat on the side of the bed. Lily, who was under the blankets, rested her head on her pillow while she primly folded her arms over her chest and looked up to the ceiling.

"It wasn't you Ian didn't believe in—it was ghosts."

"Oh, stop trying to defend him, Dani. You broke it off with Joe when he refused to believe you."

"Umm, that's a little different. As I recall, Joe arrested me and thought I should be tried for murder. I don't seem to remember Ian wanting to send you to prison."

Lily looked over to Danielle. "Okay, maybe it's not exactly the same thing. But even if he couldn't believe in ghosts himself, why did he jump to the conclusion I lied to him? Why didn't he simply trust that *I believed*. After all, people believe in all sorts of things other people don't believe in, and it doesn't make them liars."

"Remember, we talked about that," Danielle reminded her.

Lily let out a snort and scooted down in the bed.

"From Ian's perspective, ghosts are pure fiction. At least, he used to believe that. So when he sees things flying through the air, he assumes it's some sort of trick."

"And since I was sitting right there, I had to know how the trick worked."

"So? Are you going to go over there in the morning and get this all straightened out?"

Lily sat up a moment, grabbed a pillow, hugged it, and then rolled over on her side. "Nope. Like I said, the ball is now in Ian's court. He needs to apologize to me."

———

"I HATE ALL THIS DRAMA," Danielle told Walt. They sat together in the parlor, Danielle on the sofa and Walt on the chair facing her.

"I suspect Ian will probably come over in the morning and talk to Lily. They'll work things out," Walt said.

"I hope so. But Ian is not thinking clearly. I could tell when he left he's still trying to process all this. And I wonder, now that he believes—at least I think he does—is he going to start thinking about how Lily has kept this secret from him for the last year, and then start obsessing on how she hasn't been open with him?"

"I suppose that's possible."

Danielle let out a sigh and curled up on the end of the sofa, resting her head on a throw pillow. "I just want to see her happy. And...well...it would be kinda nice if she married Ian. I'd love for them to stay in Marie's house and then have a few little Ians and Lilys that I could spoil."

"You're planning Lily's family now?" Walt chuckled. "I thought women these days didn't believe a woman's destiny needed to include marriage and children in order to be fulfilled."

"It doesn't have to. I don't see anything wrong with a woman deciding not to have children. Or not to marry, for that matter. The road to fulfillment is different for everyone. But there's also nothing wrong with marriage and children. I know Lily would love to marry Ian, and I know she wants kids someday. She loves children; that's why she decided to be a teacher. And frankly, I wouldn't mind holding a baby. I could babysit."

"Perhaps…you should have a baby of your own?" Walt suggested.

Danielle glanced over to Walt and chuckled. "It would be way easier to just borrow Lily's."

LILY OPENED HER EYES. She was sitting on an oversized surfboard in the middle of the ocean, her feet dangling in the cool water. Looking down, she noticed the swimsuit she wore looked like something her great-grandmother might have worn, with its skirt and modest top.

Looking to her right, she found Walt sitting next to her. Instead of a swimsuit, he wore his blue three-piece pinstripe suit. Like her, his feet dangled in the water, the lower portion of his pants' legs submerged.

"Really, Walt, couldn't you dress for the dream hop?" Lily giggled.

He smiled at Lily. "I didn't think it was important. I might not be here long."

"Where are we anyway?" Lily glanced around. In every direction, all she could see was ocean.

"Looks like the middle of the sea. Which sea exactly, I haven't decided."

"This is some big surfboard. You could practically have a party on it," Lily said with a giggle.

She looked down at the water. "Any sharks out here?"

"Do you want sharks?" Walt asked.

Lily shrugged. "Not particularly. A dolphin would be a nice touch. I rather like dolphins."

In the next moment a dolphin swam by.

Lily nodded approvingly. "Good work."

"What kind of dream is this?" came a male voice from the other side of Lily.

She turned abruptly to her left. There sitting on the surfboard next to her was Ian. All he had on was boxers. Without a shirt, his impressive abs were on full display, something Lily had first noticed about Ian when she had initially spied him through the spotting scope from Walt's attic.

"What's he doing here?" Lily asked Walt.

Ian looked over to Lily and frowned. Leaning forward slightly, looking past Lily, he spied Walt on the other end of the board. "I really shouldn't have eaten that burrito before I went to bed," he muttered.

"Danielle was anxious for you two to work this out, so I thought I'd speed this up a little," Walt explained. "You two need to talk."

"This is like that other dream," Ian muttered, furrowing his brow.

"If you'll remember," Walt reminded him, "it was established that other dream wasn't a regular dream."

"Wait a minute, you brought us both into a dream hop?" Lily asked.

"Yes. I've never done this before—more than one person. Oh, I've invited a spirit into a dream, but I've never combined two dreams. I must say, I'm rather impressed with myself." Walt grinned.

"So Ian isn't just make-believe—like the ocean and surfboard?" Lily asked.

"Wait a minute, are you trying to say Lily isn't just part of my dream; she'll remember this when she wakes up in the morning?" Ian asked.

Walt nodded at them both. "Exactly."

The next moment there was a second surfboard. Walt no longer sat next to Lily. Instead, he sat on the second board, facing the pair. "This is much better."

"So why are we out in the middle of the ocean?" Ian asked.

"Less distractions," Walt explained.

"Unless another dolphin comes by," Lily interjected. "The dolphin was real cool. Came right up to me."

"I'm not sure I quite believe all this," Ian muttered.

"That's the problem with you, Ian, you find it impossible to believe anything!"

"I'm sorry, Lily. But whenever I've investigated a ghost story, they always came up empty."

"Ian, do you love Lily?" Walt asked.

"Of course I love Lily," Ian snapped.

"Then why did you make me leave?" Lily asked.

"I didn't want to love someone who lied to me."

Lily frowned. "You're saying you love me, but you don't want to?"

"I love you, Lily. I'm sorry for how I acted." Ian started to say more and then paused. He glanced from Lily to Walt. After a moment he looked at Lily and said, "Maybe this is just a dream. Or maybe you're really here. But it feels odd discussing this in front of —" Ian glanced at Walt "—him."

"I'd be happy to leave and give you both privacy. But I suspect the moment I go, this combined dream hop will cease to exist."

"Maybe we should discuss this when we're actually awake," Lily suggested.

"I don't want to wait until the morning," Ian said. "I don't want us to be apart anymore."

Lily smiled at Ian. "Well, if you want, we could both wake up, and I'll come on over to your house and we can...umm...discuss this in private."

"There is that little matter of Ian waking up," Walt reminded her. "Even when the dream hop ends, Ian will still be asleep."

"I can take care of that," Lily said with a smile. "I still have Ian's house key."

THE BARK WOKE HIM. Abruptly sitting up in bed, Ian looked around his dark bedroom and rubbed his eyes.

"Damn, that was one strange dream."

He heard Sadie bark again. She wasn't in the bedroom. Dragging himself from the bed, wearing only boxers, he stumbled through the darkness, heading to the doorway, his bedroom night-light lighting the way.

He heard the dog bark again. It sounded as if she was in the entry hall. When he reached Sadie, he flipped on the overhead light. Sadie sat facing the front door. No longer barking, she whimpered excitedly, her tail wagging. Someone was outside the door. Whoever it was fiddled with the doorknob. It sounded like the intruder was attempting to open it.

In the next moment the door flew open, and Ian found himself staring at Lily—barefoot and wearing only her nightgown and a wide grin.

Holding up the house key for him to see, she announced, "I told you I still had your key!"

In that moment, Ian remembered. "The dream! It was real!"

"You really need to stop doubting things!"

Ian began to laugh, and then he pulled Lily into his arms.

DANIELLE FOUND Walt in the kitchen on Friday morning. "Have you seen Lily? She wasn't in her bed, and I can't find her anywhere. Her car is still outside and her cellphone is on her nightstand."

"Is that a fact?" Walt smiled as he leisurely smoked his cigar.

"Where is she?"

Danielle had her answer when Lily and Ian came sailing through the kitchen door the next moment, Sadie trailing behind them, her tail wagging. Lily was still barefoot, wearing her nightgown, while Ian had since slipped on a pair of sweatpants and a T-shirt. By their smiles and the way they held hands, Danielle had no doubt they had worked out their problems.

"Glad to see you two together," Danielle greeted them.

"We're getting married!" Lily burst, swinging her left hand up so Danielle could see. Apparently Lily was not just wearing a nightgown. She also wore a diamond engagement ring.

THIRTY-TWO

"Good morning," Adam Nichols cheerfully greeted his receptionist, Leslie, when he strode into the offices of Frederickport Vacation Properties on Friday morning. He carried two paper to-go sacks. One he dropped on Leslie's desk.

Glancing down at the sack, she picked it up and started to open it. "What's this?"

"I stopped by the drive-through on the way here and grabbed some breakfast burritos." Adam flashed her a wink and then continued to his office.

"Gee, thanks, Adam," Leslie said as she pulled the paper-wrapped burrito from the sack. She looked up to say something else to Adam, but he was gone, already in his office.

Twenty minutes later, Adam had already finished his breakfast burrito, skimmed the morning newspaper, and downed two cups of coffee when Leslie announced a Mr. Hollingsworth was here to see him.

"I wasn't expecting you until tomorrow," Adam said when Mr. Hollingsworth walked into his office a few minutes later. The two men shook hands and then each sat down, Adam behind his desk, and Mr. Hollingsworth in a chair facing it.

"Something came up at home, and I had to change my plans, but I didn't want to put this off. So I decided to come early and was hoping we can get this thing wrapped up today. I need to get home tomorrow afternoon. I went ahead and booked a room at the Seahorse Motel for tonight."

"I have a real estate class this afternoon. But I don't see a problem wrapping this up before then. As long as we still agree on the price." Adam glanced at the clock. "I'll need to write up the contract—should take me no more than thirty minutes. After you sign it, I'll need to get it over to my grandmother for her to sign. After that, I can drop the contract off at the title company and open escrow."

"Do we have to sign at the same time?" Mr. Hollingsworth asked.

Adam shook his head. "No."

"Good. I'd like to grab a bite to eat. I'm starved; I haven't eaten today. And I need to check in to the motel. How about I go grab some food while you prepare the contract. I'll swing back by here, sign it, and then go check in. After you get your grandmother's signature, meet me at the motel. You can give me a copy of the signed contract then, and I'll give you the deposit for escrow."

"The renter has the house until the end of the month. But I don't think it will be a problem getting the close of escrow for August first." Adam glanced at his calendar and then looked back to Mr. Hollingsworth. "Make that the third. The first is a Saturday."

WHEN JOANNE ARRIVED to work on Friday morning, she walked into the kitchen of Marlow House to find a barefoot Lily clad in a flimsy nightgown, excitedly chattering away to Danielle as Ian stood silently behind her, sporting a Cheshire Cat grin. She was about to ask what was going on when Lily turned quickly in her direction and announced her recent engagement and then promptly showed Joanne her diamond ring.

After admiring the ring, Joanne asked, "Have you set a date?"

"We haven't gotten to that yet." Holding her left hand with her right one, Lily glanced down at her sparkling diamond and smiled. "This all happened so fast!"

"I wonder if Joanne realizes those two were broken up?" Walt mused from where he sat at the kitchen table.

Danielle glanced to Walt and shrugged.

"Do you know if you're going to have a big wedding?" Joanne asked. "Will it be here in Frederickport or back in California?"

Lily looked to Ian. "We haven't really talked about it, but I'd like to have it here. What about you?"

"To be honest, I never imagined having it anywhere else but in Frederickport," Ian told her.

"As for it being big, I'd rather have a small wedding, just with close family and friends. What about you, Ian?"

Ian looked Lily up and down and grinned. "Maybe you should run up and get dressed, and I'll take you out to breakfast, and we can work out the details."

Unable to suppress her grin, Lily stood on her tiptoes, gave Ian a quick kiss and ran out of the room. Joanne left the kitchen shortly after Lily. She headed upstairs to prepare the rooms for the guests that would be arriving that afternoon.

Danielle suggested to Ian they all go to the parlor. He could wait for Lily there. They hadn't yet started for the door leading to the hallway when Sadie abruptly ran out of the kitchen.

"Sadie!" Ian called.

"That's okay, Ian. She just went to the parlor with Walt," Danielle explained.

Standing in the middle of the kitchen, Ian shook his head. "Danielle, I'm trying to absorb all this."

"I understand," Danielle said kindly.

"Does Joanne know?" he asked.

"About Walt? No."

"How can't she? She's worked in this house for years. Before you and Lily even arrived. Does she have any idea?"

"I doubt it. Of course, like everyone else, she smells Walt's cigar. I suppose it's possible she's heard the same stories Kelly was talking about. But she hasn't really talked to us about it."

"She heard about the flying books," Ian told her.

Danielle smiled. "Ironically, Walt wasn't responsible for that."

"He wasn't?"

"No. That was another ghost," Danielle said cheerfully.

Ian groaned.

"Come on. Let's go to the parlor," Danielle called back to Ian as she headed to the door.

The moment Ian entered the parlor, he sniffed the air. Looking around, he said, "Walt's here, isn't he?"

"Yes. He's sitting over there." Danielle pointed to what appeared to be an empty chair. Sadie was curled up on the floor next to it.

"This is all very surreal to me," Ian muttered. His eyes on the chair, he hesitantly took a seat on the sofa. Sadie lifted her head, looked at Ian, and wagged her tail.

"As you can see, Walt and Sadie have become good friends." Danielle took a seat on the sofa next to Ian.

Before Ian could respond, Sadie jumped up, barked, and ran from the room. The next moment the doorbell rang.

Danielle stood up and glanced at the clock. "I don't think it's any of our guests. They aren't due to arrive until after noon." She left the room to answer the front door and, a few minutes later, returned with Chief MacDonald.

"I told the chief about you and Lily being engaged," Danielle said after she walked into the room.

"Glad to see you two worked it out," the chief said. "And congratulations." The two men shook hands. When the chief was about to take Walt's seat, Danielle informed him it was occupied. He took the one next to it.

"So you know too?" Ian asked the chief.

"I assume you mean about Walt?"

Ian nodded.

"Yes. I told you about my son Evan. He's like Danielle. Walt and Evan have become good friends. I'm grateful for him and Danielle. They've helped him adjust to this—gift."

"Gift or curse," Danielle muttered.

"Lily said Chris and Heather have it too?" Ian asked.

Danielle nodded. "Chris is like me and Evan in that we've been seeing spirits for our entire lives. I'm fairly certain the first time for Heather was after she moved here. It was when I was trapped at Presley House. I know you heard Heather talk about the ghost of Presley House before, and we all discounted it as Heather's overactive imagination. But it was real. Her sensitivity has increased. In fact, when she lived here, she never saw Walt. A glimpse or two, that was all. But now, she's able to see and hear him, and she's seen other spirits."

"That's one reason I'm here." The chief spoke up.

"About Heather?" Danielle asked.

MacDonald shook his head. "No. Agatha Pine. Have you seen her again?"

"Agatha Pine?" Ian groaned.

"She's been coming and going. I was rather hoping she'd move on after her funeral."

Holding his baseball-style department hat in his hands, he fiddled with it as he asked, "If you see her, I was hoping you could get her to tell you who helped her up the stairs."

Ian groaned and slumped back on the sofa. "This can't be happening. The police chief stops by Marlow House to talk to his informant? A medium who talks to the dead victims?"

The chief looked over to Ian and grinned. "Hey, Danielle is my number one informant."

"Who all knows about this?" Ian asked. "Adam? Brian? I don't think Joe does."

"None of them," Danielle said. "Actually, the only ones who know are you, Lily, and the chief."

"How long has Lily known?" Ian asked.

"She found out right after Cheryl showed up. Cheryl told her I claimed to see ghosts when I was a kid. I'd never said anything about it to Lily before. In fact, since I was a kid and told my family with such disastrous results, I'd never told anyone else. But then when I got married, I told my husband."

"Did he believe you right away?" Ian asked.

Danielle smiled. "To be honest, I don't think he ever did. Well, at least not when he was alive." Danielle chuckled.

"Did Lily believe you right away?" Ian asked.

"As a matter of fact, she did. I didn't even have to have Walt do any of his tricks to convince her."

"Tricks?" Walt scoffed. "Makes me sound like some carnival showman."

Ian smiled. "Sounds like Lily."

"I hope you mean that in a good way," Danielle said.

"I do. Believe me, I do." Ian sighed.

Ian looked at the chief. "When did you find out about Danielle?"

"It was a few months after she moved here. Danielle ran into my grandmother at the cemetery; they had a nice chat. After Danielle told me about it, I sort of figured it out."

Ian frowned. "I don't understand. What did a chat with your grandmother have to do with finding out about Danielle's abilities?"

"My grandmother had been dead for about a year when this conversation took place."

The answer left Ian momentarily speechless. After a moment, he blinked several times and then said, "Oh…well, I suppose having a son with the same ability, it wasn't as shocking to you when you found out about Danielle."

"I didn't know about Evan at the time. However, I believe my grandmother had the same ability. When she was alive, she once told me she used to visit with my grandfather after he died. I never really believed her. But I do now. And if a gift like this can be passed on, I suspect Evan gets it from her."

Ian shook his head. "Wow…"

The chief turned his attention to Danielle. "One more thing about Agatha. Remember all that money she was leaving her family?"

"Yeah, what about it?" Danielle asked.

"There ain't none."

"What do you mean? Did something happen to her fortune?" Danielle asked.

The chief shook his head. "She was never rich. All these years, she's been conning her family. Making them believe that when granny finally kicks the bucket, they'll get her money, so they better be nice or she'll write them out of her will."

Danielle cringed. "Well, if one of them was responsible for her falling down those stairs, I suppose her little con wasn't such a great idea. So, it was a lie about her husband's invention?"

The chief leaned back on the chair, resting his hat on one knee. "No, there was an invention, but it didn't involve millions. Agatha owns some property in California, which she and her husband apparently purchased with a portion of the money from the patent he sold. The rest of the money is gone."

"Land in California can be worth a fortune. Maybe her money is just tied up in real estate?" Danielle suggested.

MacDonald shrugged. "According to the attorney, it might be worth fifty thousand. It's undeveloped desert property."

"Fifty thousand actually sounds like a lot for undeveloped desert property. California has a lot of that," Ian noted.

"Apparently, so does Agatha," the chief said.

THIRTY-THREE

Ian glanced at his watch as he and Lily crossed the street back to his house. They had left Sadie at Marlow House with Walt as they went to go get something to eat. "It's a little late for breakfast. And I still need to change my clothes. Do you want an early lunch, late breakfast?"

"I don't know. I suppose we can go somewhere that serves both and decide then."

"Or maybe go to Pearl Cove for brunch," Ian suggested.

"Pearl Cove?" Lily perked up.

"I think our new engagement deserves something special. And Pearl Cove was where we had our first official date."

"I thought our first date was Pier Café after the water pipes broke."

Ian laughed. "No, but that just made me think of something."

Now on Ian's side of the street, they made their way up the walk to Ian's front door.

"What about?" Lily asked.

"In the beginning, I was the one with secrets, not telling you what I did for a living or about the story I was writing on Eva Thorndike. And after you learned the truth, you were the one with the secret."

"We've come a long way in the last year."

An hour later the two sat at a window booth in Pearl Cove, sipping mimosas, enjoying the ocean view.

"I was thinking…would you mind if we got married in Marlow House?" Lily asked.

"Marlow House? Really? I figured you'd want to do something like get married on the beach."

"I want Walt to be there," Lily said. "And that's the only way he can."

Ian frowned. "I don't understand."

"We haven't really had a chance to have a long discussion about ghosts—I mean aside from the fact they do exist. Dani explains it like this. Spirits who haven't moved on have the ability to harness their energy, which enables them to do things like move objects or interfere with electricity. But they're limited on what they can do."

"I'm not sure I understand. But I find it hard to believe random ghosts are just wandering around beside us. If they were, I'd expect objects moving by themselves would be a common occurrence. Which is one reason I had such difficulty believing any of this."

"That's the thing, if a ghost is wandering around—unlimited in where he's going—then that's pretty much what he's using his energy for. There's nothing left to move objects."

"But Walt moves objects."

"Exactly. Which is one reason why he can't leave Marlow House. He's confined there. If he does leave, he has to move on—to wherever we're supposed to ultimately go when we die."

"Why does Walt Marlow choose to stay at Marlow House?" Ian asked.

Lily shrugged. "I suppose in the beginning, before we arrived, it was because he was confused. He didn't completely understand he was dead—or what had happened to him. Actually, no one knew what had really happened to him until Dani moved in. Dani explained to me that when a spirit is confused, it makes it difficult to move on."

"He apparently understands now. Why is he still here?" Ian asked.

"I suspect he stays because of Dani."

Ian cocked his brow. "What do you mean?"

"I think he's in love with her."

"But he's a ghost?"

"Yes, he is. And please, when he's around, don't call him that. He prefers spirit."

Ian considered Lily's words a moment. He shook his head and then took a sip of his mimosa.

"So that's why I want to get married at Marlow House. Walt is a dear friend. I want him at our wedding, and if you think about it, he's partially responsible for getting us back together."

"And one of the reasons we broke up," Ian reminded her with a chuckle.

"True. But that wasn't Walt's fault." Lily grinned.

"A wedding at Marlow House could work out. We could rent rooms there for our family. It does have a nice staircase you can walk down for the ceremony. The entry hall has a lot of room."

"And it'll be convenient, with your house across the street. I assume we'll stay there." Lily took another sip.

"That's what I want to do." Ian paused a moment and then set his glass on the table. "Oh crap."

Lily frowned. "What's wrong?"

"I gave Adam my notice. He thinks I'm moving out at the end of July."

Lily shrugged. "That shouldn't be a problem. I'm sure he'll understand."

Ian shook his head. "No. Adam has a buyer for the house. I even signed some papers terminating the lease I had because the new owner doesn't want a renter."

"Adam sold the house?" Lily gasped.

"Not yet." Ian glanced at his watch. "He told me the buyer wasn't coming in until this weekend to close the deal."

Lily picked Ian's cellphone up off the table and handed it to him. "Well, call him!"

Ian dialed Adam's number, but it went to voicemail. He left a message.

"Try the office," Lily suggested.

"I don't have that number on my phone. Let's finish breakfast, and when we leave here, we can stop by Adam's office. He told me the buyer wasn't coming in until tomorrow."

"What happens if Adam doesn't want to cancel the deal? He doesn't have to. You just said you don't have a lease anymore."

"Then I guess I'll have to put an offer on the house."

Lily smiled. "You want to buy it?"

"Yes. Actually, I do. I'll simply offer more than what the other buyer offered."

"If Adam is going to sell the house, doesn't he have to sell to the person he's already agreed to sell to?"

Ian shook his head. "Not if they don't have a signed contract. One saying in real estate, an offer is only as good as the paper it's written on. If there isn't a written and signed contract, there is still a chance I can buy it."

"We can buy it," Lily corrected. "If Marie agrees to sell to us, I want to pay for half of the house. It's about time I spent that settlement on something."

WALT REMAINED in the parlor with Sadie while Danielle walked the chief out. She was standing in the entry hall, the door open, while the chief stood just outside the door, saying goodbye, when Agatha Pine appeared in the entry. If MacDonald had been like his son and Danielle, he would have seen her. But since he wasn't, he had no idea Agatha's ghost had joined them. It wasn't until after Danielle had said her final goodbye, shut the door, and turned around did she become aware of Agatha's presence. The ghost stood just four feet from her.

"Oh!" Danielle said in surprise. "How long have you been there?"

"Just a moment, I suppose. What was he doing here?"

"How about we go in the parlor to talk," Danielle suggested.

"Why?" Agatha asked.

"Because Joanne is here, and I really don't want her to walk in on me talking to myself."

Agatha shrugged. "Fine. But then will you tell me why he was here?"

"Yes." Danielle headed for the parlor, Agatha by her side.

"Where did you find her?" Walt asked when the pair walked into the room.

Danielle closed the door after them. "She showed up in the entry hall after the chief left."

"So why was he here? Was it about me?" Agatha asked.

"He's still trying to find out who took you upstairs."

"I told you I don't want to talk about it." Agatha walked to an empty chair and sat down.

Sadie, who was still by Walt's side, lifted her head and watched the unwelcome ghost.

Agatha glared at the dog. Sadie growled. Danielle didn't know what the two had just said to each other, but whatever it was, she didn't imagine it was friendly.

"It's interesting you're protecting someone in your family, especially after lying to them all these years," Danielle mused.

"I'm not protecting anyone," Agatha snapped. "I simply choose not to discuss it. And I don't know what you're talking about."

"You mean about the lying? How you conned your family into believing they would someday inherit a fortune from you."

Agatha shifted in her chair. "I didn't lie about anything."

"You certainly did. You claimed your husband had an invention that you made a fortune with, and someday your family would inherit. But first, they all had to do whatever you said, to keep in your good graces and not be written out of the will."

"My husband was brilliant, as was his invention!" Agatha insisted. "We invested the money in land. It proved to be a wise investment. After all, it cost us less than fifteen thousand, and the last time I spoke to a real estate agent about it, I was told it was worth almost fifty thousand dollars. That's not peanuts!"

"Maybe not, but it's not millions," Danielle scoffed.

Walt spoke up. "If you hadn't exaggerated your estate, you probably wouldn't be sitting here with us right now."

Agatha glared at Walt. "What's that supposed to mean?"

"A family member would not have been as anxious to push you down those stairs if they didn't think they were going to inherit millions." Walt flicked an ash off his cigar. It vanished. "Or maybe not. They might have done it anyway, considering your disposition."

"I'M SORRY, Adam isn't here," Leslie told Ian and Lily when they walked into Frederickport Vacation Properties on Friday afternoon.

"I tried calling him, it went to messages," Ian told her. He and Lily stood by the front desk.

"He's in a class," Leslie explained. "They make them turn off their phones."

"Class?" Lily frowned.

"Real estate class. He has to take so many each year or so, to keep his license active," Leslie explained.

"Any chance he'll be out soon? I really need to talk to him," Ian told her.

Leslie glanced briefly at the wall clock. "I imagine it's just getting started. Adam's had a busy day today. He left early this morning. He had a buyer come in, and then he had to get his grandmother to sign the contract. He was going to drop it off to the title company and open escrow before going to his class. And I think the class runs until around five."

"Leslie, the contract he was getting signed, this wasn't for the house Ian is renting, is it?" Lily asked.

Leslie's eyes widened; she looked over at Ian. "Oh, that's right! I forgot you rent that house. Are you leaving Frederickport or renting something else here?"

"I thought the buyer wasn't coming in until tomorrow?" Ian said dully.

"I guess he showed up early. Said something about a change of plans back home," Leslie explained.

"They've already opened escrow?" Lily felt sick.

"That's what I have to assume. Adam told me he was going to have his grandmother sign the contract and then go pick up the deposit from the buyer and get it into escrow before he went to the class."

"Maybe Marie wasn't home to sign it?" Lily asked hopefully.

Leslie shook her head. "No. Marie was home. Before Adam left, he had me call her and let her know he was on his way over there. Is there some problem?"

THIRTY-FOUR

J oanne was just driving away from Marlow House when Ian and Lily pulled into Ian's driveway on Friday afternoon.

"I really made a mess of this," Ian grumbled as he parked the car.

Lily unbuckled her seatbelt. "I'm sorry I didn't handle this all differently."

Ian glanced at Lily. "You? How is any of this your fault?"

"I should have talked to you sooner about Walt—and everything. I should have figured out some way to help you understand."

"I doubt that would have changed anything." Ian got out of the car. "At least in respect to my stubbornness." He slammed the car door shut.

"So what do we do now?" Lily asked.

"I need to find a house by August."

"You could always move into Marlow House," Lily suggested.

"I suppose that could be a short-term solution if I don't find something by the end of the month. But before we get married, I'd rather we move in together—alone. Just the two of us."

"I'd like that too."

Standing next to the car, Ian glanced across the street. "Let's go get Sadie and talk to Danielle. I need to see about renting a room."

"I CAN'T BELIEVE IT; Marie is selling the house?" Danielle said after Ian and Lily told her what had happened.

"It's my own fault. If I hadn't overreacted and given Adam my notice." Dejected, Ian slumped down on the living room sofa, Lily by his side. She patted his knee.

"Of course you're welcome to stay here until you find something."

"If he does, he'll be staying in his own room." Walt piped up from where he stood by the fireplace.

Danielle glanced to Walt. "What's that supposed to mean?"

"If Ian moves in here before those two are married, they each need to have their own room."

Lily glanced from the fireplace, where she assumed Walt stood, to Danielle. "What is Walt saying?"

"He's getting all Victorian on me." Danielle rolled her eyes.

Lily wrinkled her nose. "Huh?"

Instead of explaining, Danielle looked at Ian and asked, "How about if I talk to Marie? I can't believe she'd want to sell the house if she knew you still wanted it."

"It's too late," Ian explained. "Once that purchase contract is signed by the buyer and seller, it becomes a binding contract. Marie could be sued if she tried to back out of it. The only thing that could happen now is if it fell out of escrow."

"What could make it fall out of escrow?" Lily asked.

"If, for instance, the buyer was getting a loan, and the house didn't appraise for the selling price, or the loan fell through for another reason. In those instances, the buyer often can't secure financing to finalize the deal. Or if an inspection is part of the contract and the buyer finds something wrong with the property, then he can cancel."

"That's the buyer cancelling. How can a seller back out of the deal?" Lily asked.

"The only way I know is if the buyer isn't performing. Which would be something like failing to come up with the funds to purchase the property by the closing date."

"Well, crap," Lily grumbled, settling back on the sofa.

The doorbell rang. Sadie jumped up from where she had been sleeping and let out one bark before heading to the door. Before she reached the hallway, Walt called her back before Ian had a chance to intervene. Sadie paused, looked at the fireplace, and then reluctantly returned to where she had been napping.

Danielle stood up to answer the door while Ian glanced down at his dog. "Walt just told Sadie to stay, didn't he?"

"Yep," Danielle said as she disappeared into the hallway to answer the front door.

"I'm not sure how I feel about this," Ian muttered.

"I'm sorry, Ian. I didn't take that into consideration," Walt said. He then let out a sigh. "I suppose I shouldn't waste my breath, you can't hear me anyway." He looked down at Sadie. "Stay here with Ian. I'm going to see if our new guests have arrived." Walt vanished.

WHEN WALT ARRIVED at the front entry, he found Danielle at the open doorway, talking to three men. At closer inspection he realized who they were: Agatha Pine's grandsons. He glanced around to see if Agatha Pine was anywhere in sight. He didn't see her.

"What do they want?" Walt asked just as Danielle was opening the door wider, welcoming the men inside. He followed them and Danielle into the parlor.

"I imagine you thought you'd hear from our attorney first," Henry said when the three stepped into the parlor.

Danielle motioned to the sofa and chairs, silently offering them a seat. "I'm afraid I don't understand."

Shane and Henry each sat down on the sofa while Larry took one of the chairs across from them. Danielle sat down on the chair next to Larry.

"The wrongful death suit, of course," Henry explained.

Danielle arched her brows. "Wrongful death?"

"When my grandmother fell down your stairs, of course. We thought it would be best if we could handle this out of court, without an attorney," Henry told her.

Danielle leaned back in her chair and studied him for a moment. "You intend to sue me?"

"We really don't want to," Henry insisted. "In fact, Mother wants to avoid going to court. For one thing, it would be horrible publicity for your business. Mother appreciates the fact you were so understanding about her mistakenly taking those coins."

"Mistakenly?" Danielle said.

"She did come forward with the truth, which she didn't have to, that helped you out of an awkward situation. Even though we've explained to Mother you've cleared that slate, she still feels a debt of gratitude toward you, which is why we're here."

"Umm…so why are you here, exactly?" Danielle glanced over to Walt, who arched his brows and gave her a shrug before conjuring up a cigar.

"Like I said, to settle out of court. In the long run, it won't cost you as much. There won't be any attorney fees. And without going to court, there won't be all that bad press."

"How much exactly are we talking about?" Danielle asked.

Just as Henry blurted *four million*, Shane blurted *five million*.

Danielle glanced from Shane to Henry. "Which is it? Four or five?"

Henry glowered at Shane and then reluctantly said, "Five million."

"I'll need to speak to my insurance company and see what they say," Danielle said calmly. "But I'm still trying to figure out how exactly your grandmother got up those stairs and managed to start up to the attic when her wheelchair was still downstairs."

"Someone must have helped her upstairs and left her," Larry explained.

Danielle turned to Larry. "I understand you were on the way to take her upstairs when you left suddenly."

"Yes. I got a call from my ex-wife about our son. He had an emergency appendicitis."

"I hope he's doing okay," Danielle said sincerely.

Glancing down to avoid eye contact, Larry shuffled uncomfortably in the chair and mumbled, "Yes, he is, thanks."

Danielle looked to Shane. "You were right there when your grandmother fell. Did you see what happened?"

"I wasn't there when she fell," Shane corrected. "I came down the stairs from the attic after she was already on the floor. I found her at the bottom of the stairs. I had no idea she had come up to the second floor."

Danielle turned her attention to Henry. "I understand you were the one who originally was going to help her up the stairs. Why exactly was it you didn't?"

Henry shrugged. "I came inside to use the bathroom, got side-tracked, ended up talking to a few people. After I finally made it to the bathroom, I heard my brother screaming just as I was coming out. I was as surprised as anyone to discover Gran had gotten upstairs somehow."

"Someone helped your grandmother up those stairs. I'd like to find out who."

"Leave it alone, Danielle," Agatha snapped when she appeared in the parlor the next moment.

"Which one of these upstanding ambulance chasers pushed you down the stairs?" Walt asked as he puffed on his cigar.

"Oh, shut up, Walt Marlow," Agatha hissed.

Danielle stood up. "I'll consider what you've proposed and discuss this with my insurance agent—and my attorney."

As the four left the room, Agatha watched and then turned to Walt and asked, "What have they proposed?"

"Since they didn't get the money you promised them, now they're going after Danielle."

"They're suing her?" Agatha asked.

"For your wrongful death. Which one of them may have facilitated." Disgusted, Walt flicked his cigar into the air. It vanished.

Agatha began to laugh. "I didn't think they'd consider doing that. Joyce is so terrified Danielle will change her mind and press charges for taking the coins."

"Are you saying you approve?" Walt asked.

Agatha looked at Walt and chuckled. "Of course. They have every right to sue. I fell on Danielle's property, and it's perfectly normal to sue in a case like this. Good for them."

"So you think it's right for a murderer to seek damages from the owner of his crime scene?" Walt asked incredulously.

"Who said anyone was murdered? Accidents happen." Agatha vanished.

"That really did not surprise me," Danielle said when she walked back into the room. Glancing around, she saw only Walt. "Where did she go?"

"I have no idea. You certainly aren't going to give them any money, are you?"

Danielle let out a sigh and took a seat. "Actually, Walt, I called my insurance agent on Tuesday. He's already expecting this."

"You didn't mention anything."

Danielle shrugged. "To be honest, considering the circumstances, I wasn't convinced there would be a lawsuit. For one thing, at the time I thought the family was inheriting Agatha's imaginary fortune, and I figured if one of them was involved, they wouldn't like too much attention on the circumstances of her death. You never know what will come out in court. Plus, I figured Joyce might be hesitant to bring a case, considering our history. Of course, my insurance agent didn't agree with me, and it looks like he's right."

"Sounds like they want to settle out of court. But five million seems rather excessive. I would think if damages were awarded in a court case, it would be considerably lower."

Danielle nodded. "I agree. I know this sounds horrible, but in cases like this, when determining the settlement, the courts take into account the person's age and income potential. We're talking about an elderly woman with absolutely no income potential."

"You're right. Reducing someone's worth to what they might earn sounds horrible."

Danielle shrugged. "But it's what they do. I really don't have a problem paying a claim. If someone falls on my property, I understand I can rightfully be sued. Of course, the extent of damages is typically based on if there was some sort of negligence on my part."

"You certainly aren't responsible if someone from her own family pushed her."

"True. But the only reason we suspect foul play is how she landed, along with the fact no one has come forward to admit they helped Agatha up those stairs and left her. If someone had admitted helping her up and leaving her up there alone, it would be easier to assume she fell on her own, regardless of how she landed. Which may or may not make me liable."

"Hmmm…" Walt narrowed his eyes and stared off into the distance as he considered another possibility. "Perhaps if someone took her up there and left her, maybe they haven't come forward because they're afraid the family will sue them."

"That's entirely possible. Which would mean whoever Agatha is protecting isn't a family member."

"I find it interesting the grandsons claim they want to settle privately, insisting it will save you money, yet they ask for a ridiculous amount. Why do they imagine you'd take their offer?" Walt wondered.

"I have no idea. I'd think hiring an attorney would be more to their advantage. For one thing, people tend to take these types of threats more seriously when delivered by an attorney."

THIRTY-FIVE

"Why did you ask for five million?" Henry asked Shane. The three brothers sat together at Lucy's Diner, having a late lunch.

"I was wondering that myself," Larry said.

"We agreed a million each. We have to give Mom a million, there's no way around that. And if we cut out Martha at this point, it's just going to cause problems. She could get Mom to keep the entire thing."

"Martha didn't want any part of this, so I don't see why we need to cut her in." Henry picked up his soda and took a gulp.

"Maybe Shane has a point," Larry reluctantly acquiesced. "Sounds like Boatman is going to get her insurance company to pay the claim, and there is no way they'll pay it to us since we don't technically represent the estate. We need to get Mom to go along with us, so when she gets paid, we'll get our share. And you know there's no way she's going to cut Martha out of it."

"The tricky part is to keep Mom from finding out until after we reach a deal with Boatman. At that time, I think it'll be fairly easy to convince her not to sabotage the deal. When we get to that point, I think we'll know if Boatman is going to bring up the coins again, or let it go like she has," Henry said.

"Let's just hope Boatman doesn't make an issue of the coins.

Mom will be pissed if she ends up facing charges over the coins because of this," Larry said.

"But it will be worth it," Shane said. "And come on, Mom will be happy we did this. After all, she's not such an innocent. She did take those damn coins."

Henry laughed. "No kidding. I still can't believe she did that. Just wish she would have held onto them."

BRIAN HENDERSON DROVE FIRST to the person of interest's home. He wasn't there. According to his roommate, he had taken off with his brothers. As Brian drove down main street, he spied Larry Pruitt's car parked in front of Lucy's Diner. Making a U-turn, Brian turned back up the street and parked behind Larry's vehicle.

Just as he got out of his car, he spied the three brothers coming out of the diner. They were laughing, and Shane had just given Henry a pat on the back, followed by another round of laughter by the two youngest brothers. Larry didn't seem as amused.

"Afternoon," Brian greeted when the brothers reached Larry's car.

The three men stopped abruptly and looked at Brian. They seemed surprised to see him, unaware he had already parked behind Larry's vehicle. They each muttered a halfhearted greeting and were about to get into the car when Brian stopped them.

"Shane, I was hoping you could come down to the station. The chief has a couple of questions he needs to ask you. It shouldn't take long." Brian smiled.

"Me?" Shane frowned. "What for?"

"It's about what you might have seen during the time of your grandmother's accident. I believe the chief is talking to Ben Smith too. As far as we can tell, you were the only two on the second floor when your grandmother fell."

"Technically speaking, I didn't come to the second floor until after she fell. I was up in the attic, looking around, at the time of the accident," Shane corrected.

"I'm assuming you don't have your car?" Brian asked.

"No. Larry is driving," Shane told him.

"You can drive with me. I can take you home afterwards," Brian offered.

Larry looked at his youngest brother. "I don't have time to take you all the way over to the police station, it's on the opposite side of town. I have to drop Henry off and get back to work."

Shane glanced from his brothers to Brian. "Do I really need to?"

Brian smiled. "I'm afraid so."

SHANE SAT ALONE in the interrogation room, waiting for the police chief. When Brian had picked him up, he had been under the impression the chief would be talking to him in his office. He didn't like the interrogation room. It brought up too many bad memories. Shifting uncomfortably in his seat, he glanced over to the two-way mirror and wondered who was on the other side, watching him.

Five minutes later, Joe Morelli walked through the doorway. In his hand he carried a manila folder.

"I thought the chief wanted to talk to me," Shane asked.

"The chief is busy." Joe tossed the folder on the table and sat down, facing Shane.

"I understand you're quite the entrepreneur." Joe opened the folder and flipped through it.

"Not sure what you mean. What does this have to do with Gran's death?" Shane shifted in the chair again, unable to get comfortable.

"I understand you make a living selling things on eBay."

"Yeah, what about it? It's all legal. I mean, I'm not selling drugs or anything. I don't do that anymore."

"I see you've branched out."

Shane frowned. "What do you mean?"

"You're a blogger now. How is that working out for you?"

Shane stared at Joe as if trying to read his expression. "So I have a blog. A lot of people do."

"But a lot of people don't tell the world someone is going to die the next day, and when the person dies, the blogger is not only a few feet away, but believes he's about to inherit millions."

"Whoa…wait a minute. You think I pushed my grandmother down those stairs?" Shane sat up straight in the chair, shaking his head in denial.

"Right now we have some people at your place with a search warrant, going through your room, your computer—"

"Hey, you can't do that!" Shane shouted.

"According to the judge who gave us the search warrant, we can."

"You seriously think I not only killed Gran, but announced I was going to kill her before I did it? What do you think, that I'm an idiot?"

Joe shrugged. "Well, you did believe your grandmother was worth millions."

"And she wasn't." Leaning forward, still sitting on the chair, Shane slammed his open palm on the table. "Which means I didn't have a motive to kill her. Why would I? And why would I post about it?"

"We all know you weren't aware your grandmother had misrepresented her estate until after she died. And these days, it's not uncommon for people to boast online about their crimes. I'm actually surprised you didn't take a video of her falling down the stairs after you pushed her and then post it on YouTube."

Shane slumped back in the chair and glared at Joe, folding his arms across his chest. "You're sick."

"I'm not the one who pushed my grandma down the stairs and posted about it."

"Neither did I."

"Then why don't you tell me, why did you make that post claiming someone was going to die at Marlow House on the Fourth?"

Shane shrugged. "Marlow House is kind of a creepy place. Ever since Boatman moved in, weird stuff has been happening there, and to her. I just figured I'd cash in on the attention she's been getting and earn some money with ads. People like stories about haunted houses and curses. And you got to admit that place has to be cursed, considering the crap that's gone on there. I didn't really think someone was actually going to die, but I figured with her wearing that necklace again, something was bound to happen, and I could spin it in my next blog post and people wouldn't even care that my prediction of another death didn't happen."

"But there was another death. And you didn't seem to mind exploiting your grandmother's tragic death in your blog, did you?"

"I think I want to see a lawyer."

BRIAN HENDERSON WALKED into the chief's office, shaking his head. "I figured Shane's blog post was just a bizarre coincidence. I didn't seriously think he would be stupid enough to blog about a murder he was about to commit."

The chief closed the file he had been reading and leaned back in his chair. He watched as Brian tossed a folder on the desk and then sat down.

"So did you actually find something?" The chief leaned forward and picked up the folder Brian had just dropped on his desk.

"You know those television shows about the dumbest criminals?" Brian asked.

MacDonald opened the folder and glanced up at Brian. "Yeah. What about them?"

"Shane Pruitt could have his own series. He didn't even make an attempt to get rid of his search history. I can't believe he didn't realize he might become a suspect and we'd be looking at his computer."

"What did you find?"

"I suspect a murder mystery writer wouldn't have as many searches on their computer involving ways to kill people as he does."

MacDonald arched his brow. "He's been searching on ways to kill people?"

"One search involved a blood pressure medicine. He wanted to know what other drug—in conjunction with the blood pressure medication—would be lethal. On a hunch, I checked with the local pharmacist and found out Agatha took that particular blood pressure medication."

Leaning back in his chair, MacDonald let out a low whistle.

"There were extensive searches on methods of poisonings—antifreeze, arsenic. He ran numerous searches looking for poisons that were difficult to detect."

"But he didn't poison her," MacDonald reminded him.

"No. But he also looked up ways to electrocute someone, as well as methods of asphyxiation. And get this—he was looking up how to find a hit man."

MacDonald arched his brow. "Charming fellow. Was there anything else?"

"He was also doing searches for expensive cars and beach-front property."

"Shopping?"

Brian nodded. "It looks that way. All the searches on how to kill someone were done before Agatha's death. The shopping ones, he was still making those as recently as this morning."

MacDonald flipped through the folder. "I got a call from Danielle a few minutes ago. It seems before you found the Pruitt boys at Lucy's, they paid a little visit to Marlow House."

"What about?"

"Now that grandma didn't pan out, they're trying to shake down Danielle. They're threatening to sue her for Agatha's wrongful death," MacDonald explained.

"Wouldn't that be Joyce's place to do that? Joyce was her beneficiary, not the boys," Brian asked.

"I think that's why they went to her and asked to settle it out of court."

Brian frowned. "I don't see why that would matter."

"Like you said, they aren't the brightest criminals."

"You think the other brothers are in on this?" Brian asked.

"It's possible. From what I know about the Pruitt boys, they've had their issues with each other. Shane and Henry seem to be the closest. I know they used to work together. They had a business where they purchased used furniture and refinished it. But they had some sort of disagreement and Shane went off on his own and started selling stuff on eBay. Secondhand junk he picked up at garage sales. Larry's always been the outsider. But they are brothers, and if they went together to see Danielle, I suspect they're in on this together."

"If we bring the other two in, split them up, maybe we can get one of them to flip on the others. After all, I don't think they'll be thrilled when they learn little brother Shane was foolish enough to be posting about the murder and not clearing his search history."

THIRTY-SIX

Both Ian and Lily were still at Marlow House when the new guests arrived late Friday afternoon. They were three middle-aged couples, siblings and their spouses. One couple was from Washington state, and the other two couples lived in California. They were in Oregon for a mini family reunion and would be staying until Wednesday.

Shortly after checking in and taking their luggage to their rooms, they left to do a little sightseeing and told Danielle they intended to stop someplace for dinner before they returned.

Lily stood at the living room window and watched as the Suburban, driven by one of the guests, drove off down the street, all three couples on board.

Lily turned from the window and walked to the sofa, where Ian sat. "They seem nice."

"I wonder what they would think if they knew Marlow House was haunted?" Ian mused.

Danielle, who sat at the small desk, glanced up from the register she was updating and chuckled. "I always said a haunted house could be a great promotional gimmick. But Walt refuses to play along and provide the necessary ambiance. You know, maybe an occasional lit candelabra floating across the library. That sort of thing."

"It would be a fire hazard," Walt said when he entered the room a moment later.

Danielle shrugged and closed the register book.

Lily giggled. "Do we even own a candelabra?"

"We could get one," Danielle told her.

Tail wagging, Sadie ran into the room the next moment and went straight for Ian. Jumping up on his lap, she swiped a wet kiss across his face.

Ian greeted his dog with several pats to her shoulders and gently nudged her to the floor. "Finished hanging out with Walt? I was starting to feel like second stringer."

Lily glanced around the room. "Did Walt come in with Sadie?"

"I don't smell his cigar," Ian said.

"He's not always smoking. And yes. He's over there." Danielle pointed to the fireplace.

Walt smiled at Danielle.

"This would be a hell of a story," Ian muttered.

Lily laughed. "Well, that was quick. I was wondering when you would finally admit that."

"Of course I can't write it. I understand Danielle wants her privacy, and no one would believe me anyway. It would probably destroy my credibility." Ian sighed.

"And I thank you," Danielle said. "I don't really need that kind of notoriety."

"You know what is rather amusing?" Ian asked.

Lily glanced to Ian. "What?"

"I thought the big story I wasn't writing was about billionaire philanthropist Chris Glandon living in Frederickport under the alias Chris Johnson. But the real story—Chris Glandon the medium."

"And once again I'm shoved aside for that pretty boy," Danielle said with faux dramatics.

Lily giggled.

Danielle stood up. "Are you guys going to be here for a while?"

"What do you need?" Lily asked.

"I'd like to run down to the police station and see if I can talk to the chief. When I spoke to him on the phone earlier, it sounded like something was going on regarding **Agatha's** case. If her grandsons are serious about pursuing a lawsuit, I need to call my insurance agent again, but before I do, I want to find out if any of them was involved in her death. If so, that's going to put an entirely different spin on any lawsuit."

"Danielle, if Agatha's spirit keeps showing up here, why doesn't she just tell you what really happened to her?" Ian asked.

Danielle shrugged. "Spirits aren't that much different from living people. Being dead doesn't mean you'll tell the truth or want to answer questions. Although, after someone has died, they tend to be more truthful because the reasons for lying no longer apply. In Agatha's case, I don't doubt she remembers what happened, but for some reason she refuses to share that information. I suspect she's protecting whoever took her up the stairs—and maybe pushed her."

"Why would someone protect her killer?" Lily asked.

"For one thing, if it is one of the grandsons, he is family. Plus, she may feel guilty for manipulating them all these years and realizes she probably drove the grandchild to violence," Danielle suggested.

"If she was pushed, who's to say it wasn't Joyce?" Ian asked. "I imagine she had years of pent-up frustration having her mother live with her all those years, always so demanding."

"As far as I know, she wasn't on the second floor when it happened," Danielle explained.

"The most likely suspect, Shane. After all, he was right there. But it could have been Larry. No one saw him leave, and maybe he got that phone call after he took her upstairs. And Henry was in the downstairs bathroom. It's possible he pushed his grandmother while Shane was in the attic and Ben was in the bathroom, and he then got downstairs before Shane found her. Unfortunately, most everyone was outside when all this happened," Lily said.

"I'm going to go to the police station and see what they know," Danielle said. "Can you guys stick around until I get back?"

"Only if you return with some Chinese food," Ian teased.

DANIELLE PULLED into the parking lot of the Frederickport Police Department a little after four on Friday afternoon. Inside the station, she found Joyce Pruitt and her daughter, Martha, sitting in the front waiting area, whispering amongst themselves, clearly agitated. When the women looked up to see who had entered the building and saw Danielle, Joyce said something to her daughter, to which Martha grabbed hold of her mother's arm, gave it a little reassuring squeeze, and then stood up. She walked to Danielle.

"Hello, Martha. I didn't expect to find you and your mother here. Is everything okay?" Danielle glanced over at Joyce, who immediately looked down, reluctant to look Danielle in the eyes.

"They brought my brothers in for questioning. I believe they think one of them had something to do with Gran falling down the stairs."

Danielle looked from Martha to Joyce and then back to Martha. Not knowing what to say, she simply muttered, "Oh."

"I also found out my brothers stopped at your house earlier to talk to you about Gran's death."

"Umm…yes, they did. From what they tell me, your family is considering a wrongful death suit against me and Marlow House."

Martha shook her head emphatically. "No. We aren't. My brothers weren't speaking on behalf of my mother, and she's the one who represents Gran's estate. Mother wants you to know she has absolutely no intention of suing you."

Before Danielle could respond, a commotion from down the hall distracted their conversation. Glancing down to the hallway leading to the offices and interrogation room, they saw Henry and Larry walking in their direction, the police chief trailing beside them.

When they reached the waiting area, Larry whispered something to Joyce. She stood up and then started toward the door with her two oldest sons.

As Joyce approached her daughter and Danielle, she nodded at Danielle and then said, "Martha, let's go." Both Henry and Larry walked past Danielle without acknowledging her.

Glancing at the exit, Danielle watched as the Pruitt family walked out of the station.

MacDonald, who had escorted Henry and Larry to their mother, walked up to Danielle. "You aren't here to see me, by any chance?"

Looking from the exit door to the chief, Danielle smiled. "How did you guess? So what's the deal with the Pruitt clan?"

MacDonald nodded toward the hallway. "Let's go in my office and we can talk there."

DANIELLE SAT in one of the chairs facing the chief's desk. Before sitting down, MacDonald closed his office door for privacy.

"We've arrested Shane Pruitt for the murder of his grandmother."

Danielle arched her brows. "No kidding? Am I to assume he acted alone, since his brothers just walked out of here?"

"I suspect the brothers were in on it. But we brought Larry and Henry in, interrogated them both, and while they confirmed what I already knew—those Pruitt boys have some issues with each other and their family in general—neither Henry nor Larry were prepared to roll on Shane. They insisted they have absolutely no knowledge of Shane taking any aggressive action against Agatha."

Danielle leaned back in the chair and crossed her legs. "So why did you arrest Shane?"

"I'll admit it is circumstantial. But the fact is, according to everyone—including members of Agatha's family—there was no way she got up those stairs alone and managed to walk over to the attic stairs without help. Shane was the first one on the scene, and he had the motive."

"Walt pointed out that perhaps whoever took her upstairs isn't coming forward because they're afraid the family might sue them. It's entirely possible someone innocently helped her up there and just left her. And then she fell on her own. Which makes sense, considering she had no business trying to get around without her wheelchair."

MacDonald shook his head. "I have always considered that possibility. But after what we found on his computer, I'm afraid this is a little darker."

"What did you find?"

"I can't really discuss it right now. But I can tell you I found your mystery blogger. The one behind the Mystery of Marlow House website."

"You did? Who is it? Someone I know?"

"It's Shane Pruitt."

Danielle frowned. "Shane?"

"We were able to track down the owner of the domain. Once we found out it was Shane, we brought him in for questioning and were able to secure a search warrant to check his house and computer."

"Wow." Danielle let out a deep breath. "Well, he was at the first open house. So I imagine he's the one who took the photos that were on the blog. Did he say why he started it?"

"According to Shane, he was trying to make money off the advertising."

"That makes sense. But why blog about planning to kill his grandmother—and then actually kill her?"

"In all fairness, he never mentioned her by name, and he never said he was going to kill anyone, just that someone was going to be murdered," MacDonald reminded her.

"I know. But still. If you're going to kill someone, why blog about it? Did he want to get caught?"

"Come on, Danielle, we all know there are lots of stupid people out there. Not-too-bright criminals that think it's a terrific idea to film their crimes and then post it on Facebook. Happens more than you realize."

THIRTY-SEVEN

W hen Danielle discovered Joanne's sister from Colorado had surprised her with a visit, she told the housekeeper to take the weekend off. Marlow House was already spotless from Joanne's recent cleaning, the linens had all been changed, and there was a fresh supply of bath towels stacked neatly in the laundry room.

On Saturday morning, Lily helped Danielle set the table for breakfast and prepare the meal. They served homemade waffles, sausage, hickory smoked bacon, scrambled eggs, and sliced melon. The guests seemed to enjoy the meal, which made cleanup easier, since there were no leftovers.

After breakfast, the guests left to do more sightseeing. Lily stayed to help Danielle clean up the kitchen, and when they were finished, she went across the street to Ian's to discuss wedding preparations.

Danielle hadn't seen Walt since they had served breakfast. He had come down briefly when she was making coffee, and then he disappeared. She also hadn't seen Agatha and couldn't help wondering if she knew her grandson had been arrested. Danielle was thinking of Shane's arrest when the phone rang. It was Marie Nichols.

"Morning, Marie." Holding her cellphone to her ear, Danielle walked from the kitchen to the library.

"Good morning, Danielle. I hadn't talked to you for a few days and was wondering how you were doing. I heard about Agatha, how she really didn't have any money, and I was worried those money-grubbing grandkids of hers might be coming after you now."

"Ahh, you mean suing me because of the accident?" Danielle sat down on the library sofa and put her feet up on the cushion, stretching out. She leaned back against one of the sofa's padded arms.

"Seems like the world is sue happy these days," Marie told her.

"I guess you haven't heard. They arrested Shane Pruitt last night for the murder of his grandmother."

"No!" Marie gasped. "Are you serious?"

"Yes. They believe he was the one who took her up there and pushed her down the stairs."

"Did someone see something? They must have something if they're charging the boy."

"I think part of it hinges on the fact Agatha couldn't have gotten upstairs alone. Her wheelchair was downstairs, and Shane was right there when it happened. I suspect he would have been smarter to simply admit he had taken her up the stairs and then claimed she fell. But he's denied taking her upstairs, and someone had to have because she wasn't physically capable."

"Does this mean you won't have to worry about one of them suing Marlow House?"

"From what I understand," Danielle explained, "only Joyce can really do that, and according to Martha, she doesn't intend to."

"She shouldn't," Marie snapped. "Considering she tried to make off with your coins and you didn't press charges."

"If Shane didn't have anything to do with his grandmother's death, then I can understand the estate suing. After all, the poor woman did fall down my stairs and die. Actually, most people would sue."

"I suppose you're right." Marie let out a sigh. "So tell me, how is poor Lily doing? I have been worried sick about that dear girl."

"Lily? Oh…you mean because of her and Ian breaking up?"

"I still can't believe it. They seemed so perfect together."

"I'm happy to say they got back together. Not only that, they're engaged," Danielle told Marie.

"Engaged? Is that why Ian wanted to move out of the house? Does he plan to move someplace else now that he's getting married?"

"Actually, Ian regrets giving his notice, but he understands it's too late to do anything now. But between you and me, if your buyer changes his mind and wants to back out of the deal, I know Ian would love to buy the house."

"I told my grandson Ian and Lily would probably get back together. But would he listen to me? Sometimes I would like to give Adam a good shake."

"Me too," Danielle said under her breath, suppressing a giggle.

"Oh…just a minute…" The line was silent for a moment. Finally, Marie got back on the phone. "Danielle, I'll have to call you back. There is someone at my door."

———

"WE WERE JUST TALKING ABOUT YOU," Marie told Adam when she opened the front door a few minutes later and found him standing on the front porch. "Why didn't you use your key?"

"I left it at home," Adam said, following Marie into the house. "Is someone here?"

"No, why?" Marie frowned.

"You said you were talking about me."

"I was just talking to Danielle on the phone when you rang the bell."

"I won't even ask what you were talking about," Adam said with a chuckle. "Do you have any coffee on?"

"What do you think?" Marie started walking to the kitchen, Adam trailing behind her.

"Do you have any of those cinnamon rolls left?" Adam asked.

Ignoring his question, Marie said, "I want you to know I was right."

"Right about what?" Adam asked, now standing in the kitchen, watching his grandmother pour them each a cup of coffee.

"Ian and Lily got back together," Marie said.

"Really?" Adam smiled.

"I told you they would!"

"Okay, so you were right."

"I usually am." Marie reached into the pantry and pulled out a paper sack. She handed it to Adam.

"Yes! Cinnamon rolls." Adam grinned, pulling one from the sack.

"Oh, and you know what else Danielle told me?"

While tearing off a hunk of cinnamon roll, he asked, "What?"

"They've arrested Shane Pruitt for Agatha's murder."

"You're kidding me?" Adam popped the cinnamon roll in his mouth and listened to his grandmother tell him all Danielle had told her about the arrest.

Licking the sugary residue off his fingers, Adam frowned. "So you're telling me if Agatha could have gotten up those stairs on her own, they might not have arrested Shane?"

"I don't think it's the stairs as much as walking across the second floor alone to get to the attic stairs. I imagine it would have been possible for her to get up the stairs alone if she held onto the rail and walked slowly."

"Oh crap. I got to go, Grandma." Adam set the bag of cinnamon rolls on the counter.

"But you just got here," Marie protested.

"There is something I need to do. And it can't wait."

"What about Ian and Lily?"

"I'll deal with that after I finish what I have to do."

AFTER LEAVING his grandmother's house, Adam drove directly to his office. It took him about thirty minutes to get what he needed off his computer. From his office, he intended to drive directly to the Frederickport Police Station, but then he remembered it was Saturday. There was a good chance the chief wouldn't be there, and that was who he wanted to talk to.

Sitting in his car in front of Frederickport Vacation Properties, Adam glanced over at the flash drive he had just tossed on the passenger seat. After a moment of consideration, he turned on his ignition and started toward Chief MacDonald's house.

Adam pulled up in front of the chief's house ten minutes later and found MacDonald in the front yard with Evan and Eddy Jr., playing a game of catch. When the chief saw Adam get out of the parked car, he paused a moment, ball in hand, and watched Adam approach.

"Hey, Adam. What's going on?" the chief greeted him.

Adam flashed a quick hello grin to the two boys and then looked to the chief as he walked into the yard. "I need to talk to you a minute, about Shane Pruitt. Grandma told me you arrested him yesterday."

"Yeah." MacDonald tossed the ball to Eddy and motioned to the boys to go play so he could talk to Adam. Reluctantly they complied.

Adam held up the flash drive for MacDonald to see. "You need to watch this."

Taking a step toward Adam, MacDonald frowned. "What is it?"

"It's probably going to make your case against Shane Pruitt fall apart." Adam handed him the flash drive.

The chief let out a sigh. "Come on, let's go inside. You think this will work on my computer?"

"It should." Adam followed McDonald into the house.

"So tell me how you got this," MacDonald asked after they walked into his den.

"You know Joyce Pruitt works for me, right?" Adam asked.

MacDonald took a seat at the desk and turned on his computer while Adam sat on the nearby sofa.

"She cleans houses for you, right?"

"Right. After the incident with the gold coins…well, let's just say I had some trust issues with Joyce."

"You didn't trust her anymore?"

Adam shrugged. "In all fairness to Joyce, she's always been a hard worker. I never had a problem with her showing up when she was supposed to, and I haven't ever had a complaint about her. But over the last six months, there's been a significant increase of household items disappearing after a renter moves out. Oh, some of it is to be expected. The vacation properties are completely furnished, and dishes do break, and linens disappear. At first, it never crossed my mind that maybe Joyce took the stuff."

"And then she took Danielle's coins."

Adam nodded. "Exactly."

The chief held up the flash drive. "So what is this?"

"I had Joyce clean a property that I recently restocked with a number of brand-new household items. New pillows, beach towels, linens, silverware, dishes, and some pretty nice wineglasses. I was curious to see if…well…if she'd take any of it. I set up a security camera in the house, and when she came to clean, I watched."

"Did she walk away with anything?"

"You need to see for yourself what's on there."

THIRTY MINUTES LATER, Adam and the chief sat silently in MacDonald's den. Finally, the chief spoke.

"Well, I suppose I should call my sister, see if she can watch the boys for a couple of hours."

"What are you going to do?" Adam asked.

"I guess the only thing I can do. I need to get Shane's charges dropped."

CHIEF MACDONALD HADN'T PLANNED to come into work on Saturday. But sometimes, it was unavoidable. Sitting alone in his office, he picked up the phone and called Danielle.

"Hey, Chief, what's going on?"

"I just wanted to let you know we had to drop the charges against Shane Pruitt."

"Why?"

He then went on to tell Danielle about his morning and what he had learned from Adam Nichols.

"Adam should probably go into the video surveillance business. What is this, his third time?" Danielle asked.

"He does have a knack of catching the most unexpected things on his cameras."

"I just don't want to watch his private tapes." Danielle snickered.

"Private tapes?"

"Think about it, Chief. Just what else is Adam Nichols video recording on his cameras? The women's locker room at the gym?"

MacDonald chuckled. "I certainly hope not. That would give me a major headache. I thought you two were friends now?"

Danielle let out a sigh. "I think of him more like my younger brother, who I love to harass."

"But Adam is older than you."

"Only physically." She then sighed again and said, "I have to admit I'm rather impressed at what Adam keeps capturing with his cameras. It's kind of amusing, because he's convinced Marlow House is rigged with security cameras."

"I know. But I have to wonder if he's going to start rethinking that assumption," the chief suggested.

231

BOBBI HOLMES

"Why do you say that?" Danielle asked.

"Think about it. Is Adam going to wonder why your hidden cameras didn't capture Agatha's fall?"

"You have a point."

"Is Agatha still around?"

"I don't know. I'd like her to move on. But now this…well, I would sort of like to talk to her one more time before she does. Confront her with what she's done."

"I just wish she'd be more forthcoming about what really happened on the day she died."

"That's the thing about dead people, they can be just as contrary and stubborn as when they were alive," Danielle told him.

THIRTY-EIGHT

Danielle found herself alone Saturday evening—except for Walt. Her guests had gone out to dinner and a movie, and Lily was across the street at Ian's.

Walt was taking advantage of the empty house by watching a movie on the parlor television. It was something he couldn't do if guests or Joanne were in the house. Unless, of course, it was a movie Danielle or someone else happened to have on. While Walt enjoyed his movie, Danielle decided to go outside to the porch swing and watch the evening's sunset.

She was outside for less than fifteen minutes when she got company. It was Agatha Pine.

"You're still here?" Danielle asked.

"Obviously." Agatha sat next to Danielle on the swing.

"I thought you were going to move on?"

"I don't seem to be able to," Agatha grumbled.

"Perhaps that has something to do with all your lies." Folding her arms across her chest, Danielle leaned back in the swing, enjoying the gentle back and forth motion while gazing across the street at the orange and golden-hued skyline. The sun's edge barely peeked over Ian's roof.

"I told you, it wasn't exactly a lie about my money. Nothing but a slight exaggeration, and one I can hardly be credited with spreading."

"So was your inability to walk also just a slight exaggeration?" Danielle asked.

Furrowing her brow, Agatha looked over at Danielle. "What are you talking about?"

"You never needed that wheelchair. It was just another way to manipulate your family," Danielle accused.

"You have no idea what I needed!" Agatha snapped.

"Did you know your youngest grandson was arrested for your murder?" Danielle asked.

"Shane, arrested?" Agatha asked dully. "Why would they think he was responsible for my death?"

"If you weren't able to walk by yourself, someone had to have helped you to the stairs leading up to the attic. And since Shane was the first one to find you and claimed he was in the attic at the time you fell, they just figured he must have been the one to take you up there—and the one to help you down those stairs."

"I told you it was no one's business how I got up there! I can't imagine how they could possibly arrest my grandson on such flimsy circumstantial evidence."

"Just so you know, they dropped the charges. I can see how devastated you are that this inconvenienced your grandson," Danielle said sarcastically.

"You certainly aren't very nice to dead people!"

Danielle shrugged in response, still looking across the street at the sinking sun.

"So why did they release Shane?" Agatha asked after a few moments of silence.

"I thought you would have figured it out after I mentioned your disability exaggeration."

"You aren't making any sense."

Danielle let out a sigh. "The police know you were perfectly capable of walking up those stairs on your own. Perfectly capable of getting to the attic stairs without anyone helping you."

"How would they know that? I've been in a wheelchair for almost a year now!"

"But you didn't always stay in that chair," Danielle said. "You see, Adam Nichols installed a security camera at one of his rentals. Apparently, you accompanied your daughter to work one day. I have to wonder, why was that exactly? Did you usually go with her when she cleaned houses?"

Pursing her mouth, Agatha slumped down in the swing and refused to look at Danielle.

"It obviously wasn't to help her clean. Since, according to the chief, who saw the video, you stayed in your chair—right up to the point Joyce left the house. She was gone for about fifteen minutes, and during that time, you were all over that place. Walking as good as I do. And the moment you heard your daughter return, you were back in the wheelchair, playing the invalid."

"I wanted Joyce to take me to a restaurant. But she insisted she had to clean the house first. She didn't want to come back to our house to get me, it was across town from the restaurant, so I had to go with her. And when we were there, she realized she forgot something and had to run to the store. She wouldn't take me. Said it was too much work getting the wheelchair in and out of the car. I had to stay in the house alone. What was I supposed to do, just sit in that stupid chair and twiddle my thumbs?"

"Your little game not only inconvenienced your family when you were alive, it could have helped send your grandson to prison."

"He's in the clear now?" Agatha asked hesitantly.

"I'm not sure the chief is convinced he's all that innocent. But now knowing you were capable of getting around by yourself, he really doesn't have anything to hold him on. Of course…" Danielle studied Agatha's profile. "If you tell me he had something to do with you falling down those stairs, I suppose the chief will keep digging and try to build a case."

Unsmiling, Agatha glanced to Danielle. "He has nothing to investigate."

Danielle shrugged and let out a sigh. "Then I suppose I need to call my insurance agent."

"Why is that?"

"If one of your grandchildren didn't help you down those stairs and it really was an accident, then I'm probably liable for some damages. At least, I won't ask my insurance company to fight it. Of course, that's ultimately their call."

Agatha turned to Danielle and frowned. "Are you saying if my grandson didn't have anything to do with my death, you would welcome a lawsuit from my daughter?"

"*Welcome* is a bit extreme. I mean, who actually welcomes a lawsuit? I just wouldn't be adamantly opposed and insist my insurance company tries to fight it. After all, that's why I have insurance."

Looking straight ahead again, Agatha muttered, "I don't think Joyce will sue you. She's too afraid. It won't happen unless my grandsons get her to do it."

Agatha vanished. Danielle glanced around. Agatha was nowhere in sight.

A moment later, Danielle's cellphone began to ring.

She sat up and pulled it out of her pocket and looked at it. Marie Nichols was calling. "Hello, Marie, how are you this evening?"

"I was wondering if you and Lily have had dinner yet," Marie asked.

"Umm…yeah, we ate about an hour ago."

"Oh dear. This is rather last minute of me, but Adam is stopping over in a little bit to pick me up. We're going out to dinner, and I thought maybe you girls—and Ian—might join us."

"Gee, I'm sorry, Marie. But like I said, we already ate. We can take a rain check."

"How about if I bring over dessert after Adam and I eat?" Marie suggested. "Is Lily home?"

"Lily's across the street at Ian's."

"I'd like to see Ian too. Perhaps we could all meet at Marlow House for dessert?" Marie asked. "I have something I'd like to talk to Lily and Ian about."

When Danielle got off the phone a few minutes later, she called Chris.

"Hey, Danielle, are we still on for tonight?"

"Yes, but can we make it a little later? Marie and Adam are stopping over with some dessert."

"You want to do this another night?"

"No. I don't think they'll be here more than an hour. Marie goes to bed pretty early. And I'd rather not wait."

"What about your guests?"

"They went to a movie. But even if they show up, I don't think it'll be a problem. They'll probably go on up to their rooms."

HAD his movie not just ended, Walt would have been annoyed when Agatha materialized before him, standing between the sofa and television. Instead of impatiently asking her to move out of the way, he used his energy to turn off the set.

"What do you want?" he asked.

"I'm leaving," she announced.

"Really?" Walt sat up on the sofa, moving his feet from its cushion to the throw rug covering the wood floor.

"Yes. But there's a member of my family I need to speak with before I can move on."

"Just one family member?"

"There's only one I need to talk to," Agatha said primly.

"Your daughter, right?" Walt chuckled and leaned back on the sofa. "I imagine you want to ask her for forgiveness for all your lies. But unless she's like Danielle, she won't hear you."

"One thing I've picked up during my time here, it seems you've managed to communicate with Lily somehow. I want to know how you do that."

"Lily?" Walt shook his head. "Lily can't see or hear me."

"But she has. I know it. I just don't know how you did it."

"Ah, you mean a dream hop?"

Agatha frowned. "Dream hop?"

"That's just a name Danielle gave it. It's when a spirit enters the dream of a living person. The only problem, the person dreaming assumes it's nothing more than a normal dream—that the spirit isn't really there."

"I want to know how to do that!" Agatha said. "I need to do it before I move on."

Walt eyed Agatha. "Actually, you don't have to wait to move on in order to dream hop. It's something spirits are able to do after they leave this plane. Of course, I'm not sure how it all works after you move on, and I'm fairly certain that once you leave here, you're limited in how frequently you can dream hop."

"Why is that?" she asked.

Walt shrugged. "I assume it has something to do with preventing spirits from interfering with the living—in the same way spirits trapped on this realm are constricted in their powers."

"Then tell me how to do it. I want to know," Agatha insisted.

"You really want to make amends with your daughter, don't you?"

"Whatever I may or may not wish to say to my daughter—or

anyone else in my family—is really none of your concern. Our business is ours—no one else's."

"If I don't tell you how to dream hop?" he asked.

"Then I suppose you will have to get used to me staying here."

"I hope I don't regret this," Walt muttered before giving Agatha basic dream hop instructions.

"YOU TOLD her how to dream hop?" Danielle groaned. She stood alone in the parlor with Walt. He had just told her of Agatha's request.

"I believed her when she says she wants to move on. But something is preventing her. Considering all the lies she fed her family over the years, I think she needs to find some way to clear the air with them. And frankly, if I didn't tell her how to do it, she would eventually figure it out on her own."

Danielle plopped down on a chair. "They certainly aren't going to think it's anything but a dream."

"True. And I explained that to Agatha. But sometimes we simply need to express ourselves—to say our piece—before we can move on. I don't think this is really about Agatha's daughter. I doubt it will make any difference to her. But it will help Agatha, and if she's then able to move on, we'll all be better for it."

"Walt, you're probably right," Danielle reluctantly admitted.

"As I normally am."

Danielle let out a snort.

"Very unladylike," Walt chided.

Danielle giggled.

The television turned on.

"You want to watch a movie with me?" Walt asked.

Danielle glanced at the TV. "I don't think we have time. Marie called, and she and Adam are coming over in about an hour or so with dessert. I already called Lily. She and Ian are coming over in a little bit. Marie wants to talk to them."

Walt arched his brow. "About what?"

Danielle shrugged. "I suspect about the house. I think she might be worried Lily is mad at her for selling it. But it really wasn't Marie's fault."

"Is she bringing enough dessert for your guests?" Walt asked.

"I have no idea what she's even bringing. But I don't think it'll be a problem. Our guests mentioned they were going to the movies after they had some dinner, so I don't expect them back soon. And if they do show up when Marie and Adam are here, I have a chocolate cake in the kitchen."

THIRTY-NINE

The apple pie would taste delightful with vanilla ice cream. But then, so would the chocolate cake. Marie lingered in the bakery section of the grocery store, trying to decide on which one to purchase. Perhaps both?

"Late night snack?" came a friendly female voice.

Marie looked up and found Beverly Klein standing a few feet away.

"Oh, Beverly! How are you this evening?" Marie greeted. She then glanced at her watch. "And it's not all that late. We just finished dinner."

"I'm just teasing," Beverly said with a grin as she picked up a plastic carton of chocolate chip cookies. "I had a little sweet tooth tonight myself and decided to pick up something. Living alone now, I just don't see the sense of baking."

Marie nodded in agreement. "As far as I'm concerned, there is never a reason to bake!" She laughed and then added, "At least not as long as we have such a wonderful bakery like Old Salts in town. Unfortunately, they close around six, so we had to pick up something here."

"The grocery store's bakery is pretty good." Beverly set the carton of cookies in her cart.

"My problem is deciding what to get, cake or pie? Or both?"

"Oh my, you do have an appetite!" Beverly teased.

Marie grinned. "It's not all for me. Adam and I are taking dessert over to Marlow House and having a little visit with Danielle and Lily."

Beverly looked around. "Adam's here?"

Marie nodded. "Yes. He went over to the liquor section to pick up some wine."

Beverly glanced briefly toward the direction of the liquor section and then looked back to Marie. "How is Danielle doing since that horrible accident at her party? Although, it appears it wasn't exactly an accident. I heard they arrested Agatha's youngest grandson. They say he pushed her down the stairs."

Marie shook her head. "Arrested and released already."

Beverly arched her brow. "Really? Does this mean it really was an accident?"

"The police seem to think so. They based their original assertion on the erroneous belief that Agatha wasn't capable of getting up those stairs by herself, and since Shane was the one to find her…" Marie shrugged.

"You say they released him? Why?"

"It seems Agatha wasn't quite the invalid she claimed to be. A security tape captured her out of the wheelchair and quite mobile."

"Security tape?"

Marie started to explain how Agatha's mobility was captured with one of Adam's security cameras, yet then remembered he had asked her not to say anything. "Umm…well, that's what I understand."

"I remember when he forged his mother's signature on one of her checks," Beverly whispered.

"I remember something about that."

"Steve told me about it. Although, I don't imagine he would be thrilled if he heard me talking about it." Beverly chuckled. Marie understood that Beverly's husband, Steve, who had been the bank manager, had recently died.

"What exactly happened? I don't quite remember."

"Stupid boy tried cashing one of his mother's checks. Forged her signature. But he wrote it for more than what was actually in her account. At first Joyce denied writing the check, but when she found out who was involved, she immediately changed her story. Insisted it was all a mistake." Beverly shook her head at the thought.

"Stealing from your mother is a horrible thing to do—but killing your grandmother…" Marie cringed. "I can't imagine how he could have lived with himself if he had done something like that. After all, how does one kill a member of their family they have professed to love and then just go on with their life as if nothing ever happened?"

"Had Shane actually been responsible for his grandmother's death, who's to say he ever really loved her?" Beverly suggested.

"True. But I remember how he and his siblings seemed to dote on Agatha."

Beverly shrugged. "Or maybe he did love her, and it was just a tragic accident? Had he actually been responsible, I mean."

"I suppose that would be worse, don't you?" Marie asked.

"Worse?"

"To really love someone and then realize you're responsible for their death. And then you keep quiet about it for fear of being arrested. I'd think something like that would simply eat a person up. Maybe even drive them insane."

"Perhaps." Beverly flashed Maria a bright smile. "I need to go grab myself a carton of milk to go with these cookies! It was wonderful seeing you, Marie. Say hi to Adam for me."

"YOU THINK Marie wanted to bring over dessert because she feels guilty?" Lily asked Danielle. She and Ian sat in the living room with Walt and Danielle, waiting for Marie and Adam to arrive.

"She didn't say anything about the house," Danielle said, "if that's what you're referring to."

"Marie has nothing to feel guilty about. This entire thing is my fault," Ian grumbled. He leaned back on the sofa, where he sat with Lily.

Sadie announced Marie and Adam's arrival a few minutes later when she jumped up and started barking just moments before the doorbell rang.

Marie had decided against bringing ice cream with her bakery item. Instead, she walked into the living room with Adam, who carried a boxed cheesecake in one hand and a bottle of wine in the other.

"The chocolate cake and apple pie looked good," Marie explained as she took a seat. "But then I saw the cheesecake. And of course, I couldn't imagine the grocery store bakery's chocolate cake would be as good as Danielle's, or their apple pie as good as Old Salts. But the cheesecake looked rather tasty."

"This is very sweet of you," Danielle said as she removed the cheesecake from the box Adam held, and then set it on the coffee table.

Sadie eyed the cake, her tail wagging.

"Don't even think about it," Walt warned, pointing to the throw rug by the fireplace.

From the corner of his eye Ian noticed Sadie's subtle change. He himself was about to call the dog from Danielle's side and have her go lie down. But she seemingly decided to move in the opposite direction on her own accord, and then plopped down with an unceremonious grunt on the small throw rug. Her eyes were still on the cake, yet now she was too far away to sneak a taste.

Ian suspected Walt had given Sadie the command to move and park herself. He wondered how many times in the last year a similar situation had occurred while he had failed to notice. He chided himself for having been supremely unaware of his surroundings. How had he not noticed such odd behavior?

Picking up a stack of paper plates she had set on the table before Marie and Adam's arrival, Danielle asked, "Everyone want some cheesecake now?" The answer was unanimous, and for the next few minutes Danielle sliced up portions of the cheesecake while Adam passed out the plates.

"I brought some wine, if anyone wants some," Adam said, pointing to the bottle of wine he had set on the game table. Next to the wine bottle was a pitcher of ice water and glasses.

"Maybe later," Danielle said. "Perhaps wine and cheese go together, but I'm not so sure about wine and cheesecake. Does anyone want some water?"

"I'd love some," Marie said as she took a bite of her dessert.

"This was really nice of you two to bring this over," Lily said.

"When I heard you and Ian were not only back together, but engaged, I thought we should celebrate," Marie told her. "Congratulations, by the way."

"Thank you, Marie," Ian said.

"And I wanted to talk to you two about my house," Marie said.

"It's okay, Marie," Ian told her. "I understand you wanted to sell it, and it's my own fault for impulsively giving Adam my notice."

Marie looked sharply at her grandson. "See, Adam, didn't I tell you?"

Adam rolled his eyes. Before taking another bite of cheesecake, he said, "Yeah, you were right."

Marie looked at Lily and Ian and smiled. "I told Adam you two would be getting back together—that it was only a little lovers' spat. Goodness gracious, Adam's grandfather and I must have broken up a half a dozen times before we finally walked down the aisle. That's why I wouldn't sign the sales contract."

"You didn't sign it?" Ian blurted.

"You mean you didn't sell the house?" Lily asked hopefully.

Marie shook her head and smiled. "No. When he came over Friday, I told him I wasn't going to sign anything until I was certain Ian really intended to move. So if you still want the house, you don't have to move at the end of the month."

"Oh yes!" Ian shouted. "I love your house. And I would love to stay. But if you still want to sell, I'd like to buy it."

Smiling, Marie glanced at Adam and nodded. "See, I told you so."

Adam chuckled and then looked over at Ian and Lily. "While I'm glad you two worked it all out, part of me wishes you hadn't. Grandma is going to be unbearable to live with."

"Adam, that's awful!" Danielle laughed.

Marie shook her head at Adam and muttered, "You'll miss me when I'm gone."

Adam snatched the now empty paper plate from his grandmother's hands and gave her a quick kiss on the cheek. "You aren't going anywhere."

CHRIS SHOWED up at Marlow House in time for a slice of cheesecake. When Heather arrived, the cake was gone—as were Adam and Marie.

"I waited until after Marie and Adam left," Heather explained. She sat where Marie had been sitting fifteen minutes earlier. She glanced around.

"I wasn't about to miss dessert," Chris said with a grin. "Not when Danielle told me Marie and Adam were bringing something over."

Confused, Ian glanced around. "Are we having some party I wasn't told about?"

"I just thought it might be a good idea to do this as soon as possible," Danielle explained. "And unless our current guests decided to see a different movie, they should be gone for at least another hour."

"Do what?" Ian asked.

Chris looked over to Ian. "Now that you know about…well… you know…Danielle thought it might be a good idea if she got us all together and let you ask whatever questions you might have."

"After we catch you up," Lily corrected.

"What do you mean, catch me up?" Ian asked.

"A lot has happened this last year that you aren't aware of," Lily explained. "Learning about Walt or how Danielle and Chris, or Heather and Evan, can see ghosts—or how Walt can communicate with Sadie and Max—is just part of it."

Ian frowned. "What more could there be?"

"Well…there was Cheryl…" Danielle murmured.

"Cheryl?" Ian asked.

"I think Dani means Cheryl's ghost. But I'm pretty sure I already told you about Cheryl," Lily explained. "But then there was that time Stoddard haunted our yard…"

"And your out-of-body experience," Danielle reminded Lily.

"And mine," Chris added.

"And don't forget the ghost Chris brought with him when he showed up for Christmas." Lily grinned. "Or Lucas's visit on Valentine's Day."

"Ugh…and that creepy muse guy." Heather shuddered. "And the leprechaun!"

"The muse wasn't that bad," Danielle countered.

Ian let out a groan and sank down in his seat, closing his eyes, while those around him rattled off all that had happened in the past year—many of which had happened right before his eyes, which he had been unable to see.

FORTY

According to the clock in the hallway, it was a few minutes past midnight. The guests staying at Marlow House had returned from the movies and had since retired for the evening. Lily was over at Ian's, and Walt suspected she wouldn't be returning until morning. The only bedroom with light slipping out from under its door was Danielle's. Without knocking, Walt moved through the wall, into her room.

Walt found Danielle sitting up in bed, tucked under the covers, and leaning against a pile of pillows. Sitting on her lap was her portable computer. With her attention on its display, her fingers danced gracefully over the keyboard. Walt wondered what she was researching this evening.

Silently moving closer to the bed, he noticed she was already occupying just one side of the mattress, leading him to believe she was expecting him.

"Danielle," Walt whispered.

Looking up from her computer, Danielle smiled. "I was hoping you'd come say goodnight." With one hand, she patted the empty spot next to her. Walt accepted her invitation, and a moment later he was sprawled out next to her, his shoes already off, as he too leaned back against the pillows stacked in front of the headboard.

His attire was far more formal than hers—a light blue three-piece pinstripe suit—while she wore an oversized T-shirt and a pair of flannel pajama bottoms—its fabric adorned with cartoonish kittens. She hadn't yet unbraided her hair, and remarkably much of it remained neatly in place.

"Do you think we overwhelmed Ian tonight?" Danielle asked in a whisper.

"He did seem a bit dazed." Walt chuckled. "But he'll deal with it. He has Lily to help him."

"There were a couple of times there tonight I got the impression he thought we were pulling his leg."

Walt chuckled again. "Yes, I noticed that too."

Danielle let out a sigh and looked back down at the computer.

"What are you doing?" he asked.

Danielle grinned and looked up at Walt. "Actually, I've been working on your family tree."

"My family tree?"

"More like I'm stalking your cousin—the other Walter Clint Marlow."

"I go by Walt," he reminded her.

"But your real name is Walter, right?"

He shrugged. "Yes, but it always sounded so formal."

"Well, your cousin doesn't go by Walter either. He uses his middle name."

"Clint?"

Danielle nodded. "Yep."

"You learned that on that ancestry site?"

Danielle shook her head. "No. I found his Facebook account. Since he uses it for work, he doesn't seem to have many privacy settings on, so I can see his pictures."

Walt arched his brow. "What else have you learned about him?"

"He's engaged. Very hot lady. Wanna see?" Danielle asked mischievously.

"Certainly." Walt leaned closer to the display and looked while Danielle clicked on a link, opening a photograph. It was a picture of a man and woman at the beach—the man looked exactly like Walt, but was shirtless, wore faded denims, and was barefoot. He was obviously Walt's cousin. Next to the cousin was a tall bikini-clad blonde, her slender figure boasting a disproportional amount of bosom.

"Oh my," Walt muttered.

"From what I've read, I'm pretty sure that is the fiancée."

Danielle glanced over at Walt and noticed he continued to stare at the picture. "They're fake, Walt."

"Fake? What is fake?"

Danielle chuckled. "The breasts, of course."

Dazed, Walt shook his head and muttered something under his breath.

"I was thinking of asking him to be my Facebook friend," Danielle said.

"Why would you do that?" Walt frowned. "I thought you just said he was engaged."

"Asking him to be my Facebook friend doesn't mean I'm trying to hit on him. I just thought you might want to meet your cousin someday. Maybe he and his fiancée would like to come stay for the weekend."

Walt shook his head. "No, Danielle. I'm naturally curious about my cousin. But I don't want you to do anything rash. We don't know anything about this man."

"I just thought I could send him a friend request and tell him I inherited Marlow house, and say something about finding him on the computer when I was researching you, and then mention how much he looks like your portrait."

Walt shook his head again. "Please don't do that. At least not yet. Find out more about him. I've gone this long without seeing any family members, and people get strange when money is involved."

Danielle frowned. "Money?"

"Yes. He might argue he should have inherited my estate instead of you, because he's a blood relative."

"I didn't really consider that." Danielle wrinkled her nose. "But I don't think he'd have any legal standing."

"Let's not open that particular Pandora's box right now. I think you've had enough excitement lately."

Danielle closed her laptop and let out a sigh. "I suppose you're right. Speaking of excitement, have you seen Agatha? I haven't seen her since this afternoon. Do you think she really left?"

Walt shrugged. "She told me she intended to."

"I've decided I'm going to call my insurance agent on Monday."

"Insurance agent? What for?"

"If Agatha fell down those stairs—without her grandson pushing her—then maybe I am in some way liable. I was going to tell him the family's planning to sue and that maybe we should approach Joyce with a settlement."

"I thought her daughter told you at the police station her mother wasn't suing."

Danielle shrugged. "Well, I won't tell my agent that."

Walt nodded toward the laptop. "Are you done?"

Danielle yawned. "I guess."

The next moment the laptop lifted off Danielle's lap and drifted to the dresser.

Watching the computer, Danielle giggled. "Thanks, Walt."

The next moment, Walt was no longer next to her, but standing by the bed. "You need to get some rest. You've had a rough week."

Danielle yawned again. "I guess you're right."

"And no dream hop tonight," Walt said sternly, pulling the blankets up around Danielle, tucking her in. "You need a good night's sleep."

"Yes, *Dad*." Smiling, Danielle snuggled into the bed.

Walt grinned down at Danielle, blew her a kiss, and then disappeared. A moment later, the bedroom light turned off.

SHANE OPENED HIS EYES. It took him a moment to realize where he was. He had been here before. The attic at Marlow House. Glancing around, he saw that he was alone, standing in the middle of the enormous room. Sunlight streamed through the windows.

Dazed and confused, he stumbled to the back window. Looking outside, he tried to make sense of what he was seeing. Folding tables and chairs were set up in the side yard, as was the croquet set. Sitting at the tables, lingering in the yard, standing on the patio, and playing croquet were people—some he recognized, some he did not. He spied the table he had been sitting at with his family. The only ones there now were his mother and Martha. They appeared to be talking. Not far from his mother and sister was his brother-in-law, Dennis, who stood by the barbeque, chatting with Adam Nichols. The overwhelming sensation of déjà vu washed over him. This had all happened before.

Pressing the heel of his hand against his forehead, Shane closed his eyes and muttered, "I don't understand. How can I be here again?"

Opening his eyes, he found it difficult to breathe—suffocating.

"I need to get out of here," he said under his breath as he headed for the door leading to the stairwell.

The moment he reached the exit, he froze. He knew what was going to be on the other side of the door, and something deep inside told him not to go there. Yet he couldn't stay in the attic indefinitely.

Taking a deep breath, he reached for the doorknob, clutching it tightly. Pushing himself to keep moving, he swung open the door and was relieved to discover no one was standing there. Taking another deep breath, he started down the steps, wanting nothing more than to get down the two flights of stairs and out of this house. He wanted to get away from Marlow House—far away.

He made it halfway down the staircase when he saw her. His right hand clutching the handrail, Shane froze. The woman was looking down, watching the placement of her feet as she progressed up the steps. All he could see was the top of her gray head.

Yet Shane knew immediately who it was, just as he had the last time. Unable to move, he just stood there as she took another step up the staircase—bringing her closer to him. Finally, she stopped and looked up, her eyes meeting his. A smile turned her pale lips.

"Shane, are you just going to stand there?" Agatha asked.

"Wha...what are you doing up here? Where's your wheelchair?"

"Funny, that's exactly what you said the last time." She took one more step up the staircase.

"Last time?"

"I believe I was standing about where you are, the last time. Maybe if I get a little closer, you'll remember."

Abruptly, Shane took a step backwards, almost stumbling on a step. His right hand clutched the handrail a little tighter.

Agatha laughed. "Why do you look so terrified, Shane? I remember when you were a little boy. You didn't like going into the haunted house on Halloween. Do you remember that?"

"I think you should go back downstairs, Gran," Shane told her.

"Why don't you push me like you did the last time? I'll probably get there faster that way. Won't I?"

Shane took another step backwards—up the stairs. Agatha followed him, her pace matching his.

"You remember now, don't you?" Agatha taunted, her eyes never leaving his.

"I've got to be dreaming," Shane muttered. "That must be it."

"Oh yes, you're dreaming. But that doesn't mean I'm not here. It doesn't mean I don't know what you did."

Shane's eyes widened, his gaze locked with his grandmother's. Trancelike, he stepped toward her, placed his hands on her shoulders, and then shoved abruptly, sending Agatha's frail body tumbling down the stairs like a rag doll. She landed with a thud on the second-floor landing, her head and neck bent in an awkward position.

Dazed, Shane remained standing midway on the attic staircase, looking down at his grandmother's lifeless body. He was about to shout for help, when she suddenly jumped up and ran back up the stairs.

Once she reached him, he placed his hands on her shoulders and shoved—and once again she toppled down the stairs, landing in a lifeless heap. And just as before, when he was preparing to scream for help, she jumped up, running back up the stairs.

It continued again and again—an endless loop—pushing his grandmother, only for her to return, until he could no longer stand it and he managed to scream.

———————

SHANE BOLTED upright in his bed. Drenched in sweat, his breathing labored, he reached for the lamp on the nightstand and turned it on. It bathed his bedroom in a soft glow. His heart racing, he attempted to calm his breathing. The silence in the room was deafening. He remembered screaming in his dream, but since his roommate hadn't come barging into his bedroom, he assumed it had all been a dream, and there had been no real scream.

His breathing now steady, he glanced over to his bedroom window. He had forgotten to close the blind before going to bed. Beyond the window was darkness. Shane stared at the window, not willing to attempt sleep again and risk another nightmare. It was then he noticed a soft glow on the windowpane. Frowning, he thought for a moment someone was outside in his yard with a flashlight.

He started to get out of bed to have a closer look. It was then he saw it. His grandmother, Agatha Pine, staring in the window, looking at him.

Shane screamed. This time, it woke up his roommate.

THE GHOST AND THE BRIDE

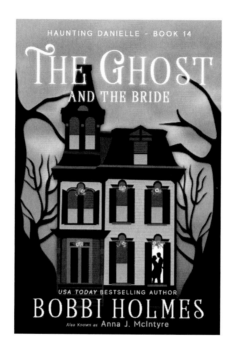

RETURN TO MARLOW HOUSE IN
THE GHOST AND THE BRIDE
HAUNTING DANIELLE, BOOK 14

Family and friends gather at Marlow House for Ian and Lily's wedding.

What could possibly go wrong?

Isn't a haunted house the perfect place for a wedding?

NON-FICTION BY

BOBBI ANN JOHNSON HOLMES

HAVASU PALMS, A HOSTILE TAKEOVER
WHERE THE ROAD ENDS, RECIPES & REMEMBRANCES
MOTHERHOOD, A BOOK OF POETRY
THE STORY OF THE CHRISTMAS VILLAGE

BOOKS BY ANNA J. MCINTYRE

COULSON FAMILY SAGA

COULSON'S WIFE

COULSON'S CRUCIBLE

COULSON'S LESSONS

COULSON'S SECRET

COULSON'S RECKONING

UNLOCKED ⚷ HEARTS

SUNDERED HEARTS

AFTER SUNDOWN

WHILE SNOWBOUND

SUGAR RUSH

Made in United States
North Haven, CT
03 April 2022

17758869R00159